GOODE VIBRATIONS

GOODE GIRLS

Jasinda Wilder

GOODE VIBRATIONS: GOODE GIRLS

ISBN: 978-1-948445-50-4

Cover art by Sarah Hansen of Okay Creations.

Formatting: Champagne Book Design

GOODE VIBRATIONS

ONE

Poppy

WALKING YOUR WAY OUT OF NYC IS NOWHERE NEAR as easy as you might think. Especially when you don't have an itinerary…or a great sense of direction. But what I did have was a box of protein bars ordered online from Costco, two extra-large Nalgene water bottles, and a huge backpack filled with clothes—mostly underwear and T-shirts and sweatshirts and socks, plus a couple pairs of jeans and a pair of TOMS shoes to give my feet a break from the hiking boots. Also, I had in my possession an extra-large purse containing my cell phone and charger, my iPad Pro with its keyboard case, stylus, and charger; my new-to-me vintage camera courtesy of Mrs. DuPuis, my erstwhile advisor from

Columbia University. I had approximately two hundred rolls of black-and-white film, and a hundred rolls of color film, divided between my purse and backpack. I was carrying four thousand dollars in cash, separated into rolls of hundreds packed in my purse, backpack, and pockets. And, finally, I had a multi-tool and a Zippo lighter.

I'd say I was traveling pretty light for someone backpacking from NYC to Alaska.

But my most valuable possession was my innate trust in the goodness of humans, balanced by a pretty reliable bullshit and creep detector.

It took me an embarrassingly long time to navigate my way on foot through the maze of boroughs and bridges and tunnels that made up New York City and then, when I thought I was making something like progress, I found myself lost in suburbia.

Dammit.

I stopped at a gas station, waited in line behind locals getting gas and buying cigarettes, and when it was my turn at the counter, the young man behind it, sporting a Sikh turban and a fantastic beard, offered me a dazzled, surprised smile.

"Good morning, how can I help you?" he said, in a lilting Punjabi accent.

"I need either a bus station or a train station," I said. "I'm sort of lost."

"No kidding you are lost," he said. "I think you should call a cab to take you to the train depot. It is many miles from here, and I am not certain exactly how to tell you to get there. I only know it is not somewhere to walk to easily."

I laughed. "Well, I'm planning on walking to Alaska, but getting out suburbia is proving pretty tricky."

"You are walking to Alaska?" He sounded so shocked I may as well have told him I was flying to Mars. "I am only in America two years, so maybe I am misinformed, but is not Alaska many thousand of miles from here?"

"Yeah, something like thirty-five hundred miles."

He blinked. "Why?"

I shrugged, smiling brightly. "I'm bored with my life, and need a challenge. Plus, my family all lives there."

"If you are bored of life, get a tattoo, or…or a motorcycle." He shook his head. "It is your business, not mine. But I feel I must say…a woman like you, so young, so beautiful, perhaps it is not safe."

"Can we speed this up?" an impatient voice said from behind me, in a thick New York accent brimming with attitude. "I got shit to do and places to go, so come on already."

I turned, offering the man my most brilliant grin. "I'm sorry to delay you on your important business, sir, I was just asking directions."

Middle-aged, tall and slender, salt-and-pepper hair, neatly trimmed goatee, wearing an expensive three-piece suit. He blinked at me, taken aback by... well, me. "Uh, yeah, no—no problem. You need directions, I can give you directions. Where you tryin' to go, sweetheart?"

It's idiotic that reality works the way it does. Being blessed—through no virtue or achievement on my part—with extreme good looks, I can grin and flirt my way out of pretty much any potential conflict. Smirk a little, bat my lashes, arch my back just so to push my boobs up, and men just...go dog-brain gaga drooly stupid.

Like this guy. When all he saw was my black ponytail, backpack, jeans, and boots, he was all Mr. Impatient, hurry up, I'm so important. All I had to do was turn around, grin, show him some tank top and cleavage, and he's tripping over his own saggy balls to help me.

"Well, I just need to get out of the city and out of suburbia."

"Yeah, sure, but to where?"

"I mean, just generally west."

He looked me over again. "Well, I'm heading

to Buffalo for business, but I could take you as far as Scranton, if you want."

I could see the wheels turning in his head. Thinking maybe he might get something out of giving me a ride. Wondering what kind of girl I am.

The question for me, then, was whether my creeper radar pinged. I in turn looked him over, assessed him. Brusque, self-important, vain, wealthy, impatient, selfish. Kind of a prick. But…mostly safe. He'd be the type, if he made an overt move on me and I turned him down, to leave me on the side of the highway.

I shrugged, extended my hand. "Scranton it is, Mr.…?"

"Zelinski. Don Zelinski."

"Nice to meet you, Mr. Zelinski. I'm Poppy."

"Ahh, if we're gonna be sharing the car together for an hour and a half, you oughta call me Donny."

I thanked the young Sikh behind the counter, and followed Donny Zelinski to his car.

After fueling his sleek silver Audi A8, we headed out of suburbia westward. He had a podcast on, something by NPR, and he turned it down when we hit the highway, offering a grin at me.

"So, Poppy. Generally west, huh?"

I nodded. "I have family in Alaska, and I'm taking the long, scenic route to visit them."

He whistled. "Alaska, huh? That's a hell of a trip."

"Well, I'm young and I'm in a bit of a transitional point in my life, so I may as well see some of the country, right?"

He fiddled with something on the touchscreen, and the A/C blew colder. "Sure. Makes sense to me. When I was your age, I took a gap year and hiked Europe with my brother."

"Yeah, I might do that next."

A few minutes of silence; the cabin of the car, wrapped in luxurious black leather, grew colder by the minute—I caught his gaze flicking subtly but consistently to my chest, and I realized why he'd turned the A/C up so high: to give me headlights. And he'd succeeded, noticeably so.

Douchebag.

Joke was on him, though, because I just tugged my flannel shirt closed to cover them.

"So, what's your boyfriend think about you doing this whole trip on your own?"

I laughed. "No boyfriend."

"You mean to say a sexy young thing like you is totally unattached?"

Ick. He was old enough to be my dad. Don't call me sexy, my dude.

"Yeah, well, I don't need a boyfriend to be happy,

and on a journey to self-discovery like I'm on, a boyfriend would just be in the way. So yeah, unattached and proud of it."

"Good for you," he said, and it was hard to tell if it was meant genuinely or not.

I let the silence extend, and eventually Donny turned his podcast back on, glancing at me to assess my reaction. I just turned the volume up a bit, to indicate I was fine with the podcast.

It was a long-winded discussion of some political thing or another, boring as hell but better than nothing, and better than trying to make conversation with Mr. Make-it-cold-in-the-car-so-your-nipples-get-hard.

I knew the move was coming, and I was prepared for just about anything. As long as he didn't get handsy, I figured I could handle him. And it would be worth it for a ride out of New York City.

He made it most of the way to Scranton. We'd started seeing signs for Scranton, thirty miles, then fifteen, and we were on our second NPR political podcast. He took an exit, one too soon by my reckoning.

"Figured we'd stop for a bite to eat before we get to Scranton. Not much there, and I know there's a nice little place at this exit."

"Oh, that's all right. I'm not hungry. But thank you."

He waved a hand. "Ah, come on. You gotta eat, you know? Keep your strength up for that long trip, right?" He winked at me. "My treat. Come on."

Here it came. Cue transition to overt flirtation…

"No, really, I'm all right. I appreciate the offer, though, Mr. Zelinski, really, I do." Emphasizing the formality hopefully would emphasize the fact that he was fifty-something and I was just barely eighteen.

He eyed me. "Told you, call me Donny. And plus, you know, the little place I got in mind happens to be close to this real nice hotel. Figured, you know, we could grab a bite to eat and grab a room."

Just like that? Where did he get the idea I'd want to do that?

I stared hard at him. "I don't think so, Mr. Zelinski. While I'm grateful for the ride, if that's what you thought this was going to be, I'm afraid you've woefully misunderstood the situation, and the kind of girl I am."

"Figured you'd be a little more grateful, that's all."

"I'd be happy to reimburse you for the fuel cost, if you like."

He narrowed his eyes. "Nah." It was a quintessential New Yorker sound of dismissal. "I guess I thought maybe you'd just play nice, you know?"

I laughed. "I think we have differing ideas of

what it means to play nice, in that case." We pulled up to a stoplight, and I unbuckled. "I'll get out here, thanks." I reached into the back seat, hauled my backpack onto my lap over the center console, and pressed the unlock button on my door. Shoved the door open and stepped out, shouldering the backpack and carrying my purse in the other hand. I gave him a friendly smile, but not too friendly, and waved at him. "Bye, Donny, and thanks for the ride!"

He just gave me a frustrated sigh. "You can't get out here. This ain't a good spot, you know?"

I looked around—industrial outskirts, warehouses, manufacturing plants, a gas station. "I'll be fine, but thanks for your concern. Have a nice day!"

I closed the door, put my other arm through the backpack strap, clipped my purse to the strap near my hip, and set off directly away from Don Zelinski's Audi A8. A moment of silence, and then I heard his engine roar, and he squealed an illegal U-turn back toward the highway. I waited until he was on the highway entrance ramp and gone, and then pulled out my phone, figured out which compass direction I was facing and which way I needed to go. It looked like finding my way to I-80 would be my best bet. It was a bit of work with Apple Maps to get situated, pinching to zoom, shifting the focus this way and that, but finally I had a decent sense of where to go.

It was the very same entrance ramp Donny-boy had used. I cinched my straps tighter, pulled my Air Pods out and cued up the playlist I'd made, a six-hour mix of all my favorite music, which was eclectic, ranging from country and bluegrass to indie pop, singer-songwriter, and even a few hard rock and classic rock songs. First up was "Ain't That Fine" by I'm With Her, which put pep in my step as I began the real work of walking to Alaska.

Up the ramp, well off to the side of the road, I followed it as it curved around and up to join the highway. Gravel liberally sprinkled the sparse crab-grass growing just off the shoulder, and the sun beat down hot. A pickup truck blasted past me, honking. I just waved and they were gone, and then I was on the freeway.

Which was much, much bigger on foot than it had seemed from the confines of a car. The white stripe on the side of the road, which from a car seemed only a few inches wide was, in fact, almost as wide as both my feet. The lanes themselves were enormous, and the highway as a whole seemed to be an entire world wide, rather than a narrow strip of pavement with a little bit of paint.

Also, it was *loud*. Very loud.

Cars, trucks, semis, car-haulers, panel vans, all roared past so fast they were barely even a blur, the combined noise of engines and movement a constant, almost deafening wall of sound. I had to turn my music up to hear it over the noise, and for the first several minutes I found myself startled every time a huge semi barreled past at seventy miles per hour, the wind battering me even when I walked as far from the edge of the highway as I could.

Now, don't get me wrong, I wasn't regretting my decision. A few miles in, and I started to get used to the noise and the battering wind of passing trucks. But…it was a little scarier walking along a freeway than I'd expected.

Some part of me, the part spoiled by growing up white, well-to-do, and pretty, expected someone to stop and offer me a ride almost immediately.

I guess it was kind of hard to tell what I looked like from the driver's seat of a car going eighty on a freeway. Whatever the reason, a few miles turned into a few hours, and a few hours turned into almost a whole day. My feet hurt like a bitch and I'd drunk almost all of my water, and I was hungry as hell.

I was in a section of freeway where it was miles and miles between exits, which meant I had no clue how much farther I had to walk before I came to a decent exit for food and lodging.

I was, at that point, beginning to question the wisdom of this plan.

A tan Buick slid past going way too slow to be on the freeway. The driver tapped the brakes, and then swerved erratically onto the shoulder. Stopped. Brake lights held, and it became clear the driver was waiting for me to get in, so I hustled my steps to the front passenger side and leaned to peer into the window.

The driver was an elderly woman—by elderly, I mean snow-white hair in a thinning bouffant spray of strands, blue standout veins on stick-thin arms and hands, eyes that could barely see over the steering wheel, and the kindliest smile I'd ever seen.

"A little darling like you shouldn't be on the side of the freeway, young lady. Get in and I'll take you somewhere safe." She patted the seat beside her and I, without hesitation, got in.

The inside of the car smelled like…well, the indefinable scent that meant "old person." She had classical music playing softly. She was wearing a matching pink crushed velvet tracksuit with Nike walking shoes as white as her hair. She wore huge chunky costume jewelry; massive square rings on several fingers and an even bigger necklace, with matching earrings that were heavy enough to make her earlobes droop.

She was one in a million, and looked as if she had driven up from Miami Beach.

"Hi, I'm Poppy," I said. "Thanks for stopping for me."

"Nice to meet you, Poppy. I'm Delia." She waved at the shoulder of the highway as we merged into the traffic. "I saw you walking there with that big backpack, and I thought of my great-granddaughter walking alone on the side of the freeway and I just had to stop. It's simply not safe. Where are your parents, young lady?"

I had to laugh, she was so sweetly earnest. She probably assumed I was a runaway half the age I really am. "Well, that's where I'm going. My whole family lives in Alaska, and I'm making a fun road trip out of getting to them."

"Oh my, that's ridiculous. You can't walk to Alaska."

"No, but I can walk and hitch rides."

"Not everyone who stops for you is going to be a nice little old lady like me, you know. Something awful could happen."

"Sure, it could. But something awful could happen anywhere, anytime. I've been living in New York City, and I'm pretty certain it's far more dangerous than the side of the highway."

"Oh, I don't know about that, but I see your point." She turned the radio down so it was nearly inaudible. "So, where should I take you? I can't take you all the way back to New York City, I'm afraid, but if you called your mother I'm sure we could work out some way of getting you home safely."

I laughed. "Oh, no, that won't be necessary. I'm perfectly fine, Delia, but thank you. My mother is in Alaska, like I said."

"Well, shouldn't you ask her to buy you a plane ticket or something? Hitchhiking simply isn't safe. Not anymore, if it ever was."

"I'm having an adventure, that's all. I'll be perfectly safe."

She huffed, not liking that answer but sensing that I wouldn't be dissuaded. "Does your mother know you're hitchhiking like this?"

I laughed. "Heck no! She'd be apoplectic if she knew. But I'm eighteen and I've been living alone in New York since I was seventeen, so I'm not about to go asking her permission."

"On your own since you were seventeen? Are you a runaway?"

Honestly, the inquisition was getting a little annoying. "No ma'am. I was in college. Columbia University."

"Well, you can't be finished yet, and it's got to be the middle of a term, right? So why are you going to Alaska?"

I couldn't entirely suppress a sigh of annoyance. "I dropped out. It just wasn't for me, for a lot of reasons. I'm an artist, and the college scene was honestly just cramping my voice as an artist, and left me no real time for painting or anything but classes and studying. So, I'm hitchhiking to Alaska and thinking about what my next step will be."

Delia frowned at me. "One of my granddaughters dropped out of college to be an artist, and now she's addicted to drugs and living in a tunnel or something in Chicago."

I sighed yet again. "I'm not addicted to drugs, and have no plans to start. I don't even like drinking all that much. But I appreciate your concern."

Delia chuckled. "Am I being a know-it-all busybody again? My grandchildren all get upset with me quite often for that. I just can't help wanting the best for everyone."

I thought about lying, but it just wasn't my style. "Honestly, Delia, yes, a bit. It's all right, I understand and I appreciate your concern. But I do promise, I'm safe and being cautious about who I accept rides from."

I mean, after all, I'd anticipated exactly what happened with good ol' Donny Zelinski.

"I only live a few miles from here. How about I take you to my home, cook you a meal, and you can sleep in a real bed tonight. And then, in the morning, I'll make you breakfast and take you half an hour in any direction you want. Preferably to a bus station, but if not, I'll understand."

Home-cooked food, and a bed?

Hello, generosity of strangers.

"That sounds wonderful, Delia. I'd be delighted to accept."

A fairly auspicious start to my trip, I'd say.

TWO

Errol

"THESE LOOK AMAZING, ERROL," MY EDITOR AT *National Geographic*, Len, was looking down, away from the screen of his laptop, at the iPad upon which my latest completed photography project was displayed. "Sienna and I will go through them and make some choices."

"Sounds brilliant." I was in an airport lounge in…St. Paul?

Maybe. Probably. I'd been connection hopping since yesterday morning, without sleep, so I was a bit cranky and more than a bit confused.

"What's next for you, then, Errol?"

I yawned. "Find somewhere to sleep."

"Well, yeah. But then what? Got a project lined up?"

I scrubbed my face, listening as a boarding call was announced. Not mine, so I tuned out. "I mean, I've had a few ideas. But honestly, this last project was pretty intense and I kinda need something more chill, you know? I like extreme stuff, but I've been hanging off the side of helicopters for the last six months. I wouldn't mind being on the ground for a while."

"So, ideas. Hit me."

"Well, I'm in the States, right? My ticket is supposed to take me all the way back to Christchurch, but the only way I could get out of Norway was through Atlanta which somehow included a layover in St. Paul…whatever, you don't care about my connections. Point is, the idea that's been rattling around in my head lately is sort of a different take on things for me. I was thinking something like a photographic essay of unusual parts of the States. The title I've got in my head is 'The Unseen America.' Sort of my own unique take. The kind of shots I'm good at, but here, Stateside. A tour of the country, no real itinerary, no plan, just…bang about with a few cameras."

"A break from the usual, but still working." Len chuckled. "Meaning, getting me to pay for you to take time off."

"Yeah," I laughed. "But you'd get a few thousand

photos out of it, at least. I just need a bit of time to recharge, you know?"

Len mused, still idly flipping through my photos, which was a collection documenting the Norwegian fjords, but most of them had been taken from the side of a hovering helicopter, or rappelling halfway down sheer vertical faces, or from a kayak...the kind of shots impossible to get—birds nesting in the cliff faces, the sea hundreds of feet below—as seen from the chimney crack of a granite face.

"How long are you thinking of spending on this?" Len asked.

I shrugged, yawned again. "I dunno. A few months, at least. Four? Maybe six."

"If I'm not getting a new project from you for four to six months, it had better be your best work yet."

"When you get it, Len, I promise you, it'll be a cover feature. You'll want to give me at least half the rag. Maybe even a full magazine special feature. It'll be brilliant, I swear. Also, if I don't take time off, my work will go to shit. So there's that."

"Sounds suspiciously like an ultimatum," Len said, smirking at me.

"It's not even a real holiday, Len. I'll still be shooting just about every day. It's just not a high adrenaline, wildly dangerous project way the hell out in the wops, accessible only by helo. I love those, you know I do. But I've been doing those back-to-back for years now. I need a little break from it, is all."

"I know, I know." Len closed the iPad and rubbed his jaw as he looked at me on his computer. "All right. Six months. Then I'm gonna need a pitch for something high octane. A real attention-grabber Errol Sylvain special."

"How about I give you the pitch now? All the highest, most challenging mountain peaks in the world, as only I can shoot them. K2, Annapurna, Everest, Kilimanjaro, Fuji, St. Helen's, Kilauea. Like, standing on the actual real highest peak? Looking down into an active volcano. The corpses marking the path on Everest. Hanging off a cliff on K2, or El Capitan. Crazy, crazy shit. I've wanted to do that one for a while, and after a nice long boring break, I'll be all geared for a new challenge."

Len's eyes lit up. "All right. If you'll do the peaks project next, I'll give you six months at full salary, and full creative control over this. No check-ins, nothing. Just take six months off, call it a sabbatical, and if you've got a killer new photo essay at the end of it, great. Beautiful. But I'll expect the peaks project ASAP following the time off."

"Sweet as," I breathed. "You're the best ever, Len."

"I know. You're lucky you're a talented sonofabitch."

"I'll ring you up in six months, bro."

"Sounds good. Have fun and try not to…what's the phrase you use? Cork it?"

I laughed. "Cark—try not to cark it." I shook my head, snickering. "One of these days you'll get the hang of it."

"Not bloody likely, cuz," he said, in a passable impression of my native accent. "I'm an old dog, and that's a new trick." He glanced to the side, lifted his chin in acknowledgment, and then glanced back at me. "Gotta go, my nine thirty is here."

"Chur. See ya."

My iPad made the disconnection sound, and I flipped the lid closed.

"Flight DL 1234 to Los Angeles, now boarding…" the PA squawked, and I began gathering my things, as that was my flight.

But now I realized I needed a new plan. My flight to LAX was a connection meant to take me home to Christchurch, where I'd been planning on kicking off a short holiday before my next gig. But now, with Len's blessing to take an extended sabbatical, I needed a new destination. I could just take the connection and figure things out from LA, but I hated LA something fierce, for reasons I always had trouble articulating. It was too…everything. And not enough of anything. See? I just didn't like it there, and I'd rather start in New York. I was more comfortable with New York, if nothing else.

So I hiked my bags onto my shoulders and headed up to the counter, where a pretty young black woman with fantastically long box braids offered me a welcoming smile. "Hi, how can I help you?"

I leaned against the counter and smiled back. "I'm meant to be on this flight to LA, but I need to reroute. Can you switch me to a flight to New York?"

She scanned my boarding pass, displayed on my cell, and then tapped at her keyboard for a while. Frowned, tapped again. "Well…not directly, or soon, unfortunately. If you can wait till tomorrow morning, you could fly directly to La Guardia at six thirty, or if you want to leave as soon as possible…no, you won't make that connection." She chewed on her lower lip, and bobbed her head. "Well, maybe. If you're quick. How do you feel about running across airports?"

I laughed. "Piece of piss. Done it heaps."

She blinked, snickered. "Piece of piss, huh? Is that Aussie slang?"

"Nah love, I'm a Kiwi. New Zealand."

"Oh. Cool. So, yeah. So you get on this flight to LAX, and if you can get across the airport to your connection in less than fifteen minutes, you can fly into Atlanta, layover forty-five minutes there, and then fly into New York."

I sighed a laugh. "Fuck me, what a mare." I wiped my face. "I just came from Atlanta, been on a two-and-a-half-hour layover here, and Oslo before that. Now back to Atlanta?"

"Man, that's a lot of flying. Only other option I see is find a room tonight and fly direct tomorrow. That's all the options I've got, Mr. Sylvain, I'm sorry."

I shook my head. "Yeah nah. I'll take the long route. Back to Atlanta, eh?"

She tapped a while longer, and then printed out a new boarding pass, handed it to me with a flirty smile. "Remember, the second that plane parks, you better be moving. Your connection to Atlanta is wheels up in fifteen from when this one lands. I hope you're fast, honey."

"Piece of piss," I said again.

She just laughed and waved me toward the jetway. "Go on, get your seat. You miss this flight, you're outta luck till tomorrow."

I boarded, found my seat, which fortunately wasn't in the very, *very* back, just most of the way back and the middle seat. I'm not a small guy, so sitting middle was the worst, but the woman in the window seat was already nodding off, and the man in the aisle seat gave me a glare that said I'd better not even ask about switching, so I stuffed my baggage overhead, took my seat, and tried to will my shoulders to be narrower and my legs shorter.

Swear to God, when I finally land in New York, I'm not stepping foot on another airplane for at least six months.

Longer, if I could talk Len into extending my sabbatical.

Despite my exhaustion, there was no way I was gonna be able to sleep wedged in the middle like this, so I slid my iPad out of my backpack and searched the internet for a suitable automobile to live in for the next six months.

By the time wheels squealed the touchdown on the La Guardia runway, I was nearly delirious, but I had a reliable line on a van I could buy…if I could find a way from the airport to upstate New York.

The trip included a horrendously expensive taxi ride to a bus station, and then a one-way ticket up-state, and then a four-hour hike on foot from the bus station along a rural highway to a dirt road, and from that dirt road to a two-track into the woods…and I'd been awake over twenty-four hours. Hadn't had a real meal in as long. If I didn't wind up with a decent, running, reliable caravan out of this, I'd pack a sad right in the dirt.

The two-track wound through towering, swaying pines, which were arrayed in neat, precise lines, which meant it, was planted forest. The deeper and deeper I walked into the forest, the more the wind soughed, the late evening sunlight dappling the sky orange-red.

Way out in the wops, this was.

Finally, the two-track twisted almost back on itself, and then the forest abruptly opened into a clearing a good full kilometer across. In the clearing was a small ramshackle house with dirty white siding, an old, leaning red barn with an attached, roofless silo, and a maze of electric wire fencing keeping forty or so head of cattle and sheep and horses separated. The moment I popped out of the tree line, a chorus of barks announced my presence, and I saw three or four large white dogs running along the fence lines, back and forth, fixated on me. At an angle to the house opposite the barn was a long low blue pole barn, the front doors opened, showing a messy jumble of farming equipment and tool chests and junked old cars; when the dogs started barking, a tall older man emerged from the jumble, spotting me.

The two-track became a narrow, rutted gravel drive leading between fenced paddocks to the house and barn, rusted gates leaning this way and that, ready to be swung across the path as needed. I followed the driveway toward the house, only to stop short of the pole barn when a fifth dog trotted out from behind the waiting man—the dog was enormous, with long dirty white fur and a deep, ripping bark. The dog stayed within six feet of the man, waiting for a command as it stood growling and barking at me.

"I'm Errol Sylvain," I said, offering a friendly smile. "I emailed you about the van."

The man, pushing sixty-five or seventy, was lean and hard with a gray buzz cut and a shaggy salt-and-pepper beard. He wore dirty jeans, a white tank top, and had a big silver spanner in one hand and a greasy rag in the other.

He made a flicking gesture at the barking dog. "Colby—hush."

The dog immediately went silent, glancing at his master. The man stabbed a finger at the ground. "Colby, heel."

The dog trotted to his master's right leg and sat down, panting.

"Good boy, Colby." He extended a hand to me. "Dillon Hendrick."

"Pleasure to meet you, Dillon. I'm Errol."

He eyed the sky. "Gettin' on to evening. Took your time getting here."

I shrugged. "Well, I had to get a bus from the city and then walk here from the bus station."

Dillon blinked at me. "Damn, son, that's a hike. If you'd'a emailed me, I'd have picked you up."

"Now you say," I laughed. "No worries, though. Have you got the van?"

"Yeah, it's in here." He aimed the spanner at the pole barn. "Been giving her a once-over, makin' sure it's all here and in working order."

"All good, then?"

"Oh yeah. I put a new belt on, the old one was squeaking. Could use an oil change and a new set of tires if you're planning on going anywhere far."

"Well, I'm actually planning on living out of it for the next six months or so."

He nodded, scratched his jaw with the greasy rag. "I got some newer tires in there somewhere, and some oil. If you wanna cop a squat for an hour or so, I'll do it for you."

"That sounds choice. I'm beat, and got no clue where I'd get that done anyhow."

"My missus could fix you something to eat, if you're hungry."

"Well, I wouldn't want to impose, but I could eat."

He flipped the spanner in his hand. "As long as your money's good, we're good."

"Eighty-eight hundred, yeah?"

"That's what we agreed on," Dillon said, nodding.

No stranger to potentially risky cash deals in remote areas, I had the appropriate amount of cash pre-counted and in an envelope, which I dug out of my back pocket and handed to him. "All there. Can I see the van before we call it done, though?"

Dillon took the envelope and it disappeared into his own back pocket without being counted. "Sure thing, man. In here."

In the pole barn, but just inside, was the van—a 1976 Westfalia camper van. Bright green, with a yellow peace sign painted on the back that was probably new when the thing was new in the mid-seventies. Not in mint condition by any stretch of the imagination, it had spots of rust around the wheel arches, and on the bumpers, but it was straight, and he'd claimed in the ad online that it had pretty low miles and had been well maintained by him, the original owner. I'd be getting a hell of a deal, if it all proved out.

The sliding door moved open smoothly, and the interior was clean and intact, if more than a bit dated. Green plaid cloth, a tiny kitchenette, pop top, rock and roll bed, plenty of storage. A bit worn, a bit faded, but clean and neat and in working order. The engine bay was open, showing the tiny motor. Dillon slid into the driver's seat, one leg hanging out the open door, twisted the key; the engine coughed once, sputtered, caught, the tailpipe belched a bit of white smoke, and then it set to purring quietly.

"If I fixed the rust on the arches and bumpers and redid the interior, I could get a few grand more for it, but I ain't got the time, honestly. Rather just take what I can get and be done with it, you know?" He patted the dash as he shut the motor off and slid out. "Me and the missus bought her together back in '76, followed the Grateful Dead around in her for a couple years. Lotta good memories in the old girl, but we won't be doin' any road trips any time soon, so we figured it was time for someone new to love her. Keep an eye on the oil; she's got a leak somewhere inside. Just burns up, don't drip none, but every once in a while she'll need a top off. Pop top opens nice and easy, bench folds flat, all the kitchenette stuff works just fine. Wipers, lights, all that, it's all good. New headlight lamps recently, I should mention." He leaned in the front door, tapped a part of the dash. "Only thing I've done was pull the cigarette lighter and replace it with this one-ten outlet, so you can plug in a cell phone. Don't connect to nothing but power, but it'll keep your phone charged while you drive."

"Smart touch, that." I felt a shiver of something

slither over my spine. Excitement. This was the start of a new kind of adventure. "Looks great, Dillon. Real great."

He nodded. "So we've got a deal?"

"Sure have."

We shook hands, and after signing the title I became the owner of the van. I figured there were hurdles yet to face regarding the legality of driving it in the States as a citizen of another country, but I had a legal and valid NZ license. I'd just have to muddle through the rest. Dillon had a shouted conversation with his wife—the missus—about fixing something to eat, and then Dillon and I shared a beer while he changed the oil and put on newer tires which he procured from somewhere in the middle of the maze of parts and old cars and tractors and implements cluttering the interior of the pole barn. I asked him what else I'd have to do to legally drive around, and he explained registration and insurance requirements to me, and honestly it sounded like a real pain in the ass, but I was going to be living and driving in the van for the next six months, so I'd have to just grin and bear the process.

The missus turned out to be a female version of Dillon—tall and lean and willowy where Dillon was tall and lean and whipcord hard. Her graying hair was tied back in a loose ponytail, and she wore colorful clothes that had probably been new when the van I now owned had been new. She brought out hamburgers with wheat bread in place of actual buns, and crumbled potato crisps. It was delicious, being home-cooked and the first non-airline food I'd had in two days.

By this time, Dillon had finished the oil change and tire replacement. We ate, and chatted, and by this time it was near dark.

"Well, I'd best be off," I said. "Thanks for the hospitality, Dillon."

"Where ya headed to?" he asked.

I shrugged. "No real destination. Just exploring. I'm a photographer for *National Geographic*."

"You on some kind of assignment?"

I shrugged. "Sort of. My project is something I'm calling 'The Unseen America.' Weird stuff, out of the way places, unusual perspectives. That kinda thing.'

Dillon laughed. "Well, it's a big ol' country, friend. You could spend a lifetime and not see a quarter of it." He scratched his jaw. "We saw a hell of a lot of it when we were Deadheads, doing sorta what you're doing." He eyed me. "If you got no plans, you want an idea to start you off?"

"Sure, bro. Hit me with it."

"Head down to the Mammoth Cave in

Kentucky. It's a nice drive down from here, and the caves are worth seeing. From there, you're in a good spot to head north, south, or straight west. My advice to you, if you're interested in unusual and unique perspectives, and ain't in a hurry, is stay off the freeways. Stick to state and local highways, the little two-lane ones. Ain't the most direct route anywhere, but that's where the real America lives. Won't see shit going eighty on an interstate."

I smirked. "Will the van even do eighty?"

Dillon laughed. "If she will it won't be for long. I wouldn't do more than sixty-five, if you want to keep her healthy."

"Brilliant advice, my friend. Thanks again for everything."

"Pleasure. Safe travels to you, Errol."

Still exhausted, but refreshed by the break and the home cooking, and energized by the prospect of a whole country to explore, I tossed my gear into the back of the van, shook Dillon's hand, and headed out. The radio was tuned to a local country music station—weird stuff, you ask me, but I didn't mind it, mostly,—and I heard a phrase: "…get in my old Bronco, point the headlights south…"

No clue about the band or song, but it fit, so I turned it up and did what song said: pointed my headlights south, consulting my phone's GPS for directions—sticking to the small highways, county lines and two-lane roads in the open country.

Windows down, stars overhead, bitter American drip coffee in a Styrofoam cup from a gas station, munching on oily crisps and jerked beef, nowhere to be, no one to please but me.

I'd a feeling this was going to be a great holiday.

THREE

Poppy

I HAD A STUFFED-TO-BURSTING BELLY, THANKS TO DELIA insisting on making a three-egg omelet, a full pound of bacon, and two thick slices of homemade bread, along with coffee so thick I wasn't sure she measured the grounds so much as poured with her eyes closed. She also insisted I call my mother while she drove me, as promised, thirty minutes west from her house.

"Poppy! How nice to hear from you, honey."

I couldn't help but smile at the sound of her voice. "Hi, Momma. How are you?"

"Oh, I'm spectacular, darling. In between showings, grabbing a bite of breakfast with Lucas. What are you up to?"

I hesitated over my answer, especially when Delia gave me a hard, expectant look. "Oh, well, you know. I, uh, officially dropped out of Columbia yesterday. Thought you should know."

"I suppose this is a bit odd coming from your mother, but I must say, it's about time. So what are you doing?"

"I'm traveling and exploring my options." A nice, neutral answer.

"Exploring your options." She sighed. "I suppose that's teenage code for something I probably wouldn't approve of if I knew the full story."

"Pretty much."

"Just make me a couple promises, Poppy. No stupid stuff. No hitchhiking on the side of the highway at midnight. If someone gives you the creeps, you run fast and far. You get into trouble, call your momma. Just be smart, Poppy. Just because you're young doesn't mean you're invincible. And honestly, with your looks, you need to be even more careful."

"I'm careful, Mom. No creepers, no dumb risks."

"A huge part of me is screaming to demand you get on the next airplane to Ketchikan, but I know better. I think I did a little too good a job of raising you girls to be strong and independent."

"By the way, I gave my art department advisor, Mrs. DuPuis, your address. She gave me her old vintage Minolta, and I'm going to be mailing my rolls to her to develop, and she's going to mail the processed photographs to you to hang on to for me until I get there."

"Am I allowed to look at them?" she asked.

I laughed. "Yes, Mother. Just don't get fingerprints on them."

"Darling. You do know film cameras were the only kind of cameras we had until rather recently, right?"

"Yes, Mother."

"Will there be anything in the photos that will shock me?"

I hummed. "I don't know. Maybe? Probably not, but you never know."

A pause. "Is this the right thing for you, Poppy? Is this going to bring you joy and happiness and purpose?"

I didn't answer right away, because when Mom asked a question like that, she expected a thoughtful answer. "I mean, it feels like it. I was suffocating in New York. Artistically, I was being hamstrung at Columbia. I had friends; you know I've always made friends easily. But…I'm leaving them all behind and they don't seem to miss me nor I them. I don't know. I'm not going to say I'm looking for something, I'm just…"

"Eighteen and spreading your wings."

"Something like that."

"Just be safe. That's all I ask."

"I will."

I ended the call and slid the phone into my purse, and then looked at Delia. "Satisfied?"

She shook her head. "Well, I wouldn't have let *my* daughter go hitchhiking across the country at eighteen, but then I'm old-fashioned."

"If you think about it historically, though, this is the way of life, Delia. You strike out on your own. Find your own way. It's all I'm doing."

"Men did that, dear—we women stayed home and raised babies."

I snorted. "True. But there were women who did go out on their own. And anyway, it's what I'm doing. I really do appreciate your concern. I know you mean well."

We drove a while longer, and then we reached a junction where two highways met. Delia pulled to the shoulder and put the Buick into park. She pointed one way. "That way takes you to US-40, which will take you to Ohio." She pointed the other way. "That way takes you to US-119, south toward Kentucky by way of West Virginia."

I looked around—four-lane highways, a Sunoco, a maze of entrance and exit ramps; endless possibilities.

"This is perfect, Delia. Thank you for setting such a wonderful tone for my trip."

"I think what you're doing is foolish, and you ought to go home straight away. But I'm also a bit jealous, if I'm honest. I was never brave enough to do what you're doing."

I leaned across and hugged her. "Thank you again for everything. Be well."

She patted my cheek. Reached into the pocket of her cardigan and held something in her hand—she took my hand in hers and pressed something into my palm. "Take it and no arguments, if just to soothe my conscience that I've done everything I can to help you be safe."

It felt like cash rolled up, and I knew I couldn't refuse it. So I pocketed it and shook my head. "It's not necessary, Delia. But thank you."

She just patted my hand. "Be safe. Be smart."

"I will." I got out, shouldered my backpack and arranged everything properly. Waved. "Bye, Delia."

"Goodbye, dear. Safe travels and Godspeed."

She pulled a U-turn and headed back the way she came, and then after a moment was out of sight and I was alone. Ohio, or Kentucky? North or south?

Either direction was the wrong way for my eventual destination, but for some reason my gut said south, so south I went.

I followed US-119 on foot, on the shoulder, for a long time. Hours. Miles. A truck stopped for me, about three hours into the day, then later on a cube van marked with the logo of a local plumbing service pulled over. The gentleman within was middle-aged, rounding, balding, sweating, smelling of chemicals and tobacco. The interior of his cab was cluttered with Mt. Dew bottles, empty cigarette boxes, and McDonald's bags, but his brown eyes were kind and he offered to take me three exits down, a good forty-five minutes drive for him and hours of walking for me. He told me about his daughter, my age, a journalism major at Penn State, who had a serious boyfriend he didn't like, and about how she was a cheerleader and he went to all the football games just to watch her cheer even though he was more of a basketball fan…I had a feeling he was talking about his daughter more to put me at ease than anything, which was sweet. He eventually got around to introducing himself as José, and I told him my story, leaving college to explore as I headed for Alaska on foot.

I got the usual disbelief and warnings and such, but then José started telling me about when he was sixteen and living in Mexico and his parents decided to emigrate here to the States. They got separated at the border and he ended up going through immigration alone, and how hard he worked for his citizenship and how he built his plumbing company on his own from nothing…

We reached the exit, and he stopped at the stop sign at the top of the exit and I got out, said goodbye, and headed back onto the highway.

So it went. Hours on foot, a ride for a few miles or a few hours, conversation with interesting people. A long-haul trucker named Jerri—with an I—took me from West Virginia halfway through Kentucky, and good grief Jerri was interesting. Jerri didn't identify as either gender, and wore…his? Her? Their?—Their, I suppose, hair in a long, thick, wavy, mass of glossy blond that wouldn't have been out of place in a shampoo commercial, but also a heavy stubble beard, lipstick and eyeliner, masculine tattoos on burly arms, a girly pink tank top with a jean skirt… it was confusing, but Jerri was sweet and soft-spoken and bought me lunch at Sonic and talked my ear off about everything from how *Rogue One* was the best *Star Wars* movie, to the effects of political policy on living as a nonbinary transgender person.

Along the way, between rides, I walked. I ended up discovering that I was much happier sticking to local county highways than interstates and major highways. It was safer, for one thing. Fewer semis barreling past at seventy-five, less risk of some distracted asshole veering out of their lane and turning me into toothpaste. Perhaps, being more remote and less traveled, the smaller county highways carried a bit more risk of being picked up by skeezeballs and creepers, but hey, there was a trade-off to everything, right?

And the other benefit to sticking to small, deserted, rural roads was that there was a hell of a lot more interesting stuff to photograph. I got cool shots of all sorts of things. Roadkill twisted into pained contortions, old abandoned cars on the side of the road off in the tall grass with stickers and wheels missing and weeds growing out of the wheel wells, toppling old barns that had probably been standing since the Civil War, giant six-foot-tall sunflowers growing by the acre, all angled to face the lowering orange sunset; I photographed ancient oak trees standing tall in hayfields like lone sentinels, tiny farmhouses next to industrial-sized barns and silos, and train tracks like endless fingers vanishing into distant points, and trestles over rivers smeared with impossible graffiti, and overpasses like abbreviated tunnels casting patches of shade on the sunbaked asphalt.

I shot at dawn and dusk, noon and midnight, mostly in black and white. Compulsively, obsessively. I shot the cars that picked me up, the semis as they waited for me to climb up, I shot the drivers (with hand-scribbled releases in case I ended up turning the photo into a sellable piece) as they smiled at me awkwardly or naturally, with even white teeth and meth-fucked gaps.

I reached Louisville at four in the morning in the cab of a long-haul dairy trucker named Jeb, who let me off at a motel he knew was safe and cheap and near a nice little local trunk line that would put me through to Missouri, eventually. The next morning, or, rather, late afternoon, I mailed several dozen rolls of film to Mrs. DuPuis and purchased more from a local supermarket.

I then set out on foot, feet aching and legs tired, but finding a bizarre joy in the journey. The long hours on foot shooting everything I saw was sparking my creativity; there were a number of shots I'd taken that I just knew would end up on canvas. I was more inspired than ever to paint, which was tricky since I'd sent my painting supplies to Ketchikan. I had my iPad and stylus, so I could sketch and do digital stuff, but it wasn't the same as putting on my dad's old white button-down and standing in front of a freshly stretched canvas.

I wasn't even lonely.

Mostly.

I had lots of fascinating conversations with lots

of fascinating people. The only real skeezeball I'd encountered was Donny, that first day. Everyone else who had stopped for me and given me rides had been kind, generous, honest, and good. Jeb, the trucker who had taken me to Louisville, had been one of the most foul-mouthed, vulgar, strange, and offensive people I'd ever met in my life, but it wasn't directed at me, it was just…him. Every sentence featured at least two F-bombs, minimum, and everything he saw and thought was verbalized through a filter of vulgar jokes. It was honestly fascinating, once I realized he wasn't being intentionally offensive, he was just a lonely old man who lived his life in the cab of a semi talking to himself and occasionally to the other truckers via CB radio.

I wasn't lonely.

I was horny, though. Good shitting mother of demons, I was horny. And no mistake, I took the time to alleviate the pressure on my own frequently. I'd discovered masturbation at thirteen, and until I'd managed to get myself a vibrator at sixteen, I'd learned a lot of creative ways to pleasure myself. Mornings were for coffee and jilling off. Of course, waking up in a motel was not exactly conducive to coffee access, and without consistent Wi-Fi access, I couldn't reliably find any visual stimuli. And god knew my memory banks of hot sexy times were a little fuzzy, seeing as the last time I'd had sex with a boy was my dumb ex four months ago. I'd sworn off men at the time, and then I'd been so caught up in the drama of what I was doing with my life, and my art, and if I was meant to go to college at all, that I'd avoided hookups to focus on sorting myself out. And now, this road trip. And no, I was for damn sure not about to get jiggy with a long-haul trucker in the back of his sleeper cab. Most of them were old enough to be my father, for one thing.

I mean, if I managed to meet a hot guy that didn't feel like a skeeze, I'd possibly be willing to let some fun times roll, but mostly I wanted to just do my walking, and find rides with truckers, and take my photographs. But god, I was horny.

I needed something more than my own fingers, more than my little silver bullet vibrator, which was the only sex toy I'd felt was easily transportable. I needed a man. But I didn't *want* to need a man.

I also didn't have the emotional energy to deal with hardening my heart and mind for a one-night hookup, which I mostly loathed. I'd do it if I got desperate enough, but I preferred to cultivate…temporary, short-lived, low-emotion flings. The barista at a coffee shop away from my usual stomping grounds, for instance. Or the TA of a class a friend was in. Or a construction worker doing welding on a building I passed on the way to the subway station. It wouldn't be a one-night hookup but, instead, a couple days or a couple weeks of decently arousing fucking that didn't involve a lot of exchanges of life stories or anything. And when I was done, I could alter my routine a little, and that particular fling would be over. No phone numbers, no texting, no explanations of why this was only temporary.

On the road like this, hookups were the only possibility and I just wasn't feeling it. I needed something more. Something better. Something different. What? I had no clue. Thus the problem.

Would I have to wait until I arrived in Alaska to find what I was looking for?

What was I, in fact, even looking for?

God, I had no clue.

All I knew about myself at the moment was that I liked walking the county highways taking photographs. I liked hanging out with long-haul truckers and old grandmas and kindly plumbers. I liked blue skies and cheap motels and greasy diner food. I liked being on my own. I liked the feeling of an endless world to explore.

What I didn't know about myself was how to fill the hole where my heart was, or even how the hole got there. How had I'd gone eighteen years without realizing there was a giant, gaping hole in my soul.

Further mysteries included why I had to be cursed with a wickedly, insanely, mind-bogglingly out-of-control sex drive, but also with a fiercely independent nature that refused to depend on anyone and refused to ask for help and refused to let me even, for a moment, let anyone in to see the soft tender center of my soul.

I didn't have any answers to any of that.

I also didn't want to admit I'd possibly started this wild-ass adventure in search of answers to questions I didn't even know how to articulate.

FOUR

Errol

THE ONLY THING THIS VAN DIDN'T HAVE THAT I KNEW I'd miss was a shower. But being a bachelor, I didn't mind going a while between bathing. Also, I was a photojournalist used to living in remote locations with scant access to civilized amenities like western bathrooms, and often went long periods of time smelling like yak sac. I mean, the only person I had to impress with smelling good was myself, right?

I'd stopped in the next major town closest to where I'd bought the van and spent several angry, frustrating hours negotiating a maze of impenetrable bureaucracy getting basic insurance so I could register the vehicle and not get pulled over by local law enforcement. I found a grocery and stocked up on basic food items, meat and cheese and bread and beer, mostly.

Then, I'd hit the road. Headed toward the caves my mate Dillon had mentioned, by way of two-lane roads winding through the countryside. Good old Google told me it should take me about twelve hours driving time to get to the caves from where I was outside Utica, but the slow winding back roads route I took added several hours to that. Plus, I stopped to snap photos of whatever caught my interest. For the first time since I'd started working for Nat Geo, I wasn't hyper-focused on one thing. And there was no adrenaline. It was nice, actually. See a nice old barn? Stop for a photo. Stretch the old legs, bask in the sun and enjoy the peace and quiet and solitude.

I was in no hurry to get anywhere, so if I saw a likely looking detour, I took it. If I saw a side road or turnoff that burbled my curiosity, I followed it. Sometimes it took me to a dead end or a big circle out of my way through rural nowhere dirt roads, but I always got some good shots out of the detour, so it was never wasted time.

I already knew what my favorite shot was so far. I'd taken exactly one such detour—a two-track dirt road off the already remote county highway I was on, which took me through cornfields and then through a stand of trees, on the other side of which was a fenced-in pasture containing a few dozen head of cattle.

It was a quaint, pleasantly pastoral scene, so I parked the caravan, tossed my trusty Nikon over my shoulder, and my backup Canon over the other, and hopped the fence. The pasture was several hectares of open grassland, rolling hills here and there with a few tall old spreading oaks. The cows were clumped hither and yon lowing softly, shaking great shaggy heads. These were no Holsteins or the familiar breeds I knew, but rather great furry, longhaired ones with curving horns and broad flat foreheads. A few of them ambled over to me, sniffing warily, accepting forehead scratches, which told me they were used to human interaction. I snapped a few photos of them as they clustered around me, curious and gentle.

Then a massive old bull with huge horns and small beady eyes trotted over, reddish-gold hair, curly and shaggy. He, the bull I mean, did not appreciate my presence in the least. A point he made very clear by angling toward me, shaking his colossal head with those wicked curving horns, making angry noises at me. I backed away from him toward the fence, but that wasn't good enough for the touchy old fucker.

Oh no, he wanted me *gone*, so the closer toward the fence I got, the more earnestly he chased me, bellowing what I was certain were the cow versions of curses. I didn't dare turn my back on him, so I did my best to run backward and, of course, I snapped shots of him from the hip as I went.

And then my heel caught on a huge pile of shit, and down I went, ass over teakettle, cradling my cameras out of instinct. By the time I hit the ground, Mr. Bull was on top of me, staring down at me, head shaking and nodding. I lifted my camera, clicking the shutter as fast as I could as he bore down. I was, clearly, a photographer first and a human with a normal sense of self-preservation second.

A normal person would leave the cameras and run, but not me, oh no. Huge angry bull weighing thousands of pounds coming at you all hooves and horns and flaring nostrils? Take a dozen snaps first, then run—shooting as you run, hoping a few of the backward shots were usable.

I hopped the fence, and the moment I had the fence between him and me, I spun around and got face to face with him, and got the money shot—his head lowered, nostrils wide and dark, beady dark eyes angry under a curtain of reddish-gold hair, horns curving toward the center of the shot like spears.

I pulled up the last shot, and what a beauty.

Captured the great old bloke in all his angry glory, mere inches away, and even on the screen he just exuded protective threat.

He bellowed at me all the way to my van—*that's right, bitch, you better run!* That's how I heard it, at least.

I continued on that way, making slow progress to Kentucky. I took a six-hour detour to get a single shot of a rock face, risking life and limb as I hiked off the highway and through scrub forest and dense brush until I was at the base of a mammoth rock face some fifty feet high, a sheer outcropping of gray weathered granite. Not content with a shot looking up, though. Hell no, not me. I climbed the damn thing, despite the multiple signs warning of danger and advertising legal action if caught. I just had to not die and not get caught, that's all. I mean, I'd once donned a "borrowed" HAZMAT suit and hiked into Chernobyl and filled an entire memory card with highly illegal and medically hazardous photographs. So hiking a tiny little outcropping of rock? Child's play. I was an experienced mountaineer, rock climber, and rappeler, so this was very literally a walk in the park. But still, worth it for the straight-down view from the top of the rock face, which Google image searches told me was a pretty well-known tourist attraction in the area.

Forty-eight hours after leaving Utica, New York, I finally reached Mammoth Cave, Kentucky, and arranged a private tour before the caves were open to the public—a perk of being a Nat Geo photographer.

God, the shots I got. The guide assigned to me was, fortunately, a young woman newly hired just weeks before, and if I knew anything besides photography, it was how to flex my admittedly ridiculous good looks to my advantage. Flirt, banter, tell tame but thrilling stories of embedding with a unit of SAS on assignment in Afghanistan, making stepping a bit beyond the designated safe areas seem just plain silly. The best shots were ones my guide protested the most, where I had to climb off the path and clamber across slick rock surfaces and cling like a spider in precarious positions with the camera clutched to my face clicking off shots so fast it was almost machine-gunning. Worth it, though. Even when my foot slipped and I almost slid into a crevasse, only catching myself on a stalagmite at the last moment, to the mortified, horrified, frozen-helpless terror of my so-called guide.

Once back on the path, I pretended my heart wasn't beating out of my chest, offering her a winsome, breezy grin. "Piece of piss, yeah?"

"Ohmygod I'm going to get into so much trouble," she gasped.

"Nah, love, not if you don't tell. As far as anyone needs to know, we stayed on the path the whole time. It's all good."

"But you just almost died."

"Yeah, but I didn't, did I?" I pulled up the shot I'd gotten for my trouble. "Plus, look at this. Worth it, I'd say."

She leaned against me to look, and bless her for the down-blouse glimpse I got. "Wow, that's amazing."

"Oh, just wait till I get it into Lightroom and touch it up a bit. That's gold, that is. My editor's gonna love that one."

We walked back, and she stuck a bit closer to me than was strictly necessary. "So, now what?" she asked.

"Well, now I find somewhere to have brekky."

"Have what?" she asked, laughing.

"Breakfast."

"Oh. There's a nice cafe in town. I'd show you, but my shift just started."

Damn, damn, damn. She was a cute little thing, too. Smiling up at me. A few more of my better stories and I'd have her eating out of the palm of my hand. But, sadly, I felt the highway calling me, louder than my need to linger till her shift was over and see what trouble we could get into.

"And I'd hang about town till your shift was over, but I gotta get a move on." I shrugged, offering a sad smile. "Thanks for the tour, though."

She seemed bummed, but smiled back at me. "No problem. Glad you didn't, you know, die in the cave. I'd have gotten fired for sure if you had."

"I always know the risks I'm taking. No worries." We were at the gift shop by then, so I said goodbye to her, picked up a little shot glass as a souvenir, and hit the highway.

No direction, no itinerary, no one to rendezvous with, just…freedom.

St. Louis. The arch, some urban exploration. Old warehouses, litter-ridden streets, and glitzy high-rises. I found an abandoned manufacturing plant in a district outside the city where I was fairly certain I was not entirely safe, pulled my van into a tiny alley behind the plant where it was less likely to be stolen or ransacked. I spent several hours shooting the plant, climbing dizzy heights up into the rafters to get bird's eye and tilt-shift shots, slid under machinery and climbed over it and squeezed behind things, ducked through broken glass windows and yanked open rusting doors.

By the time the sun had set, I had thousands of great shots. Once the sun started setting, though, some primeval instinct had me hightailing it for my van and I made tracks out of the city before dark found me in what felt to my well-honed instincts as being sus as hell.

I found a single track that dead-ended at a signal tower off in the wops miles from the highway, parked my van and caught some sleep. Dawn found me wide-awake, so I heated water for some pour-over coffee, lit my camp stove outside and rustled up some eggs. On a motorcycle trip across the wild interior of Russia, I discovered that if I stopped at a little farm somewhere, I could usually buy a dozen or two fresh eggs, which would keep unrefrigerated for months, and I'd continued that habit anywhere I went, and the rural expanses of America were no exception, and speaking the language made it easier than it'd been in Russia. I used the Westfalia's tiny fridge to keep meat and veg in, and left the beer warm because I'd rather have warm beer and fresh beef.

An hour past breakfast, I was zinging along a picturesque two-lane through cattle pastures, singing along to a Harry Styles song, and yes, I realize some may call my masculinity into question over it, but question it to my face if you dare—you'll be choking on your teeth if you do.

And that's when I saw her.

We can meet again somewhere/somewhere far away from here...

She was on her knees on the side of the highway. Bent forward, crouched, hunched. All I saw was the finest backside the world has ever known, spread out in a floral skirt, leather boots peeking underneath, a lush man of raven-black hair.

Yes, I saw the skirt, the boots, the hair, the rounded arch of her back in the ribbed white "wife beater" tank top, and god we need a better term for that shirt, don't we? I saw *her*, but I was going seventy and all I saw was that ass.

Round, juicy enough to make my jaw drop even as I hurtled past at seventy. Thick, firm. Fuck, that ass. It was...god, there are no words. Just a damned perfect bottom, so perfect my foot was mashing the brake and my hands were steering the Westfalia off onto the shoulder, because I didn't care what the situation was, I had to—*had* to—meet the owner of that ass.

Out of habit, as I exited the driver's side I yanked my camera off the passenger seat and slung it over my shoulder, because I wouldn't feel naked if you stripped me to my Jandals and not a stitch else as long as I had my camera, but without it I'd feel naked as a jaybird even if fully clothed.

She was taking a photo. In the dirt of the highway shoulder, elbows braced on the ground, bent over to get the angle, shooting a wildflower growing improbably tall out of a crack in the blacktop.

"You're in my light," she said, in the distracted tone of someone utterly focused and annoyed at disruption.

Indeed, I was casting a shadow across her shot, so I moved so I was out of the way, and watched her work. She shifted to the side, and I heard the real click of a shutter, noticed her camera was a gorgeous antique Minolta. She shuffled around on her hands and knees a bit, to get the blacktop in view I assumed, checked her settings, adjusted her ISO a tweak, snapped. *Click click click…click…clickclickclick.*

I could almost see the shot she had—the tall lavender petals with the brownish center reaching for the heavens, probably a nice strong bokeh keeping the blacktop blurred. A great, great shot, if she was worth shit as a photographer.

And, judging purely by the way she shot and shifted and shot and shifted with precise and measured movements, she was. You can tell an amateur just by the way they move, the way they hold the camera.

She was shooting manual too, because a camera that old was *only* manual. In the age of DSLR cameras worth several thousand dollars that could all but press the shutter button for you, working with an antique manual film camera meant you were either very, very serious about true classical photography, or you were a dipshit hipster who thought using a manual made you cool as you referred to yourself as a "photog."

This lovely thing was, if not an actual pro, certainly not an amateur, and was not using the vintage for imaginary cool points. An amateur would take, maybe, half a dozen shots of that flower and figure they had some good ones and move on. A pro would take a whole roll, at least.

And, indeed, as I leaned against the wobbly metal post holding up a dented, .22-pocked Deer Crossing sign, I watched her shoot and move and shoot and move, tirelessly, switch rolls with easy familiarity and speed, and shoot a whole second roll.

I had no problems watching her shoot, even though she spent a good twenty, maybe even closer to thirty minutes on that one flower, from all possible angles. Partly because I could see in my mind's eye each shot as she took it, cataloging them as good or nah. The other factor that made it rather easy to just stand and watch her was because she was bent over most of the time, leaning forward, wearing a tank top, and not wearing a bra. And behold, it was evident that she had been blessed by God and nature with the most massive and natural and beautiful breasts to ever grace womankind.

I exaggerate very little, if at all.

They were fucking glorious.

Granted, I'd spent the past six months and some weeks on the lam, far from civilization, and women in particular, so perhaps I was feeling the effects of six months of near-total celibacy—near-total because there had been a brief and aborted rendezvous with a willing farm girl outside Bergen, but her father had discovered us and chased me off before we got anywhere fun, and thereafter I'd been focused on the job. The tour guide in Kentucky had been willing enough, but number one I hadn't been sure she was even eighteen, and I know America has laws about that and I have my own moral standards, and plus, there was just something else telling me to keep going. I have no real explanation for the feeling, because you'd think me being a horny twenty-four-year-old heterosexual male on a six-month dry spell, I would jump at the first opportunity to get laid. Maybe it was fate nudging me, because fate knew I was about to meet this girl.

I mean, I'd not even seen her face yet, not fully, but I'd seen enough of her curves to know I wanted to know more just from a visual standpoint, but there was something else. Something less…tangible. Call it a woo-woo feeling, I don't know. I was just drawn to her. Drawn to the fact that she was alone on the side of a remote rural two-lane road in the wops of Missouri, spending half an hour on her knees and elbows taking several rolls of film worth of shots of a single wildflower. Something about that just…spoke to me, on an artistic, emotional, personal level.

So, you know, it wasn't just the wondrous glory of her tits and ass. Just so we're clear.

But holy shit, the tits and ass on the girl.

Finally, she pushed up to sit on her knees, capped her lens—which, I noticed, was a 50mm prime lens, ratcheting my respect up a notch—checked the count on her roll, and then stood up, letting the Minolta swing around to bump softly against the swell of her hip.

She eyed me, assessing and scrutinizing. "Anyone ever tell you it's rude to stare?"

I shrugged. "I wasn't staring, I was watching. Call it professional curiosity." I lifted my own camera in gesture.

She rolled her eyes. "Professional curiosity had you standing where you could see down my shirt, too, I suppose."

I grinned. "Nah, that was just a bonus."

"So you were looking down my shirt."

"I mean, if the look is there to be had, I ain't gonna pretend to not enjoy it. No point in taking the piss about it."

She blinked. "I have no idea what that means."

"It means don't be fuckin' unreasonable."

"Maybe things are different in Australia, but around here, if you get busted looking down a woman's shirt, you apologize."

"First, I'm from New Zealand. Second, I don't see why I should apologize. I wasn't staring. You were bent over and you knew I was there, and you know how you're dressed, and I'm guessing you're right capable of figuring out what I'd be seeing just by being stood where I am. You're looking right skux, as we say back home, and I admit I checked you out. But I don't agree I was being rude or creepy. Also, you need a ride somewhere?"

She laughed. "Skux. Should I be offended by that?"

"Nah. It just means you're looking hot. It's a good thing, and not offensive. If my mate is dressed nice and looking cool, I'd tell him he was looking skux. A girl I like is dressed hot, I'd tell her she looks skux. Not dirty at all."

"Oh." She looked past me, at my van. "Nice ride. Where are you headed?"

"Thanks. I just bought it a few days past. I'm not really heading anywhere in particular. Generally west, I guess, but I'm really just exploring the country, and doing it mainly through this," I said, tugging the strap of my Nikon.

"Is that a D6?" she asked.

I nodded. "Yeah. I quite fancy your Minolta. What year is it from?"

She laughed. "Actually, I'm not certain. It was a gift from my advisor when I left Columbia. She bought it used herself back in the early nineties, so I'd guess it's probably from the eighties, maybe even the seventies."

"When you say Columbia, do you mean the country or the university?"

"Um, the university in New York."

"I don't mean to offend, but you seem a bit young to be graduated from uni already."

"I am, and no offense taken. I left. Dropped out, really. It wasn't right for me."

"I know you're not supposed to ask a lady her age, but…"

She rolled her eyes. "Eighteen. Nineteen at the end of September."

Phew. Not a kid, this one. All woman, and no bullshit, I could tell already.

"And how old are you?"

"Funny to exchange ages before we know each other's names. I'm twenty-four, just turned last month." I extended my hand. "I'm Errol."

"Like Errol Flynn?" she asked, shaking my hand.

I sighed. "I dislike the comparison, given his reputation, but yes, I'm named after him. My dad and my granddad used to watch *The Adventures of Robin Hood* every weekend together when my dad was young, and Errol was my granddad's favorite actor, so I got named after him."

"I agree about his reputation, but it's still a cool name, though."

"Thanks." I waited. "And you are?"

"Poppy."

"Short for anything?"

She snorted. "What would it be short for? Poppins? Poppina?"

I laughed. "Yeah, just Poppy then, like the flower?"

"From whence comes opium, yes."

"Well, only one particular species of poppy produces opium—Papaver somniferum. And all of the various species of poppy are beautiful, as, I might add, are you."

She laughed. "Smooth."

"And genuinely meant. You're damned lovely."

"Thanks." No demurral or deflection, but no ego about it, either, just a dignified acceptance of a compliment. Striking, that trait. She locked eyes with me, and I could tell she was deciding whether or not I was safe to ride with. "So, you're not heading anywhere in particular? Which means you could, in theory, take me pretty much anywhere."

I laughed. "I mean, I don't plan on punting off to Mexico just yet, but if you're going somewhere I could probably take you that way."

She smiled. "I'm heading in the general direction of Alaska. But I'm not in any hurry." She lifted the Minolta. "Like you said about yourself, I'm just sort of exploring as I go, seeing as much of the country as I can, through the viewfinder."

"Well, Poppy, we've got that much in common at least." I gestured at the van. "Shall we?"

She hesitated another moment. "Well, despite the inauspicious beginning, I don't get creeper, serial killer vibes from you, so yeah, let's go."

She reached down, grabbed her large, bulging backpack, hiked it onto a shoulder, and headed for my van. I admit I may have held a step back just to watch her backside sway in the skirt. Yeah, definitely every bit as fine as it had looked from the van at seventy mph. Better, since my view was closer and it was now in tantalizing, swaying motion.

"Quit staring at my ass," she said, without turning around.

"Not staring. Just appreciating."

Now she paused at the tail of the van, glancing back at me with droll disbelief. "Right."

I laughed. "Fine, I was staring a little. This time, I will apologize for staring."

"Apology accepted," she said, her voice crisp and arch.

And she continued toward the front passenger side door, and unless I was greatly mistaken, she'd accentuated the womanly sway of her hips. Whether for my benefit or to bait me, I wasn't sure, but either way, it worked, because I did indeed look again. I mean shit, an ass that nice, you gotta look twice.

She opened the front passenger door, slid the huge, overland-hike backpacking style bag in the footwell and tried to slide in with it. I stood at the sliding door, waiting for her to come to the realization that the footwell just simply wasn't big enough for that. After a moment of struggling to fit herself and the bag into a too-small space, she slid back out and glanced at me as I stood at the open sliding rear door, an amused grin on my face.

"Yes, Errol? Have something to say?"

I shrugged. "Yeah nah, I was just thinking you might like to set it back here. A bit more room, eh?"

She blinked at me, stifling a laugh at herself as she hefted the bag by the straps and set it behind her seat, taking a moment to glance over the interior. "Super nice. It's like an RV."

"We call it a caravan, where I'm from. Or a campervan. I call it home away from home, for now."

A moment later we were on the road, headed west, the radio tuned to whichever local country station came in clearest.

I examined my new ride-along partner: fucking *breathtaking*. Five-seven, maybe? Not tall, not short—just bang in the middle. Thick, long, wavy black hair—she had just the pieces that would get in her face tied up and back, the rest down and loose, and saying her hair was *black* is like saying the Pacific Ocean is *wet*, or the Great Wall of China is *long*. Black is a poor descriptor. Dig into your favorite tropes and clichés, and they're all insufficient. Jet black. The exact shade of a raven's wing, with the same purply glint in the sun, as if you could almost see your reflection if it would just polish up a bit. It wasn't just stick straight, pin-straight, like Wednesday from Addams Family. A roiling cloud of inky waves around her shoulders. Soft, hazy almost. Like wisps and shreds of storm clouds. Glossy elsewhere. I could go on and on just about her fucking hair.

Eyes? Same story. I could say they're *brown*, like liquid chocolate bubbling in a Swiss chocolatier's vat is brown. I've seen that, and it's one of those memories with a vivid scent, one I can recall on command, almost smell it just thinking about it. Her eyes are that exact shade. Darker than milk chocolate. Not your shitty American bars of cocoa-flavored turd, oh no. I'm talking real Swiss chocolate handcrafted in copper vessels by tenth-generation artisans. That kind of chocolate. Molten, churning with sweet heat, the kind that melts the moment it touches your tongue. That's Poppy's eyes.

Skin…god, how do I describe her skin? Sun-kissed bronze? Too romantically melodramatic. To say her skin looked soft was, again, an egregious understatement. Sun-kissed was right; she wasn't the type to tan or lay out, but she didn't languish away under fluorescent lights either. It was impossible. Her skin just begged to be touched, kissed. So perfect it didn't seem she could be real.

She had the straight white teeth of someone with great genetics and a stellar dentist she saw regularly.

An easy smile, the corners of her lips tipped up as if life had just blessed her and she was happy to simply be alive.

And, yes, those curves. Contained in a plain white tank top, her breasts threatened to spill out the sides just sitting still, and if she moved just so? Lordy lord, I got teases of heaven. Like, fuck me, but I wanted to rip that damned shirt off and just stare at her. How dare she malign the gifts they were by hiding them? They were meant to be viewed like art, but only by me.

Damn, though, where did *that* come from?

They were fucking incredible, for real. And real, which I was certain of, because you just didn't get that kind of movement from silicone or saline, not that I had anything against implants mind you, they were very nice as well, but Poppy's were just…nature's bounty, barely veiled behind not quite see-through white cotton. I couldn't quite make out areolae, but glimpsed a hint of darker flesh at the center of those glorious mounds beneath the shirt.

Hips defined by stretched skirt material spoke of mouthwatering curves; squishy, lovely round hips that would fit just so, in my hands, against my own hips. The skirt swirled around her ankles, but as she shifted to cross one knee over the other, I caught a slice of calf, a hint of under-thigh, strong and tan and flawless.

In short—I don't think smitten is an exaggeration. Stunned that such flawless human female beauty could be found on the side of a remote Missouri road, sitting next to me, looking at me with open curiosity and—if I'm honest—appreciation for what she saw.

"So, Errol." A smile, friendly, casual. Not flirty, not yet. "What's your story?"

I laughed. "What, like the whole thing, sad bits and all? A bit much for having just met, I think."

"You can leave out the sad bits, if you want."

"Not much to tell, in that case," I said. "Nah, only joking."

I wasn't actually really joking, because there were more sad bits than not in my life story, but you don't get a pretty girl in bed with you by sharing the tragedies you've suffered because, believe it or not, sad girls aren't horny. So no, not sharing the sad bits is a vital strategy in getting laid.

"Where's home? Innocent enough place to start?"

I laughed. "You'd think. I don't actually have a permanent home. I'm a photojournalist for Nat Geo, and I'm on assignment pretty much permanently. So I don't really keep a proper home, as it'd be empty all but a few days of the year."

She glanced back into the interior of the Westfalia—clothes, a few camera bags, a pair of gum-boots, a hoodie draped over the backrest of the rear bench seat, a leather jacket, a couple other bags, and odds and ends…

"So that's, like, everything you own?"

"Yeah, pretty much. I've got a storage unit in Christchurch I rent, and I've got my dad's old Rover there, some stuff of my mum's, a few other things I can't really travel with. But, day to day, yeah, this is it. Pack it all up right quick and I'm on a plane in the next minute."

"Photographer for *National Geographic*, huh?"

"Yep."

"So you're, like, a nature photographer?"

"Sort of." I scrubbed my hand through my hair. "I get the odd shots, the ones that make you go 'bloody hell, how'd he get that one?'"

She squinted hard, thinking. "You know, my roommate's mom gave her a lifetime subscription to *National Geographic*, so she had crates of old issues, and the newest one was always laying around." She grinned sheepishly. "It was what we looked at in the bathroom, actually."

"Not your phone?"

"I mean sure, but I once read that taking your phone into the bathroom with you is actually really gross, due to the way germs move around in bathrooms, so I've tried to not do it as much." She waved. "Point is, I've probably seen your work."

"Most people don't really pay particular attention to the photographer byline, so no worries that you don't know the name." I grinned, making a joke out of it. "Did you see last month's issue?"

"Yeah."

"Did you read the article on natural sinkholes?"

"Yeah, actually. Wait, that was you?"

"The photos, yeah."

"Like, the one from the bottom of the giant sinkholes in the forest? That was a great shot."

"Sarisarinama. Those are in Venezuela, yeah. To get that shot, I rappelled down the hole, for which I had to get special permission from the Venezuelan government."

"Any others I might immediately recognize?"

I shrugged. "I mean, I've done loads of features."

"So you've been all over, then."

"God, yeah. Everywhere. I haven't done Antarctica yet, but I did one on the break up of the ice in the North Pole, where I got lots of cool shots from on top of these huge icebergs just off the ice shelf."

"Oh shit, yeah, I saw that feature! The underwater one, where you can see how much bigger it is under the water? That one was incredible."

"Yeah, I spent like three days in a dry suit getting that shot. Took maybe a thousand photos and finally got that one, the rest are just fuckin' rubbish. All you could see was the top and the water. Still dunno what made the difference, but the water just cleared up at the right moment, and I got the shot."

"Wow. Pretty cool."

"Froze my sac off, you mean. Even in a dry suit, that water is *cold*. Had to get out every so often, warm up, let my camera warm up, and then get back in."

"The whale in the one shot toward the end of the feature? How cool was it to be so close to a whale like that?"

"Cool? Try terrifying. I about pissed my pants, I was so scared. She just came up out of nowhere, about knocked me clear out of the water with her tail, too. Like, you're just swimming along trying to get a shot of the berg, then just bam, there's this great big fuckin' whale the size of a building swimming past you, silent as a fuckin' ghost, and you just…you realize just like *that*, you do *not* belong in that world. You're a tiny, fragile, weak little thing that belongs on land, and even just swimming past innocent as anything, she could kill you. The current of her swimming past some ten or fifteen feet away sent me spinning as it was, and if I hadn't had the camera clipped to my webbing, I'd have lost it. You don't know what it's like, you really don't. So yeah, it's cool, like it's a memory I'll never forget as long as I fuckin' live, but fuck me, it was scary."

"You got the shot, though."

"Hell yeah, I got the shot. Second I felt her going past I had the shutter going."

"Is that the scariest thing that's ever happened to you?"

I cackled. "Not even almost. My whole job is scary shit. It's what I do."

She had her camera on her lap and fiddled idly with the focus ring. "So you're a professional adrenaline junkie."

"Yeah, that's about right. But it's not about the adrenaline as much as it is the rush of getting a photo no one else has ever got, or will ever get."

"Oh. Well, that I understand, to some degree. I bet you have some cool stories."

"People tend to assume I'm making them up to sound cool, so I usually downplay the truth a bit, if anything."

"Really? Like how?"

"Well, this one time, I was between assignments for Nat Geo and sort of just bumming around the Eastern Bloc, this was…two years ago? My editor is friends with the editor at *Time* magazine, and there was talk about trying to do a feature on some of the super remote places special forces operators get assigned to over in Afghanistan. Like, places where they've likely never seen a white person before, and then suddenly it's all a big shootout with the Taliban. There was a team of guys from the British SAS and the American Army Rangers going way deep in country, right, like leaving Germany that week and it was gonna be the last opportunity to get someone embedded for the story. All of *Time's* best photographers were on assignment in places where they couldn't get to Germany in time to make the embed, and I was already in the Ukraine, so it was a no-brainer when my boss told the *Time* editor I was available. So I got loaned out and sent to Afghanistan with this mixed squad of SAS and Rangers, these blokes who were just the most badass humans I've ever met. I spent three months with them, and I was either bored out of my mind, exhausted, or scared spitless. I can't really say what their directive was because number one they didn't tell me, and number two they're still over there doing it and I'm sworn to secrecy. That part sounds bullshit, but I swear it's not. I can say they were hunting Taliban, but that's generally it. I think they were after someone in particular, but I don't really know. It turned out a mint piece, though. Some of my most brilliant shots, if I do say so myself."

"So you've done literal, actual war stories?"

I shrugged. "Yeah, I guess you could call it that. There were times I thought for sure I'd catch one. Mainly because the only way to get the good shots was to ignore my handler and put my head up when he was telling me to put it down. I learned bullets make different noises depending on how close they get to your face. I learned mortar shells don't whistle before they land. I learned you don't get thrown backward when bullets hit you. I learned you may not even notice your mate's been hit until he's already bled out beside you."

Shit. Too heavy. Way too fuckin' heavy. Stupid ass, Errol. Stupid.

She was quiet a while.

"Sorry, Poppy. Went a bit too far into the sad bits, there."

She eyed me. "You know, I think I'd rather you be real than feed me just the cool stories."

"Why don't you tell me a story, now?"

She rolled her eyes. "I got nothing that can compete with actual war stories."

"Ain't a competition, though." I grinned, hopefully winningly. "Hit me with one."

"I'm actually more of a painter than I am a photographer, that's the first thing to know. I discovered in, like, fourth-grade art class that I just sort of...*got*... oil painting. My hand, my eye, my brain, they all just...do things and I go along with it. Give me a canvas, palette, and brush, and I'm in my happiest place."

"What style do you do?"

"Oh, I've tried them all. If I'm going to just do something for fun, I'll probably veer into Van Gogh's world. I like the not quite abstract, you know? Smears, lots of paint. If I want to spend a few days or weeks on something, I'll do a reproduction of a classic. Vermeer is the hardest, by far. Everyone knows he's a master, one of the greats, but until you understand technically how good he was, you just won't get it."

"Sort of like black-and-white photography and Ansel Adams."

"Exactly. You know his prints are just...sublime. Anyone can appreciate that. But go get a black-and-white camera and stand in the exact spot he stood and take the same photograph, and you'll be like, 'ohhhh, shit, now I get it.'"

"Because your shot will be shit, which is why he's famous and you're not."

She laughed. "Yes, exactly. But with trying to paint like Vermeer? It goes deeper. He could do things with light and depth that are just...you can't explain them."

"And you can paint like Vermeer?"

She shrugged. "I mean, you won't mistake mine for his, no. I'm no van Meegeren, that's for sure. But it's fun to try."

"I got no clue who van Meeg-whatever is, but what you're saying without saying is that you're a talented as hell painter."

"I *did* get a full ride to Columbia University's art program on the basis of my portfolio alone." She smirked. Not *too* humble, then. "Van Meegeren was famous for forging Vermeer. It's a whole art history thing. A cool story, but not the point."

"What's the point, then?"

"It was my second semester at Columbia, and I was still trying to cram my homework, classes, my own painting projects, art department projects, and a social life into twenty-four hours. Basically, not sleeping hardly at all. Like, three or fours a night, and I am *not* that person. I need eight hours or I'm a serious bitch. So, I was doing classes, going out partying with friends half the night, then cramming for tests till four in the morning, and waking up for an eight a.m. class."

"Yikes. That doesn't usually last long."

"No, and it didn't. I'd met some friends way the hell uptown at this stupid hoity-toity Upper East Side bar, a real swanky place where everyone dressed up all fancy and the drinks were like fifteen dollars a pop. Not my scene, but they'd been invited by these guys they'd met and they dragged me along. So the night wears on, I'm getting sloshed—"

"Wait, wait, wait," I cut in. "You said you're not even nineteen, and I know for a solid fact the drinking age here is twenty-one."

She looked away, shrugged, hiding a smirk. "I don't *look* eighteen, and I have an ID that *says* I'm twenty-one, and it's nearly perfect."

"I see. Naughty, naughty."

"I didn't use it much. Mostly one of our friends

who *was* of age would buy for us and we'd hang at someone's dorm or apartment. But sometimes my friends would go out and the hell if I'd let something as pesky as my age keep me from the fun."

"Well, I can't say much on that, I've been drinking since I was fourteen or fifteen."

"Sounds like a story there, too."

"Yeah, but that one's got sad bits, so let's focus on yours."

"Right. So, it's way late. I'm sloshed. I lost my friends, I took a cab there so I have no idea where I am, and I used most of my cash at the bar. Guys are hitting on me left and right, trying to get me to go home with them, into the bathroom, you name it. I know I'm way too far gone to be doing anything like that, so I need to get home. Only, we're in a dead zone as far as cabs go, and I'm nearly broke besides, so I figure I can find a bus. Right? Wrong."

"This sounds sketchy."

"Ohhhh boy, *so* sketchy. I leave the bar. Start walking. I figure I'll find a bus, a subway station, something. I got an MTA pass when I first moved to New York, because I did my research on living there before I got there, thinking I'd be this enlightened, sophisticated Manhattan socialite in no time, right? I was a sixteen-year-old girl with her head in the clouds, thinking living in New York would be the start of my rising star."

"From what I hear, New York eats up and spits out those dreams a dozen at a time."

"You have heard correctly, my friend. It's a ruthless place. It's everything you've heard and more, good and bad."

"So where'd you end up?"

"I passed out on the subway. Ended up in Coney Island at six in the morning when a conductor realized I was still on the car and woke me up."

"What does that have to do with you being a painter instead of a photographer?"

"Huh?"

"When you started the story, you said the first thing I should know is you're more of a painter."

She laughed. "Oh. Well, I was going to tell a different story."

"So tell me that one."

"Nuh-uh. It's embarrassing."

"I'll trade you for an embarrassing story of mine."

"Fine. But this is, like, true mortification."

"Mine involves involuntary public defecation in a *very* conservative country."

Her eyes widened. "Wow, I think you'll win. But okay, here goes. You know the old trope about art students having to do nude portraits, right? It's a thing. And it *is* real. It's not like in the movies, usually, but you get to a point where you do end up drawing someone nude. Usually it's all very professional, and not really that exciting or titillating, after the first few minutes of your first one, at least. So, I was in this private studies track, me and a handful of other students selected by the department head. The assignment was to do portraits of each other. But it was a competitive thing. The winning portrait, as selected by our advisor—the same woman who gave me the camera, by the way—and her colleague who owned an art gallery, would be displayed for purchase in a showing. Big time bragging rights, huge for your portfolio, huge for your resumé as an artist, plus the chance to get real money for a piece of art you made. A big deal. So, you couldn't just do any old portrait, like a typical bust portrait or whatever. You had to have an angle; you had to demonstrate your voice as an artist. And you also had to pose for a portrait of you, right? Took the competition to this whole other level, because you were competing with each other, but also posing for each other.

"And let me tell you, sitting for an oil portrait? It's a very intimate process, especially when it's a one-on-one thing rather than a classroom setting. You don't just sit once; you sit for hours, several times. There was no stipulation about what kind of portrait, just that it had to be a portrait of someone in the class.

So we all spent days figuring out what we were going to do, who we were going to have sit for us, and then scheduling things so we all had time to sit *and* to paint."

"When does this get embarrassing?" I asked.

She rolled her eyes at me. "Momentarily, trust me. So, there were two girls in the class, me and Avril Galloway, and three boys. We're none of us professional artists, but we are art students. Nudity in art is a whole different thing. Because, like, it's *art*, you know?"

I nodded. "Sure. I've done some portraits. I'm not formally trained, so I've never done any classwork, but I know what you mean."

"Wait. You're not formally trained?"

"I also don't have a degree. Strictly speaking, I shouldn't be able to work for them like I do. How I got in is a whole other story, and—"

"That part has sad bits in it too," she surmised.

"You guessed it."

"Short version?"

"My mum was a photographer. Did work for Nat Geo, Getty Images, AP. One of her best friends was an editor at Nat Geo. My mom, uh…well, she was in a position to ask this friend, this editor, for a favor that he could not refuse, because of…circumstances. Her favor was that he look at my photography. He did. But

I was just a kid at the time and had nothing but stuff I'd shot around the house and neighborhood on her old Leica. Nothing even close to good because shit, I was twelve, but he was a good sport and looked. Was very encouraging. Gave me some real gems of advice on pro shooting like he was taking a likely young buck under his wing, things I've never forgot to this day. So then, fast forward six or seven years, I was in a bar in the Netherlands, and I was real pissed, like way deep in the bag. Meaning, drunk as a skunk.

"And who do I run into but my mum's old mate, the editor? I had my camera, and my laptop full of photos I'd taken over the last few years on tour with my dad's band, right? I'd gotten good, and I asked him to look. He knew me, knew why I was traveling with the band, he'd been there with Mum at the end, and he was the best sort of sport there is, so he looked at my stuff again. And this time, I had stuff worth looking at. He said publications have rules and regulations as for needing college degrees and a minimum experience requirement and specialization and all, but I had something that can't be taught in college and can't be learned in any amount of experience...that being raw golden talent."

I sighed, thinking back to those days, fondly but also with a heavy patina of bitter pain. Poppy was rapt, so I continued.

"I'd already developed a specialty—the adrenaline shots. We traveled all over Europe—we being my dad and the band he was in—and I'd hang off railway trestles to get the steam off a stack as it passed under me, climb up the outside of a high-rise to get the sunrise off a particular window at a specific angle. I was crazy. I liked the danger. I figured I had no reason to be careful, so fuck it, right? Get the shot. If I cark it, I cark it, so what, who the fuck cares. Right? And my portfolio showed it. Jerry knew it, and he remembered the promise he'd made to Mum, and he knew it wasn't to humor a twelve-year-old boy who liked to play with cameras. He knew Mum had seen my natural eye even then, and so old Jerry took me in. He used seniority or some corporate shenanigans to get me on salary despite being eighteen with not even my level one qualifications, much less any higher education. He says he just showed them my amateur work and it spoke for itself, but the corporate world doesn't work that way, which means the old bugger pulled some very serious strings to keep his promise to Mum."

She was quiet a while. Eyed me seriously. "There is a whole hell of a lot to pull out of that story, Errol."

I focused on the road. Shrugged. Studied the

way the yellow lines flashed past in dot-space-dot rhythm, the trees here and there, a cluster of cows browsing, an underpass…anything to avoid seeing her work through to the realizations of what I'd hinted at—the ugly tragedies which had shoved me out into the world alone as a kid posing as a man.

I didn't want sympathy or understanding. That led to people thinking I needed to be *healed*. Thinking I needed *help*. Thinking I was this poor damaged thing that needed to be given sweet succor. Nah, mate. Bullshit. I made it through. I like my life. Sure I've got shit that keeps me awake some nights, but who doesn't? And the problem with sharing the sad bits is people stop seeing you as *you*, they just see you as you-plus-tragedy. Then the you-plus disappears and, in their eyes, you're just the tragedy that defines you.

I refuse to be defined by my tragedies.

Keep your sympathy and your succor, thanks, and fuck off.

That's where the stories come in, the cool, swashbuckling tales of embedding with special forces and skydiving into volcanoes with a high-speed camera machine-gunning and hanging off the side of a freight train as it barrels along a mountainside in remote, rugged China.

It's all real.

It's no smoke screen.

But if it distracts from the shit I don't want you to know about? Great.

So why the *fuck* was I getting into that shit with this girl?

FIVE

Poppy

GOD, HE WAS FASCINATING.

Hot as *fuck*.

I don't mean to sound like I'm all stuck-up and snotty about what I look like, but let's just say I've gotten into some pretty highbrow, high society Manhattan parties simply because I look like I belong there—I'll splurge on a blow-out, have my friend Zeke, the makeup artist, do my makeup, and put on my trusty LBD, and I can bluster my way into just about any party. Point of this little aside is that I've rubbed elbows with some wealthy, fascinating, famous people. Some of whom have in fact graced the covers of magazines, and been named sexiest men alive. So, when I say Errol Unknown-Last-Name is hot as fuck and interesting as hell, it is with some level of objective authority on the subject.

He's a golden god, of the devil-may-care surfer variety. Tall, over six feet for sure, lean and hard. What he's said of his profession makes sense of his build—he's not bursting with gym-rat muscle, he's not some skinny-fat pud, nor is he an ultra-shredded IG fitness douche. He's powerfully built, with broad shoulders and a thick chest and strong arms, but it's the kind of power and strength you can only get by living hard, being outside, and doing hard physical things. Like climbing mountains, rock climbing, hiking for miles on end with a backpack full of gear. His is functional power, not simply aesthetic muscle. And maybe it's just me, but damn is it sexy.

His hair is longish, not quite to his shoulders but long enough he could tie it back or put it in a man-bun, wavy and messy and curly and a sun-bleached dirty blond. At the moment he had it down and loose, and strands stuck to his beard, which was somewhat less than a real beard of the lumbersexual variety, but not just heavy stubble. It's the short beard of a man who rarely cares or has the time to shave, but also has neither the time nor the interest in maintaining a fancy beard. It's masculine, and sexy. Run your fingers over it and it'd be soft and scratchy at the same time. I bet it would tickle if he kissed me, and burn so good if he went down on me.

His eyes, the glimpse of them I got from behind his care-worn Wayfarers, were blue as...well, honestly, metaphor fails me. The Greek island of Santorini is famous for many reasons, chief among them being the white houses with vividly blue domed roofs. Errol's eyes were the exact shade of those rooftop domes. The color of the Aegean at noon on a cloudless day.

I wonder if he's been there.

"Have you ever been to Greece?" I asked.

Because that seemed a hell of a lot safer than diving into the details of that story he just told, which was just brimming with untold tragedy.

He blinked at the unexpected conversational shift. "I...yeah. I did a piece on the locations of Greek mythology, like the actual mountaintop said to be Olympus, and where the oracle of Delphi was said to be, stuff like that. I worked a cool angle, too, because I found these guys who built wooden boats in the style of the ancient Greeks, and we went from location to location in that boat, and I did some features on locations from the *Odyssey* and the *Iliad*, using the latest archaeological data. It was a fun piece to do, actually. There's just heaps of fascinating history in that area. I've had an idea of doing a piece on the actual route taken by Philippides, the soldier who ran from Marathon to Athens to deliver the news of the victory of the battle at Marathon, creating the sporting event. I just can't get Jerry to sign off on it yet."

"That sounds cool," I said. "Why won't your boss let you do it?"

"Because he said my job is the high octane stuff the sissy old fart photographers are too scared to do." He laughed. "Nah, I'm just kidding. They're all wicked talented and manage photos I couldn't even dream of. Jerry just likes to assign me the wild stuff that takes a certain amount of 'don't give a shit adrenaline junkie bravado,' and figures that piece is too fluff for a man of my specific talents."

"So, then, what are you working on here in the States?"

He passed his hand through his thick mop of messy hair, pulling it away from his cheekbones and jawline, checking traffic as we reached a junction where the highway we were on crossed paths with another. He gestured at the intersection. "Straight, left, or right? Up to you."

"I don't know. Which way are you going?"

He glanced out the window at the sun, which was to our left and behind us a bit. "North, maybe?

I don't know. I've not really been paying super close attention, to be honest. I just sorta go where the road goes until I find a new road that looks like more fun driving."

I perused the options—ahead, more open highway, cow pastures and cornfields and silos; left, more of the same; to the right, a sign cautioning that the road became winding, and the promise of something like hills. "I'd say right. No idea where it'll take us, but it looks more interesting."

Errol nodded. "Woman after my own heart, you are. Exactly what I'd pick."

God, that fucking accent. Could it get any hotter? If I were to be wearing underwear under this skirt, that accent would make them all wet. I wasn't, though, so I just got all squishy and warm between my thighs every time he spoke.

He turned right, and within a mile we were winding through a forest of rolling hills, sunlight dappling us in staccato flashes of brilliance.

"You never finished your story," he said, smirking at me. "Don't think I forgot. The one about the portrait."

I winced. "I had hoped you'd forgotten."

"Not even almost."

"Fine. But your story had better be seriously embarrassing, if I'm telling you this."

"Oh, it is. And it ain't the only one. There's the time I spent two weeks in a Malaysian jail over a situation involving a prostitute, a poor translation, and me being a right cad sometimes."

She blinked. "I don't even know where to start with that."

"All's I can say is, it's not what you think, which is why I landed in jail." He chuckled. "I'd have to be a mite more pissed to tell *that* story, though."

"Pissed meaning drunk?"

"Yeah, 'xactly." He jerked a thumb behind us. "There's a little white chilly bin back there with cold drinks in it, if you're thirsty. And one of the cabinets up top has snacks in it, nuts and crisps and the like. Help yourself."

I unbuckled and moved carefully to the rear of the van, found the cooler and fished two bottles of water out of it—it was more water than ice at that point, but it kept the bottles chilled. In the cabinet I found a box of prepackaged mixed nuts, and brought some of those forward as well.

"What was it you called it? A chilly bin?"

He arched an eyebrow at me. "Yeah, chilly bin. Cooler bin, if you like. It's what it is, ain't it, a bin that keeps things chilled?"

"Well, yeah. It's just funny to me for some reason."

"What would you call it? A *cooler*?" He faked an American accent, making the final -er syllable exaggeratedly pronounced.

"I mean, it's a Yeti. If you have a Yeti, you call it a Yeti."

"You Americans are weird, bro. Who gives a shit what brand it is? It's a chilly bin, just call it what it is." He twisted the top off his water and sipped at it. "Now. Story time. Embarrass yourself, if you please."

I popped a salted almond into my mouth. "Well." I chewed, swallowed, washed it down, and continued my story. "There was this guy in the class with me."

"Ahh, now we come to it."

I snickered. "You have no clue. Just wait. But yes, like all good embarrassing stories, it was brought on by my own thirst. His name was Teague, and he was from this super-wealthy Upper West Side family, and he literally could have walked off of the set of a Hollywood teen rom-com as the pretty asshole villain. He was actually a nice guy, though, and a crazy good painter. His work with chiaroscuro was damn near genius, but he couldn't do hands for shit. Anyway. I had a stupid crush on him, as in I'd maneuvered myself into that particular track not entirely for him, but partially. And I had it on good authority that he was just over a breakup, so I figured it would be a good time to make my move. We agreed he'd sit for me first, and since I didn't have a swanky penthouse condo like he did, I had to reserve a studio at the college. My portrait of Teague was in the style of the grand old portraits of kings and generals, I had him wearing a full French army uniform from the Napoleonic Wars era, with his hand in his shirt and a big ol' codpiece and the cavalry sword and all that. It was so fucking cool. Then it was my turn to pose for him. He'd said he hadn't decided what he wanted to do, so just come ready for anything."

"Now comes the good part, yeah?"

"Yeah, oh yeah. So I take an Uber to his condo, which was probably worth triple the house I grew up in, in Connecticut. Big, open concept, super modern, all black and white and stainless steel, couches worth more than cars, the works."

"Sounds hideous."

I laughed. "Honestly, it was. But it screamed money, which was the point."

"I knew a guy from Dubai," Errol said. "Family was worth billions. He said something I'll never forget—if you've got to talk, walk, dress, act, and drive like you've got money, then you don't have *real* money. He had a garage chockablock with supercars, like a quarter-mil minimum for the cheapest one. And his condo was a penthouse, and his clothes were nice, but if you didn't *know* he was worth several fortunes, you wouldn't know. Screaming 'I've got mad money' just means you're only rich enough to fake it."

I thought about that. "You know, that sounds about right. His family had enough to own penthouses in New York, which cost enough that they had pretty serious money, but not billions. That's a different level." I waved a hand. "It impressed me, is the point. Growing up, we weren't poor, not by a long shot, but not, like, *rich*, not on Teague's level, and certainly not your Dubai friend's level. We were comfortable and certainly privileged. But this condo had my jaw dropping. You could see most of Central Park from it, which is a pretty enviable thing. So I get there, and he's got a whole, like, wing of his condo set up as a studio, with custom ventilation, an industrial canvas stretcher...and this whole huge cyc setup like he was about to film an ad for, like, Apple or something."

"A psych?" He asked. "What's that?"

"C-Y-C, cyc, short for cyclorama. The plain white backgrounds they use in videos and such so it looks like you're in an all-white room. It's a huge piece of white cloth, essentially. You can rig one lots of ways in a pinch, but a pro cyc setup costs serious money, and he had a pro set up. Including a chaise lounge for me to sit on, covered by the cyc."

"So he wasn't fucking around."

"Showing off, you mean. That should have been my first clue. I'd come prepared for just about anything, but I was hoping he'd say nude so I could use that as a jumping-off point for the seduction part of the day. And he did not disappoint. He got this big smirk, like a real shit-eating grin, and he was like, 'so, you up for a nude portrait?' I thought it was a shoo-in. Pose nude, he'd like what he'd see, we'd have some fun, and I'd be over the stupid crush."

"He batted for the other team?" Errol suggested.

"What, like he was gay? No, I knew for a fact he liked women—as I said, I had it on good authority, meaning I'd spoken to his ex, who had been more than happy to share details. So no, he played for my team. So, I say sure, I'll pose nude. Strip down, sit on the chaise lounge. He goes to work, does the sketch, and then starts painting. I'm waiting for him to make the move, right? I provide the in, he just has to take the hint. Like, why the hell else would I agree to pose nude for a classmate for a portrait assignment? I knew his style, and he didn't go in for shock stuff, he was super classical. The day wears on, and I'm still just posing, a pretty conventional portrait pose, you know, lounging on the chaise, thigh over the other so you can't quite see my hoo-hoo, elbow just here. Hours of posing. Like, when do we get to the fun part, right?" I sighed. "Never happened. He just went, 'okay, I'm done, you can go.' But he had this smirk. I was like, 'So that's it? We're just done?'"

"He didn't take the hint?"

"No, and I was still buck-ass naked, like, I could not have been any more obvious."

"Had to be gay, in that case."

I frowned. "What? No, I already told you—"

"Yeah, I know what you said," Errol interrupted, "but I submit that no heterosexual male, faced with *you*, naked, all but throwing yourself at him, could or would remain unmoved. Therefore, gay."

I eyed him sidelong. "You haven't seen me naked, though."

"More's the pity, and not for wanting," he muttered, and I wasn't sure I was meant to hear it. "So what the hell was his game?" he asked.

"I wasn't sure myself until the day we all turned in our work. He was last to present his. We all had these prepared presentations, right? Like talking about our influences and the style we chose and all that, but Teague? Walked up, stood next to the easel that had his portrait on it, covered with a piece of canvas. He hesitated for dramatic effect, and then whipped the canvas off." I paused, recalling with uncomfortable clarity my horrified mortification at the time. "He'd done it as a direct copy of Titian's *Venus of Urbino*. Which if you don't know art history, is one of the most famous and scandalous nude portraits in history." I slid my phone out of my purse and Googled the painting in question, the Titian version, I mean, and showed it to Errol.

He glanced at it, back at the road, at the image on my phone again, and then at me. "I see why it was scandalous."

"The frank, unapologetic look in her eyes? The position of her hand?"

"And she's not facing away or semi-modestly arranged. Just laying there all like, 'look at me, I'm naked!'"

"Right. I'd assumed he'd do the modest version. Oh no. He did the *Venus of Urbino*. And he went further. He made it look like my fingers were unmistakably *not* just resting demurely over my crotch." It was still embarrassing to think about. "And he exaggerated…certain features, like, into cartoon-level absurdity. Made me look like a porn star with beach ball-sized tits, fingering myself."

Errol glanced at me. "Why exaggerate perfection?"

I looked at him—no grin, no jokey smirk. He was dead-ass serious.

He looked at me. I looked at him. *Why exaggerate perfection?* Three words, a genuine compliment. But the way he looked at me right then took it somewhere else. Not hitting on me. Something beyond that. Not undressing me with his eyes—nothing so simple or pedestrian as that.

I was going to fuck the blue out of his eyes, I realized. It was going to be world-class sex.

Not yet, though. I mean, I had to at least give it twelve hours from hello to naked. But with compliment comebacks like that, how could I refuse?

I mean, shit, all he'd have to do is look at me with those devilish blue eyes and say something clever in that delicious Kiwi accent, and I'd be naked and screaming in no time.

It would be purely physical, though. Purely. My heart had nothing to do with this whatsoever. I was traveling, he was traveling—our paths intersected for a while, we'd get some mutual satisfaction out of it, and then we'd go our separate ways and that would be that.

It felt like our eyes met for an eternity, felt like sparks flew thick and fierce as if someone had thrown a log on a campfire. In reality it was a matter of seconds, a mere heartbeat, and then he wrenched his eyes away and back to the road. Hand passed through his hair, he blew a sigh, scrubbed his beard, glanced back at me again ever so briefly, and if I wasn't mistaken he mumbled something like *"Gonna be in deep fuckin' trouble with this one, ain't I?"*

Oh yes, Errol, you are. The best kind of trouble.

A long silence.

"He was a bastard." Errol growled, eventually. "Pulling a cheap trick like that. What was his game?"

"His game was he was just an asshole. Thought he was nice, but I was mistaken. His ex told me he was a real asshole, but I chalked that up to her being a bitter ex. He'd caught wind somehow that I liked him, and figured he'd have fun with it. I was nowhere near his social status, and that meant I was not even worth sleeping with. I guess he only slept with girls who were his social equals, or nameless nobodies, and I was neither, so he just…had his fun fucking with me. Led me on, painted me, embarrassed me, and then didn't give a shit. He got a shitty grade for the piece because Mrs. D knew exactly what he'd done and why, but he didn't give a shit. He didn't need the degree—he was set for life. He was just taking classes for something to do until Daddy gave him the keys to the family business and the unlimited credit that went with it."

"What'd you do? I mean, I know we only just met an hour ago, but you don't strike me as the type to take that lying down."

I chuckled. "Oh, I didn't. I snuck into the art department, and repainted his codpiece to be much, much smaller. And I used the technique where, from most angles, it looks like there's this odd smear on the painting, but from a specific angle it's actually, like a skull or something. I put the word 'prick' under his feet so if you stood to one side and below it, you'd be able to read it. And then I borrowed a ladder from maintenance and hung the painting from the ceiling so, as you entered the art department, that word would be the first thing you saw."

"You do *not* fuck around with revenge, do you?"

I laughed. "That was just the start of my revenge. I got his ex to help me steal and unlock his phone, and we made him a Grindr account soliciting dick pics to his personal cell number."

"Oh, mate, that's *cold*."

"I snuck in after our finals were turned in and stole his final work, and hid it behind some props in the theater department. Got busted for that one, but it was worth the ten percent she docked from my final grade. That painting had been his opus for the year, he'd been working on it for months. I would never have harmed the thing, I'm not that much of a monster, but when he thought it had been stolen, he was sick with panic. He knew it was me, too. I played dumb until campus security showed Mrs. D footage of me sneaking around after hours. Messing with someone else's work was a no-no, so I did get into trouble, but it was worth seeing that dickhead become a laughingstock."

He laughed. "Still laughing about the Grindr thing."

"Oh he was *pissed*. I guess he had been presenting in another class, using his phone connected to the projector to display something or other, and a giant dick pic popped up on the screen. Like, a big veiny monster cock, in a lecture hall full of students. He was the TA for the class, and he got fired for it. Couldn't prove it was me, but he knew." I cackled. "I did shit like that to him for months. Wrote his number on the stall wall of a bathroom, and I guess his phone blew up with strange-ass propositions all day for weeks until he figured it out and changed his number. Finally, he hauled me aside after class and apologized and begged me to stop. I told him he had to give me the painting, for one thing. And then I strongly hinted that a truce could be arranged if a Birkin bag somehow found its way into my possession."

"You bribed him?"

"Sure. He embarrassed me, manipulated me, led me on, and pissed me off. Am I proud of myself for bribing him? No. Do I regret the pretty little Birkin that's currently waiting for me at my mother's condo in Alaska? Also no. Don't cross me. I'm not nice when I'm angry."

"Clearly," Errol said, his voice droll. "Did you honor the truce?"

"Of course I did," I said, aghast. "I'm an honorable woman, in my own way. If I give you my word, it's good as gold. And I gave him my word—if I were to find myself suddenly in possession of a Birkin, the malicious sneak attacks would cease immediately and permanently."

"And you have the painting?"

"Sure do. At Mom's with the rest of my stuff I couldn't travel with."

"You kept it?"

I laughed. "Yeah, because it *is* a technically amazing piece. He's a talented artist; he's just an amoral cock-hair. I couldn't destroy a work of art, no matter how personally embarrassing it is."

Errol guffawed. "Amoral cock-hair. That's a good one." He glanced at me. "So what are you going to do with it?"

"I have no idea. It's wrapped up and boxed and sealed, and my mother has orders not to open it under threat of death and dismemberment, because I did tell her the basic story. When I get there, I'll probably get drunk with my sisters and show it to them, and then I'll let them decide what to do with it. It certainly should never see the light of day. But, if I'm being even a little objective…it *is* kind of funny." I pointed at him. "So. Your turn. You mentioned involuntary public defecation. Or would I rather hear the one about the prostitute and you going to jail?"

He laughed, shook his head. "Oh no, not telling that one."

"Come on. Please?"

He shook his head. "No! It's awful. Stupid, horrible, and awful, and I'm not telling it."

"Errol. You can't drop hints of a great story like that and not tell it."

He sighed. "Fine." He scrubbed his jaw again, muttering under his breath. "Gotta be munted to tell this one." He shook his head. "It's not really all that complicated. I was on my way to China for a feature on the crazy topography they have over there, and figured I may as well take a detour and see Kuala Lumpur. I hired a guide and a translator, same guy, got a two-for-one deal. Turns out the deal was he didn't know shit about the city and couldn't speak either language—joke's on me. I didn't know he didn't speak Malaysian for shit, since I don't speak it myself. Sounded like he did, and what do I know?

"I told him I wanted dinner, so he brought me to a nice little place he knew, good food, didn't get sick, everything was alright, so we continued on. Told him I wanted somewhere to sleep, but first a drink to relax. And that's where the trouble started. He misunderstood what I meant somehow and brought me to a brothel. Didn't realize it at first, being jetlagged and not the sort to go visiting brothels anyway. Asked for a room, and got shown a lineup of girls, and I was like what? No, not what I meant, just a room, just for me, *alone*. Lots of not understanding each other, me and the madam in charge of the place. Guess she thought I was saying none of the girls were what I wanted, I dunno. So she brought out a guy. And I was like *NO!* Jesus, not that either, lady, I just want to fuckin' sleep, been traveling for days and I'm wrecked, just totally ready to fall asleep standing up. I'd had a few drinks as it was, and that was making it all worse being half-pissed. And then, worst luck ever, who should bust in but Malaysian police, busting the place for trafficking and prostitution, which is actually illegal there. I got swept up in the bust, arrested, and held until I managed to get hold of Jerry who cleared the situation up. Moral of the story is…well, I dunno what it is. Don't hire shitty translators, maybe."

I was laughing, because I could see a half-drunk Errol trying to tell a madam he didn't want the male prostitute. "What was the jail like?"

"Horrifying. Worst bugger-all experience of my entire fucking existence. Even compared to the time I got plane wrecked in the Gobi desert and had to walk out. This was worse than that. Standard-size jail cell, but there were easily fifty of us in there, with one toilet overflowing with shit. Got fed scraps I wouldn't feed a pig, and that was when they felt like feeding us at all." He shuddered. "The misunderstanding is funny in hindsight, but ending up in a Malaysian prison is not fucking funny at all."

"Yikes." I blinked at him. "Plane wrecked in the Gobi desert? What the hell, dude? You sound like Indiana Jones."

He laughed. "Not hardly, I've just had a few runs of shit luck. We were flying over it, landed a few times to take photos, and we were heading out. Nearing the edge of it, something goes munted on the engine; pilot tries for an emergency landing. It's the desert, nice and flat, right? Hits the only fucking rock in half a mile, we go spinning and bouncing, flip over. Engine catches fire, the pilot is out cold, and I'm bleeding like a pig from a stupid little head wound." He points to a small cut on his forehead, over his left eyebrow, now just a thin white line, almost invisible. "I get the pilot out, he comes to, and realizes we're stranded, radio's on fire with the rest of the damn thing, night is only a few hours away, we've got half a liter of water and a melted Snicker's bar between us. Fortunately, we were only a few kilometers from a ranger station in the national park, but shit, what a walk that was. First I was gonna bake to death, then die of thirst, then freeze to death, all in a matter of half a day. Didn't, obviously, but I learned then always carry extra water, extra clothes, and a satellite phone that works almost anywhere on the planet."

I shook my head. "Now I understand what you meant when you said you tone back the truth."

"I could be lying. I coulda got that cut playing army as a kid, you don't know." He grinned, laughed. "Only joking. It's all true. I can show you the photos from the Gobi when we stop. I took photos of the wreck and along the walk, figured shit, if I'm wrecked, might as well get some good photos out of it."

"Did the shots of the wreck make it into the feature?"

He laughed. "You know they did. Turned it into the main event—*Stranded in the Gobi*, Jerry called it. One of my most well-known pieces, matter of fact. I took lots of video on that one, too, and Jerry pitched it as a mini-feature on the cable network channel. I'd actually recorded the crash itself, as I'd been interviewing the pilot when it happened and never stopped. Caught the whole thing, by some miracle. I'm not really a videographer, but I like to experiment sometimes, and that was an experiment. Fairly successful, I guess."

"You've been on TV?" I asked, incredulous.

"I mean, yeah. It was a little half-hour special that aired at midnight on a Tuesday in February. Nothing to go nuts over. I'm no David Attenborough."

"Still. It's cool."

He shrugged. "I mean, yeah, I thought it was mean as to be on the telly, but I'll take not being in a plane wreck if given the choice. Makes a good story, but it wasn't exactly fun at the time. Thinking you might not make it home is never a fun thing."

I frowned, considering that. "Yeah, I can see how the possibility of dying would put a damper on things."

Conversation wandered naturally and casually after that, from topic to topic as easily and freely as if we'd been old friends for years. He'd discovered an appreciation for American country music on his journey—I don't mind country and will listen to most songs if they pop up in a playlist, but it's not my favorite. He introduced me to the fact that other countries had their own local favorite bands and famous singers—which seems like a duh, but I'm a self-centered sheltered American and never really considered the notion of New Zealand having its own crop of artists of all genres. Discussing artists and using references that are unfamiliar to me was something I had never explored. He had a whole playlist of favorites, and we spent a good two and a half hours listening to the playlist and discussing the songs and styles and comparing his New Zealand bands to my favorite American counterparts.

Eventually we found ourselves passing through a middling-sized town with a few decent places to get a real meal, and with only a minor amount of good-natured squabbling over fast food versus sit down, we ended up at a sit-down place eating burgers and fries and drinking sweetened iced tea, which Errol had never had before and found bizarre but good, in an eye-wateringly sweet sort of way.

"It's like a fizzy, without the fizz," was his remark.

"Fizzy?"

"Soft drink. Soda."

"Oh." I laughed. "You have funny terms for everything."

"Only funny to you because you're not from New Zealand," he said. "And honestly, I'm rarely in New Zealand these days, so I don't really use all the latest slang, plus traveling abroad like I do, the accent is fine but I gotta be understood by people for whom English is a second or third or fourth language. So I can't really say things like what time is brekkie and how much are those sunnies and are you here visiting your rellies, and chur bro let's bowl round the pub for a piss up…it kinda makes communication harder, so I try to drop the lingo and use basic English. Sometimes an old word will slip through, especially now that I'm in America and most people can sort out what I mean."

I wasn't going to tell him that I found the slang fucking adorable and hysterical at the same time, in a highly arousing sort of way. But then, what about him didn't I find attractive? Not a damn thing. The way he drove was sexy, the way he slid his fingers through his hair was sexy, the way he talked was sexy, the way he looked at me was sexy…

He was just…sexy. But not in a trying too hard way. He was cool, smooth, easy to talk to, a good listener. He rode a very fine line between arrogant and confident, and the ability to straddle that line was, in some ways, the sexiest thing about him. I mean, yeah, everyone knows we women find confidence sexy but outright arrogance a turn-off. A man who can fit somewhere in between? A unicorn, as far as I'm concerned. And, so far, Errol seemed to be a unicorn with the biggest sparkliest horn of them all.

No, I don't mean *that* horn, but if he was as hung as the rest of him was sexy? Ooh lordy.

Question was how and when it would happen. I didn't want to seem too thirsty, or so easy you can doink me with a little grin and a wink of those blue-blue eyes.

But then, I'm just not into games. I want someone, I'm not gonna drag it out for funsies. I want you, you want me, we're both adults so let's just have some fun and be mature about it.

Simple.

I knew he'd be game—I saw the way he was looking at me. The way his eyes flicked from the road to my boobs when he thought I wasn't paying attention. I wondered if he'd make the move, or if I'd have to drop the obvious hints, like shoving my hand down his pants.

Afternoon turned to evening, and sunset found us rumbling down a dirt track somewhere just over the state line in Iowa, just to see where it went. Which was nowhere. After twisting and turning through cornfields, and between cow pastures and through stands of swaying cottonwood, it narrowed further to barely a deer track big enough for the van, and then dead-ended at a small pond buzzing with dragonflies, smooth as a mirror and the color of brine-worn green sea glass.

We got out, engine off, and stood with our feet bare in the muddy shore, algae sticking to our ankles.

Errol glanced up, around, at the muted red-purple of late sunset as it bled into lowering dusk, and then at me. "So the question here is, do we turn around and find a motel for the night, or do we camp here?"

I looked around. "I dunno, I'm sure this is private property."

"Yeah, but there wasn't a tire track in the dirt newer than a few weeks, so I'm guessing if it is private property, it's seldom visited, and if someone does take exception, we can just apologize and move on."

"So you think it would be safe to just stay here for the night?"

He nodded. "Yeah, she'll be right."

I inhaled deeply. "Then let's just stay here. It's quiet, peaceful. I'll bet we'll see the stars real well out here."

"Oh, no doubt. They'll be nice and bright. I don't think there's anything like even a village for miles in any direction." He eyed me. "What about sleeping arrangements? The caravan has a tent top, but I've not tried to use it. The back bench folds down and that's where I sleep, but it'd be proper cozy for a pair who've just met this morning."

I slid him a slow, coy smile. "We can figure something out, I'm sure."

Oh, he caught the subtext all right. "Yeah, I'm sure we can." He gestured up at the sky. "I mean, it's a warm, clear night. If nothing else, we can just sleep out here." A glance at me. "You ever sleep outside under the stars?"

I shook my head. "Suburbanite city girl born and raised, my friend. Closest to camping I've ever been is glamping with my family the summer before my dad passed."

"Your dad's passed, too? Sorry to hear." He blinked at me. "What's glamping?"

I laughed quietly. "Ah-ha! A slang term for you! Camping is, like, tents and sleeping bags and those little unfolding stoves and stuff, right? Glamping is when you have a big RV and you sleep in a bed and cook in a kitchen and all that, but at an RV campsite. Glamorous camping. Glamping."

He snorted. "That doesn't even count as camping." He gestured to the van. "So is this glamping, then?"

"Nah. Not swanky enough. I'm talking the RVs that are like decent-sized apartments on wheels."

He nodded. "Sleeping rough under the stars? Nothing like it. You're never so alive as when you fall asleep watching the stars go 'round and the moon go over, and then waking up to a pink horizon."

"Best sunrise you've ever seen?" I asked, wading a little deeper with my skirt hiked up around my thighs.

He stayed where he was. "Word of advice? I wouldn't go much deeper. Bound to be leeches in water like that." He laughed as I made an abrupt U-turn right out of the water, checking my legs as I went.

"Best sunrise, hmm? Hard to pick one—I've seen some truly incredible sunrises. Last project before posting up here in the States was a piece on the fjords in Norway. We went over the whole coast, near-about, from Oslo all the way up around to the Barents Sea and the national park up there, which I still can't pronounce properly, way up where Norway curls over the top of Sweden and meets Finland. Varangahol…something near that, leastways. I don't know. Gorgeous country. Cloudy there a lot of the year, but when the sun does come out? Really makes you believe in God, I'll say that, and I'm nowhere near a religious person. I slept out rough with my guide more than a few nights, in the bed of the truck we used on the journey, and you watch the stars and then the sun comes out and it's huge and red and gold like the molten, freshly minted coin of some great giant god, I dunno. It's…there aren't words for it."

He went back to the van, tugged open the sliding door, reached in and rummaged in a backpack, pulled out an iPad protected by a rubberized case that looked like it could survive being dropped from ten thousand feet without a parachute. And, from what I knew of Errol so far, it wouldn't surprise me if it had.

He opened the iPad, tapped, swiped, and then

scrolled through a rotating display of photos until he came to a particular section, and then handed me the iPad. "There aren't words, but there *are* photos. Swipe left."

I swiped.

And gulped.

His photography was…breathtaking. I know I've seen his stuff in the magazine, but you assume that's all been professionally retouched and such before publication, and things always look different on the glossy pages of a *National Geographic*. But…seeing his raw, unedited photos? Fucking stunning.

"This is all the rough stuff, mind," he said, as if he had to qualify what I was looking at. "I sent something like ten thousand shots to Jerry and he had to cull it down to a dozen or so for the feature. I went through them myself before I sent those on, and after he picked, I cut what was left to my personal favorites. I've got cloud storage by the ass-load, of course, and I keep all the originals on the memory cards I shot them on, but what's here is my personal collection of untouched photos that aren't straight rubbish."

"Shut up," I said, "I'm admiring."

He laughed. "All right, then."

One shot in particular I had to stop and just soak in for several minutes. It was taken from the back of a small fjord, where two spits of land angled away and then curved back toward each other until they nearly touched. The sun was perfectly framed between the points of land, and the sea was nearly still. The shot was taken from low to the sea, and a small fishing vessel was backlit by the huge golden-red half-sun, a net in the process of being cast caught in perfect clarity mid-throw.

"Jesus, Errol."

He looked over my shoulder. "Oh yeah, that one. I stood waist-deep in the freezing water for an hour to get that. I was on the beach before sunrise, and those fishermen were getting ready—there's a little fishing village just out of the frame to the right, and I watched them most of the morning. I knew the shot I wanted, and I knew there's this moment, real early, when sometimes the water is just still like that. I mean, it's never like glass like you'd see on an inland lake, but it goes quiet like that, just around dawn, but only sometimes. I was hoping and praying it'd be one of those mornings. I waded out as far as I could, and I had to wait for the ripples to stop and the sun to come up and the fishermen to go out. And it was just straight up luck that they stopped to cast out just *there*, while the sun was just *there*."

"All good photography is art, but that's just... sublime."

He grinned, rubbed his hand through his hair. "Thanks. I am proud of that shot."

I swiped through a few more, and then handed him the iPad. "Better give that back before I get lost and just keep swiping."

He pulled out a little folding camp stove, and browned some ground beef, sliced up some fresh tomatoes, set out a little bag of shredded cheese, and a package of tortillas. When all was ready, he gestured at the spread. "Not fancy, but it'll fill ya."

I gaped at him. "Seriously? You can just… whip up fucking *tacos*, from a van, in the middle of nowhere?"

"It's no great magic, Poppy. There's a little fridge I keep the meat and cheese in, fresh tomatoes I got from a farm stand day before yesterday, and the tortillas I got at a petrol station dairy last week."

"Petrol station dairy?" I puzzled that one out. "A gas station with a little grocery store?"

He chuckled. "Got it in one."

"Dairy. Why dairy?"

He shrugged. "I dunno. They sell dairy products? Just what we call the little convenience stores like that."

We ate his magic tacos, which were not fancy but were delicious and filling; by the time we were done and things were cleaned up, it was getting dark.

Errol climbed into his van and dug around through his stuff, coming up with a sleeping bag, two pillows, and a tightly rolled fleece blanket bound by a small bungee cord. The sleeping bag was the super expensive mountaineering kind, but the pillows seemed suspiciously like they'd come from a hotel; I couldn't have said what gave me that impression, but they were not pillows from anything like *home*.

When I mentioned it, he laughed sheepishly. "Yeah, I sorta nicked 'em from a hotel in…where was that? Bergen? Oslo? Norway, somewhere. They're nice pillows, and I'd forgotten mine, so I packed 'em up and took 'em with." He held up the sleeping bag in one hand and the blanket in the other. "You pick. I've used both and they'll both keep you plenty warm, 'specially on a night like this."

I looked around. "We're just gonna sleep on the ground?"

"Yeah. Bit firm at first, but you get used to it."

I made a face. "A bit firm. The *ground* is a bit firm, you say?"

"Yeah nah." He stomped on the earth, no hint of sarcasm on his face. "Nice plush grass here, no rocks. I mean, you want to get fancy about it, you could go cut some branches and make a little nest."

I snorted. "How do you say it? Yeah, nah."

"You say it in all one go—yeah-nah." He laughed.

"But that's not really how that one works. It's…well, it's complicated. It can mean heaps of subtly different things, but it usually doesn't mean yeah, no like you used it just then."

I sighed. "Oh."

He laughed all the harder. "No worries, you'll get it."

"I'll take the blanket," I said, reaching for it.

He unfurled the sleeping bag and lay it in the grass near the van, sat in the open doorway of the van and unlaced his boots, which were well-worn Salomon hiking boots—he tossed the boots into the van and shucked his socks off, which he carefully laid out beside the boots. He was wearing gray-and-blue board shorts with a plain heather-gray muscle shirt, which combined with the hiking boots gave him an air of someone who could hop onto a surfboard and ride some waves, chuck on his boots again and then go free-climb a mountain face. He'd been wearing his Wayfarers till the sun set, and then he'd shoved them up onto his head, using them to hold his hair back from his face.

I noticed he was wearing a necklace made of shark teeth; each tooth separated by a complicated knot of the hemp the necklace. Errol being Errol, I just knew there was a fantastically, unbelievably cool story to go with it.

Realizing I was standing with the blanket and pillow in my hands, blatantly staring at him, I flung the blanket onto the ground a bit more forcefully than necessary and lay down on it, twisting to unzip my boots and kick them off, and then slid my thick, sweaty socks off with them.

"Bit of advice?" I heard Errol say.

"Sure?"

"Put your boots in the van and lay out your socks like I did."

"Why?"

"Well, I don't know for sure what sort of creatures live around here, but nothing you want taking up residence in your boots. And the socks, if you want them dry by morning, leaving them all crumpled up like that won't do you any favors."

"If there are creatures that might crawl into my boots, what's to stop them from crawling on *me*?" I asked, squirming uncomfortably.

"Because they can sense you're a living thing, and not a place to hide."

"Oh." Somewhat mollified, I tried to banish the creepy-crawly feeling I had imagining something slithering over my skin when I thought of something with too many legs crawling on me. I did as he suggested with my boots and socks, and then lay back down on the blanket.

For the first time since we met this morning, there was silence between us. I shifted, he shifted. A cough. Rustle. Feeling the cool setting in, I tugged the blanket out from under me and covered myself with it.

I heard his breathing shift, falling asleep.

"Poppy?"

"Mmm."

"I sleep light, so you know."

"'Kay?"

"So, you know, you're safe."

I huffed a laugh. "Honestly, it never crossed my mind that I wasn't."

"Good. Because you are."

"Thank you, Errol."

And holy moly, did that notion set my brain to whirling.

It literally did not for a single second cross my mind that I might be unsafe, sleeping outside in the middle of nowhere with a total stranger.

Because…he was just…safe.

I was safe with him.

A total stranger.

A man five years older than me, who very obviously felt a serious amount of lust for me.

I was absolutely safe with him, as safe as if I'd been at home in my apartment in New York. Safer, maybe.

Fucking *weird*.

I stared up at the stars for a long, long time. I'd never seen such a sight, a countless billion, trillion points of light twinkling and scintillating like diamonds lit from within, scattered across the sky in washes and sprays. I picked out the few constellations I knew—the Big Dipper, and…well, that was about it, actually. But just lying there, watching the stars turn overhead, I did, as Errol had predicted, feel strangely alive, a frisson of wild energy surging through me, as if rising up from the earth and into me.

And all the while, I was hyperaware of Errol, snoring gently and softly beside me. Close, but not too close.

Safe.

What a weird thing to feel with a stranger.

SIX

Errol

I WOKE UP ABRUPTLY, AND TOTALLY. DEAD ASLEEP TO FULLY awake in a split second, but unsure what had woken me. It was predawn, between dark and graying to light, the air chilled and still and dew-laden.

Then I heard it, a snuffling, shuffling. *Errrrrrfff. Rrrrrrowwwwwfff. Chuff chuff.*

A bear.

I saw it, less than six feet away, ambling opposite us and the van toward the pond. Huge, black, shaggy head swiveling, paws padding quietly.

"Mmm." Poppy, sensing something, stirring. Not trained to wake up quickly and immediately like I was.

I wiggled closer to her, leaned over her, placed my palm over her mouth and hissed her name. *"Poppy."*

Her eyes flew open and her hand latched onto my hand, twisting against the joint with a vicious yank that spoke of self-defense classes.

"Poppy," I hissed again. *"It's me."* I kept my palm over her mouth, used my other hand to point at the bear.

Her eyes widened, and her defensive grip slackened. I shushed her again, and she nodded, so I let go. She twisted in the blanket, watching as the bear prowled lazily down to the water and drank, pausing to look around and listen, and then drink again. A few rounds of drink-pause-drink, and then it continued on around the pond, vanishing into the forest. As soon as it was out of sight, it was so quiet there was no indication that it had been there at all. A bird whistled, another answered, and then the forest was alive with the song of dawn.

I was still leaning over her, pressed against her thigh to chest, the thick squish of her breasts flattened against my chest. With an utterly natural gesture, she rested her palm against the outside of my bicep, her eyes on mine. The sliver of air between her face and mine blazed and crackled with chemical energy, the reactive pulse of mutual desire. A centimeter of space between her face and mine.

Her lips and mine.

Even her lips were beautiful. Plump, with a deep Cupid's bow, naturally pink. Delicate and kissable.

I had no hope of not kissing her. Futile to even consider it. She was soft; her skin was warm where her arm touched mine, where her hand slid up my bicep. Her breasts spilled sideways out of her shirt, and if she moved just so either way, one or the other would spill out. I wouldn't complain if they did, but I wasn't going to push my luck by helping them along. Not yet, anyway. For now, I slowly let gravity pull my mouth closer to hers, and she blinked up at me, held my gaze, and then her lips parted with a sigh as the last paper-thin millimeter vanished, and I felt her mouth on mine, wet warmth melding and melting on me, and her sigh turned to a murmur turned to a moan as the kiss gradually deepened.

Her palm floated up my arm, over my shoulder, graced into my hair and held me into the kiss, pulled me closer. Hers was the first tongue to quest out, but I eagerly met hers with my own, and then somehow our bodies were melting together, clothed but melding, fitting just so, angles into curves, softness into muscle.

How long did we just kiss? I don't know. Time stopped. Melted along with my lips on hers, my chest against hers, her hip against mine. The only thing that didn't melt was my cock, becoming a hard ridge between us—and her nipples, pebbling against my chest.

I wanted...

A complicated thing.

To delve into this, with this woman. To know how she tasted, every inch of her. To plummet into pleasure with her. Here, in the predawn gray, with bear tracks dimpling the grass mere feet away, with pink staining the horizon.

But for once in my fucked-up life, I didn't want to rush into it.

Always before I've been after getting to the good bits right off. Kiss to touch to come, goodbye. Not because I don't care or don't want to know, but because I haven't got the capacity to care, to know a person beyond hello and goodbye. Beyond the shape of curves and sounds of sighs, beyond a sleeping form under covers of a dim hotel room as I shoulder my bag, leaving the keycards by the TV, paying for the room as I leave.

Just jumping into the rough exploration of naked flesh as fast as I can get her there, into what makes her scream hardest, soonest.

Because if all I've got is the moment, let's make the best of it before the next bend in the metaphorical road calls me onward.

As it always does.

Yet here I am, with a willing woman under me, kissing me fit to devour, all but silently begging me to strip her naked and show her what she's been missing all this time…and I find myself slowing us down.

Resisting the siren song of her breast as it sags with heavy natural weight nearly out of the side of her tank top, resisting the slip of her thigh between mine.

Wanting to enjoy the ascent to the peak, not just the mountaintop high.

I pulled away from the kiss, and she was baffled. "Errol? I…I thought…"

I was just as confused, and now I had to make sense of it to her. Leaning up on an elbow, I made no bones about devouring the allure of her curves with my eyes. "Poppy, I…"

She bit her lower lip, fingers brushing at wayward locks of my hair. Familiar, intimate, affectionate—delirium-inducing. "I wasn't going to stop, Errol."

"I know." I was still hunting for an explanation that would make sense.

"So why'd you…why'd you stop?"

"I…it's…" I sighed in frustration. "Not sure how to explain it, honestly."

"Well, try, before I start feeling rejected. And pro-tip, I don't deal with rejection well, buddy."

I sucked in a slow breath, held it. Stared down at

her—golden skin bathed in the soft pink of new dawn light, black hair like an ink spill on the pillow under her head, molten cocoa eyes searching mine, not hiding her confusion or desire, the generous cleft of her cleavage taunting me, sideboob swell on either side of her tank top strap drawing my eyes and begging for my lips and my palms, her floral print skirt hiked up around her knees, blanket shoved aside, bare feet cute and sliding against her calves and my knee.

"God, you're fucking gorgeous," I breathed, the truth drawn from my lips. I brushed a fingertip over her forehead, sliding a thick sheaf of black hair aside. "I'm always rushing into things," I said. "Always running from one thing to another. I never stay anywhere long. Never hang around any one person for long. But for some reason, with you, I don't want to rush right into things. I can't explain it even to myself, Poppy. But the truth, as best I can verbalize it, is that I want to enjoy the process of getting there, with you. I don't know what that means. I just know I've never met anyone as fascinating or as beautiful as you, and I know I probably will never meet anyone like you again, and I want to just…I don't know how to put it…*savor* what we have for as long as we have it."

"Oh," she breathed. "That's a good explanation." Something haunted flickered through her expression, however.

"What?"

She shook her head, faking innocent confusion. "What, what?"

I sat up, and so did she. We sat facing each other—I was sitting crisscross and she had her knees hugged to her chest. "I saw that look. Dunno what it meant, but it wasn't nothing."

She laughed. "You don't miss a thing, do you?" A sigh. "It's just…weird. Because I was thinking the same thing. And it's just weird. I've never *not* wanted to rush into things before. And it's weird to think about, and weirder to talk about."

"So, how about I make some coffee and we can do one of two things—ignore it, sweep it under the rug so to speak and not worry about it and just go with it since we both feel the same way—whatever that is and whatever it means." I shrugged. "Or we can hash it out and just deal with the weirdness."

Poppy laughed. "Is there an option C?"

I stood up and began rolling the sleeping bag. "I mean, not as far as I can see. You see one, please, let me know what it is."

"Coffee first."

I pointed at her. "I knew I liked you for a reason."

She smirked. "I thought you liked me for two reasons."

I let my eyes rake down to her chest. "I mean,

those are some seriously world-class reasons to like you, but I'm not actually as shallow as that." I grinned. "I guess I'd have to investigate the matter further before I can say whether those are the only reasons I like you."

She tugged the shirt up by the straps, lifting her breasts tantalizingly, but also settling them into the shirt more fully as well. "I thought you were about to *investigate* just now, but you stopped."

I growled as I hopped up into the van and got out the supplies to make coffee. "I was. I want to, even right now. I told you, I don't know how to explain it. It's not like me, at all."

"So normally we'd both be naked right about now, you're saying?"

I didn't dare look at her, instead focused on counting out scoops of coffee beans into the manual grinder. "Well, if you're asking how I usually do things…no. *You'd* be naked. I'd probably still be mostly dressed. I'd have a mess all over my face, and you'd be on your second or third orgasm."

Profound silence.

I looked at her then. Had to. Her nostrils were flaring, and her fingers were knotted together on her lap. Her nipples were drawn to pointed peaks against her shirt, and for the first time I noticed two dimples to either side of the outline of her nipples—she had piercings. Shit, shit, shit. I've always been curious about that, what it was like to get my mouth on a woman with pierced nipples.

Fuck.

Her eyes were heated. Almost angry, or something like it. She was breathing deeply, slowly, as if measuring out each breath to keep her composure. Each breath made those breasts swell, which did nothing good for my own composure.

I don't mean to wax on about them, but her breasts made me crazy. Not just because they were big—and make no mistake, they were *huge*—but because of their shape, the way they hung against her shirt, the totality of them. I'm not obsessed with the biggest breasts, I like small ones too. All breasts are good breasts in my opinion, and I've enjoyed all shapes and sizes. But hers were just…fucking *glorious*.

And when she took those big slow breaths, the way her shirt stretched and showed the hard peaks of her nipples and the bumps of her piercings…I about went nuts. About abandoned the idea of going slow, wanting to just rip that damn shirt into shreds and bury my face between those lush silk mounds until I suffocated.

Idiotic, I know.

Shallow and rabid and macho and testosterone-fueled moon-headed stupidity.

And I only just barely restrained myself.

She was glaring at me. Staring at me, drawing in those slow deep breaths and fixing me with a hot hard look I didn't know how to begin deciphering.

"Poppy? Are you mad?"

"American mad, or British mad?" She asked, her voice pitched low and husky, almost hoarse.

I chuckled at that. "Both? Either?"

"I feel like you're playing with me, Errol, and I don't like being toyed with. I'm an upfront sort of girl. What you see is what you get. I don't play games. I don't play hard to get. I know what I want, and I take it, and when I'm done, I'm done." She stood up, began rolling the fleece blanket into the same tight package as I did, found the bungee and looped, hooked, and set the rolled-up blanket on the edge of the van's open doorway, not getting within reach of me, as if I was a dangerous animal. "You want me? Say so. Better yet, show me. I'm not easy, but I've got no qualms about going for what I want when I know I want it, and I know exactly what I want where you're concerned, Errol. So, when you kiss me like that, and get me worked up, and I start thinking things are going to happen, and then you back off like you *don't* want me, or like there's some reason we shouldn't hook up…and then you're all like 'I want to take it slow' but you can't explain why…and then you say some shit like *that*? What fucking game are you playing, dude? So, am I mad? Yes. And feeling a little of both senses, actually."

I growled. "I can't fault you for that. But I also can't change what I feel. I'm not playing games. Swear I'm not."

She huffed but said nothing else; I wasn't sure if my answer had mollified her or made it worse.

I had an electric kettle, and at the start of the process I'd poured water from a sealed bottle and set it to boiling while I measured and ground the coffee beans. Then, when the electric kettle clicked off as it reached a rolling boil, I slowly poured it over my Chemex. Coffee being such a vital part of my morning routine, I had no issue reserving space in my limited gear for the kettle and Chemex, because as long as I had potable water and electricity, I could make coffee. And I always carried a small solar battery so, in a pinch, I could boil the water when I was away from the grid…and I always carried a portable filtration system so I could be sure my water was potable. Yeah, I'm serious about my coffee.

When it was ready, I poured the piping hot black liquid into camp mugs and glanced at Poppy. "I hope you take it black, because I don't have milk or sugar."

She snorted. "Guess I'll take it black, then." A grin. "I do drink it black, though, so it's all good."

"You missed your chance to practice sounding like a Kiwi. That was a prime spot to say 'no worries, mate.'"

"I thought that was an Australian term."

"Well, there's a bit of overlap." I handed her a mug and sat in the open doorway. Sipped.

She blew across the top, took a ginger sip, sitting in the doorway beside me, but not too close. "Damn, Errol. This is fucking fantastic."

I smirked behind my mug. "I was in Indonesia recently, I think I told you that, and while I was there I made a point of visiting a few coffee farms. Ended up doing this little freelance puff piece on organic coffee farming for a tiny international coffee roasters e-zine. Upshot is, one of the farmers personally roasted a ten-pound bag just for me. I mean, I helped pick the cherries, helped wash them, helped out the process from pick to roast. Fascinating process. And now I'm addicted, so I'm gonna have to end up flying all the way back to that one particular farm so I can get more, because plain old store-bought garbage ain't gonna cut it anymore."

"No shit." She shook her head and laughed.

"What's funny?"

"You. You literally have a story for *everything*. Nothing you do, nothing you own is just…normal boring bullshit. I bet even your shoes are interesting."

I glanced at my boots where they sat beside me, feeling self-conscious, now. "Well, I mean…"

She laughed, a shriek of disbelief. "There is! I knew it! Even your fucking shoes have a cool story."

I sighed. "Not *that* cool."

"Not buying that for a second."

"Fine. Short version is this—I was doing a piece on archeological digs in Brazil…last year, I think. Maybe end of the year before. I was deep in the jungle, me and the writer I was working with, some archeologists, our guides. It was a big group of us. We were making our way out, actually, the piece wrapped up and we headed for civilization after something like three weeks in the mosquito-infested jungle, getting rained on and bitten, snakes crawling all over you inside your fucking tent somehow, boots soaked, socks soaked, fucking miserable, actually. Ready for a hotel and a bed and a meal I didn't cook myself over the camp stove."

"This is the short version?" she interrupted.

I laughed. "Fine, I don't have a short version. I'm a long-winded bag of self-important hot air, okay?"

"Now we come to the truth," she said, laughing at me over the top of her mug.

"Hey, you asked."

She nodded. "Indeed I did. So? What happened? Bandits stole your boots and you had to fight them off barefoot with only a machete and your belt?"

I rolled my eyes. "Not quite. I got stuck. Our ute got stuck to the arches in mud, and it took all of us pushing and pulling to get it out, and in the process my boots came right off while I was knee-deep in mud. Boots, socks, the whole lot. Just sucked right off. I'd packed light, so those were my only pair." I snorted. "So, I did the only thing I could—went mud diving. Had to hunt around in two, three feet of mud for half an hour, but I found them. Of course, it was days before they were clean and dry enough to wear again, and the boots I had to borrow were two sizes too small, but still. I rescued them, and I've been wearing them just about every day since."

She shook her head. "See? Stories for everything."

"You hungry?" I asked.

She lifted a shoulder. "Um…? Yeah-nah."

I cackled. "You're getting it. Assuming you mean you're not really hungry, but you'll eat if I make something, but don't feel like imposing by asking."

"Wow. That is a very specific nuance of meaning." I nodded. "But largely accurate, actually."

"I'm not much for brekkie either, so if you're cool, I'm cool. We can finish our coffee and head out."

She just nodded, sipping at her coffee.

After a few minutes, she looked at me over her mug. "So we're avoiding, then."

I reached behind me, grabbed the Chemex and refilled her mug and mine. "I'm not playing games with you, Poppy," I said again. "I swear by anything I'm not."

She watched mist writhe on the surface of the pond, swirling as a pair of ducks scudded down from the tree line, wings curved and legs extended, to land with soft twin V-trails on the green water.

"So you do want me."

"Too much, maybe."

"But yet you stopped when I was clearly ready to go all the way with you."

"You're making me feel a bit stupid for it."

"I just don't know…" She shrugged, shook her head. "It's new. It's different. I'm absolutely not some…shrinking violet or…or prudish virgin who needs you to tiptoe around my feelings and be all sweet and gentle. I hope you realize that. I've never had a guy just…pull back like that. So I don't know what to make of it."

I scraped my hair backward. "I…shit. I don't know how to make sense of it because it's not like me, which I've said more than once now."

"Try."

"I fuckin' am, alright?" I winced. "Sorry, don't

mean to snap." I took a too-big swig off too-hot coffee, scorching my throat. When I could speak again, I was a little hoarse. "Fucking hot, holy shit."

I paused to sip slowly, swallow, and then start again.

"When I was a kid, Mum and me would go for ice cream after she was done in the studio, and I'd have mine gone while she was on her third bite, and I always, always promised myself I'd go slower next time. But I never could. Then one day, I did. I chomped down that first bite, and then I was like, 'no mate, savor it,' so I forced myself to slow down. To really *taste* it. Each bite was slow, deliberate. I tried to make it last as long as possible. And, I fuckin' swear, I'll remember that ice-cream cone for the rest of my life."

"So I'm like ice cream." Her tone was…not flat, but I couldn't decide how she felt about my metaphor.

"Sort of. Metaphorically." I chewed on the inside of my cheek. "I mean, yeah. Creamy, delicious, and something I want to devour, and have to make myself slow down and enjoy it properly."

"And you don't usually do that." She held my gaze, keeping her poker face on, not letting her feelings show. "Take it slow. Sexually, you just…chomp it all down as fast as you can."

"You want the real, honest answer?"

She nodded, sat forward and fixed me with a serious, fierce expression. "Every single time, Errol. Always. There's not much I hate more than a liar. Lies of omission, flat-out lies, lies to spare feelings, lies to avoid uncomfortable conversations, all of it. I'll take the brutal truth over a pleasant lie every time."

"So then, yeah. Normally I'm an all-in, right-off sort. Like I was as a kid with ice cream. And yeah, I get that impulse sometimes, that voice that tells me to slow down and savor things a bit, but I never listen. I can't. With that, with sex, slowing down is…"

"Complicated? Or maybe it's more accurate to say complicat*ing*?"

I nodded, sighing in relief. "Yeah, exactly. Complicating."

"So I guess I get all that. But the question is, then, why me? Why slow down with me?" She stood up, paced away, mug held in both hands. Stood barefoot at the edge of the water, so the glass-still water licked at her toe-tips.

I held my place. Thought about it. Really, I did. Hunted for a reason that made any kind of sense, that fit into the puzzle of words. "I wish I knew, Poppy. But I don't. Shit of me, maybe, but I just can't explain why you." I huffed. "I like metaphors, so here's another one for you. It's like coffee. When I've got average coffee, I'll drink a pot quick as anything. Three, four mugs, not even thinkin' about it. It's just coffee. But this?" I held up the Chemex, with the last inch of black swirling around the bottom of the handblown glass. "This isn't just coffee, it's an experience. I sip it slow. Taste the flavors. One cup, maybe two, trying to make the bag I've got last as long as possible, trying to make each cup last as long as I can without it going cold."

She turned to face me, still at the water's edge. "First I'm ice cream, now I'm coffee?" A tiny, telltale smirk, just a shadow of a smile at the corner of her lips, a subtle twinkle to her eyes.

"I mean, yeah. My two favorite things are ice cream and coffee." A pause. "Favorite things in the world of food and drink, I mean."

"I see." She paused. "So what you're saying is, I'm not just any old regular coffee, I'm *special* coffee."

"Not just special. You can buy *special* coffee, it just costs more. You can't buy this. To get *this* exact coffee, you have to visit *that* farm on *that* hill outside Jakarta, and have *that* roast master roast the beans just so." I held her gaze. "Not just special. So unique, so incredible, to waste it by rushing would be…it'd be a crime."

She huffed, dropped her head, shaking it, hiding a grin. "Okay…that was good."

I stood up, set my mug down. Crossed the space between us, halting when a few scant inches separated us. "It wasn't a line. Wasn't meant to impress you or sound good. I was just telling you the truth. It's what you wanted."

"What I *wanted* was some nice hot, slow morning sex. What I got is blue balls, and you talking the smoothest game I've ever heard in my life."

"I'm not talking a game, Poppy. I told you, I don't play. You wanted to know why I stopped, and I'm trying to tell you."

She stared up at me. Mug held between us like a shield protecting her virtue. I held her eyes, and hoped she saw the genuineness in me. Saw that I wasn't fucking around with her.

I don't know what she saw, but it apparently seemed to mollify her, to some degree.

"Fine." She pushed past me, set the mug down.

I turned to watch. "Fine? What do you mean, fine?"

"I mean fine, I'll play along." She laughed.

"I've said, I'm not—"

"I know," she cut in. "I just mean we can do things your way. For now."

"I don't know what the hell I'm doing, though, just so you're aware."

Another laugh, but it was low, soft. Her eyes flicked

to mine, slid down my body. Her tongue dragged over her lips as she looked at me, as if her hunger for my body was a nearly irresistible force. "Just pretend I'm ice cream," she suggested, smirking at me with hooded eyes dancing with innuendo. "Take your time eating me."

The blatant suggestion set fire to my blood. I prowled across the grass to her. Stood over her, close enough that her breasts brushed my chest. "You know how I eat ice cream, now?" I whispered. "As slow as possible. I eat it one…slow…lick…at a time." Her breath caught, hitched, and she swallowed hard. "But I don't just *lick* it. Oh no. I use my whole mouth. Tongue, lips, teeth. I've usually got *ice cream* all over my mouth when I'm through. All messy. Then I wipe that away with my fingers and lick it off one by one." I snagged her wrist, brought her index finger to my mouth, slid it in, closed my lips over it, and dragged her finger slowly through my lips, tonguing it every inch of the way. "Like that."

Her nipples hardened against my chest. "You must really like ice cream."

"I fucking *love* ice cream." I still had her hand in mine, and I now set about licking between her fingers, licking suggestively at the V where they met. "But you know, traveling like I do, I don't get to have it for long periods of time. For example, it's been *months* since I've had ice cream. And I'm fuckin' *dyin'* for it."

Another hard swallow, her throat bobbing, lashes blinking slowly, eyes searching, flicking. "Holy shit, Errol."

I'd talked myself into trouble. Not trouble, because there was no reason we couldn't do what we wanted, both of us being sober, consenting adults. I just…I was slavering for her, now. All the talk of ice cream, the suggestion, the innuendo, and now the teasing weight of her breasts against my chest and the dimpling hard nubs of her nipple piercings…

Fuck.

I needed…*something*.

One hand crept out, touched her hip over her skirt. She held my eyes, didn't move—just waited me out. Slowly, I gathered the thin soft cotton of her skirt material in my hand, lifting the hem ever so gradually. Just on one side, with one hand. I let my eyes slip down to where the rising hem bared her ankle, then calf, then knee, then lower thigh, then hip. I kept expecting to see the lace or cotton of her underwear, but as I held the bunched fabric in my fist, her entire buttock, hip, and thigh bared in profile, I realized she wasn't wearing any. Not a stitch of undergarment, not a bra, not underwear. Daring girl. I released the skirt and cupped the outside of her hip—smooth, warm, soft. The softest, most delicate skin I'd ever touched. She inhaled quietly, a short intake of air through her nose, eyes remaining on mine, otherwise utterly motionless.

I let that one hand curl around to cradle her ass cheek…and at the hot silken heft of it in my hand, my cock went ramrod stiff. I knew she felt it, the way our bodies were touching, thigh and hips and chest. She gave no indication, didn't move, but her eyes widened.

I held her buttock in my hand, just savored the feel of it, the reality of this extraordinary privilege, to be able to touch this perfect woman, this gloriously gorgeous creature, this woman with a body that could start wars. I kneaded the flesh, the muscle. Smoothed it. Then brought my touch away, around to her hip, because as amazing as it was, her ass wasn't what I wanted in that moment.

What I wanted wasn't to take, but to *give*.

I couldn't help but lick my lower lip in anticipation as I slowly, gradually slid my hand around the outside of her hip, over hipbone. No, not a scrap of underwear, just smooth bare skin under that thin skirt. Close-trimmed fuzz where her thighs met—I felt it scritching under my fingers.

She sucked in a harsh breath, then, as I turned my fingertips downward, and delved between her thighs—her skin everywhere was silken, but there? Her upper, inner thighs, where they touched to hide her delicate, soaked center? What's softer than silk?

What's smoother, more delicate, more fragile, more lovely? I don't know. I just know I've never felt such skin as hers. She swallowed, blinked finally, eyes wide, searching.

She moved, finally. Her left foot slid aside, and her hands lifted to rest on my shoulders, and just like that, her core was exposed to my touch. Welcoming. Inviting.

She held her breath as I traced a line over her sex. I held my own as I drew that line downward, over her seam. And when I held my breath, she hissed hers out. I growled low in my chest as I drew my finger up, then, over her sex again, and delved in. That was when she whimpered, hips shifting forward eagerly, impulsively.

God, such delicate wet beauty, to touch her like this. Such a wild privilege, to feel her. Such brazen, brave boldness, the way she let me slowly explore her this way.

Slicking in, delving in. Pulling out and smearing the juices of her arousal over her plump, taut lips. Over the tight hard nub of her clit, making her shiver, flinch, groan.

It took a moment, maybe two. A swipe, a delve inward, another circle, and she was gasping, writhing against me.

"Already?"

She nodded, biting her lip. "Yeah." Another helpless whimper. "But don't let that stop you."

Even in the throes of a slow, rolling orgasm, she had that quippy attitude.

"Stop me?" I grinned down her. "I'm just getting warmed up."

She groaned, and her forehead thunked forward against my chest. "Oh thank fuck."

SEVEN

Poppy

Holy mother of orgasms, Batman. Like, whoa.

Maybe it was the fact that it had been several months since I'd had an orgasm that I didn't give myself, and to be totally honest, the ones I've gotten out of Mr. Buzzyguy and the Fingers have been pretty fricking lackluster lately. Boring, low-intensity. I've been saving my data and battery life on my phone for emergencies and navigation, which means I've been relying on my memory bank for visual and sexual stimulation. Which, normally, is pretty effective. I have a super vivid pictorial memory, and some pretty hot experiences to draw on. But for some reason, the farther I wander from New York, the farther away it all seems.

Another, more significant issue is that most of my more recent sexual experience worth even remembering were with Fucking Asshole Reed Piece of Moldy Dog Shit O-Fucking-Reilly. And I refuse to honor his memory by jilling off to him. I have vowed to purge all memories of him from my mind, heart, body, and soul, now and forevermore, amen. Fuck him. Fuck him with a Saguaro cactus. Shove it sideways up his cheating prick asshole. Which sucks, because sex with Reed was fantastic. Until I found him—

No.

Nope.

Forget that memory.

There is no Reed O'Reilly. There is no Shannyn Mallory. There is no Yvonne Johnson. None of them hold any place in my memory.

I was mentally wandering from the feel of Errol's fingers—trying to retain some sort of emotional objectivity because good motherfuck, in all my sexual life I've never come so hard, so fast, from such little stimulation. He literally touched me, like, twice. A slow wandering touch of his fingers over my thighs, up my seam, and inside me, a swirl around my clit, another, and I was coming so hard I could barely stand up. I had to cling to his shoulders, had to hope if my knees buckled he'd catch me.

"Stop me?" His whisper was a low raspy growl, a seductive leonine hiss of sexual promise that hit my arousal like a freight train. "I'm just getting warmed up."

Was it possible to come just from a man's voice? The fucking accent. The confident smirk that said he knew *exactly* how to make me come and keep me there. The roughness of the pad of his fingers, the strength in his hand—made my clit harden to a diamond point, made my nipples ache so bad if he would just brush them with his finger or his lips, I'd come again, even harder. The wild hunger in his eyes that made me feel like not only the only woman in the world, but the most incredible thing he'd ever seen, something he couldn't go another damn second without.

I've been *told* I'm beautiful all my life.

Made to *feel* beautiful? Desirable?

Not as common.

Had I ever felt this way? Had any man ever made me like this?

The resounding *NO* that klaxoned through my mind actually sort of worried me, scared me.

His fingers were exploring my sheath, two of them now, slipped inside my sex and gathering my essence, slicking in and sliding out, a poor imitation of the penetration I needed, wanted. HIM. More of him.

The slow in-and-out of his fingers, the way they scissored inside me, the way they curled inward to scrape those rough fingertips against me deep inside in that secret spot so few male fingers ever seemed to find—which he found with unerring accuracy, as if he just *knew* my body, as if he'd fingered me before, as if I'd been his and under his spell before—his touch slashed through my wandering, distracto-pony thoughts and demanded my full attention.

"Poppy," Errol murmured.

"Y-yeah?" I gasped, my hips beginning to move again, subtly, slowly, as he set a gentle and undemanding rhythm.

"You need to come again."

"Fuck yeah, I do." I pressed my chest against him, twisted and writhed, seeking friction against my piercings.

His other hand, the one not manipulating me slowly upward toward the knife-edge of another climax, was resting on my hip. Not where I wanted it. I rested my forehead against his chest for balance as I rolled my hips into his touch, pulled my breasts away from his body. I let go of his neck with one hand, grasped the thick wrist of his free hand, guided his palm to slide up over the swell of my hip, along the curve of my waist, pressed his huge strong hand to cup my breast.

He moaned as the delicate, heavy weight of my breast filled his hand. His thumb immediately swiped over my nipple, his fingernail catching on the ball of my piercing, sending a searing jolt of lightning surging through my whole body, drawing a breathless, teeth-clenched scream from me.

"Jesus, Poppy. Fuckin' sensitive there, aren't you?"

I lifted up on my toes, drove my nose into the side of his neck, and sank my teeth into the thick tendon of his shoulder, growling like a caged lioness as he dragged his thumbnail over the bar through the nipple to catch on the balls capping either end.

He snarled at my bite, but didn't pull away, didn't push me off—instead, he did three things all at once: pinched my nipple, pressed the sandpaper fingertips of three fingers over my clit and circled hard and fast, and rocked his pelvis against my thigh so the hard ridge of a monster erection pressed against me.

"Come for me," he grunted, low, rough, commanding. "Come, *now*."

Obedience to his command was involuntary, a physical, visceral response to his touch, the feel of him, the sound of his voice in my ear, the hard wall of his body providing a safe harbor for me to shelter in as I rode the hurricane waves of orgasm, my throat squeezing as I screamed through it, the sound muffled against the bulk of his shoulder and soft warm skin of his strong neck.

I clawed at his back as I climaxed, for sure leaving reddened marks as my nails dragged over the cotton of his muscle shirt. The moment the peak of climax released me from its clenching, pulsing grip, I raked my fingers down his chest and traced the outline of his erection, greedily seeking to feel the shape of it, the length of it.

"My fucking god, Errol," I breathed into his ear, awed at what I felt. "You're fucking *huge*."

He just laughed. "Glad you like what you feel."

"I'd like what I feel a hell of a lot more if it was naked and in my fist." I bit his earlobe. "Or better yet, inside me."

He growled, palming my tit, lifting it, the bulk of my breast still behind the ribbed fabric of my tank top; he hadn't even bared my boobs yet, and I'd come twice, harder than I'd believed it was possible for any human being to come—standing up, fully clothed, to boot.

Yeah, I needed Errol to fuck me the same way I needed my next breath.

At that exact moment, tires crunched to my right, brakes squealed, and a car door opened. "The hell are you two doing on my land?" A deep, irritated male voice, with a distinct *Missourah* twang.

Errol pivoted to put himself between the other man and me, surreptitiously withdrawing his hand from under my skirt, tugging my shirt in place, and then turning to face the pissed-off owner of the pond—I knew he had to be sporting a visible erection, but if he felt any embarrassment over the fact, he didn't show it.

"Sorry, mate," Errol said, keeping me entirely shielded with his body. "We were driving late last night, got a bit lost and ended up here. It was late, it was pitch dark, and our phones had no service, so we just parked the campervan and stayed here for the night. We weren't aiming to trespass, and we didn't even light a fire. We'll be gone straight away, alright?"

The man towered even over Errol, but was skinny as a flagpole, hunched forward as if his height was too great a weight for his spine to support. He was wearing baggy overalls stuffed into knee-high muck boots, a flannel shirt unbuttoned and flapping open to show a bare chest behind the overalls, with a dirty green-and-yellow John Deere hat sitting high and back on his head to show tufts of graying blond hair. He had a double-barrel shotgun broken open over his elbow, and a battered brown Chevy pickup truck that been old the year I was born idling behind him.

"Well, I guess there ain't no harm in that, but I'll thank you to get a move on." He eyed Errol up and down. "Looks like I caught you at the wrong moment, didn't I?" he asked with a crooked, teasing grin.

Errol laughed, good-naturedly. "Yeah, you did, at that." He glanced over his shoulder at the pond. "Sweet spot you've got here, though. Beautiful."

"Sure is. And now, this bein' private property, ya'll better get along."

"Sure thing, mate," Errol said—and I had the impression he was playing up his accent a bit. "We're good as gone. Have a good one."

He turned to put his back to the man, still keeping himself between the shotgun-wielding property owner and me and pushed me gently but firmly to precede him into the van. I climbed into the open sliding door and slid into the passenger seat, fastening the seat belt as Errol slammed the slider closed, hopped behind the wheel, ignited the motor, and did a three-point turn. The property owner was in his truck already, pulling forward into the clearing to make room for us on the narrow track through pine forest.

Neither of us spoke a word, tension from the encounter rattling in the van like a marble in a soda can. Radio off; the only sound our breathing, the tires, and the hum of the engine. Despite his story about being lost, Errol navigated back to the highway without error, and without consulting GPS. We hit the highway, paused with our front tires on the paved road and our rear tires in the gravel. A brief glance left and right—the highway was empty at this hour, just past dawn—and then he hooked left to continue on the way we'd been going before making the turn-off.

"You put yourself between me and him," I said, eventually.

He glanced at me, seeming a bit confused, if anything. "Well…yeah. Of course I did. He had a gun and I'd no way of knowing how friendly he'd be."

"I just…thank you for that."

"Don't make it out to be some kind of great act of chivalry. It was instinct."

"To protect me."

He nodded, his expression serious. "Yeah. I mean, I protect things that I value."

"Most guys I've known wouldn't have done that—stood between me and the threat."

"Then you've never met a proper man, have you? Only a sissy-fuck little boy would do anything but shield you in a situation like that. I'm not sayin' this to sound like I've got antiquated notions of gender roles or anything, but it's a man's job to protect a woman. You can handle yourself just fine, I see that clear as anything. But if there's danger, I'm not gonna sit around with my thumb in my mouth, I'm gonna nut up and take it on so you don't have to."

That was fucking hot. I shifted on the seat; now that the danger was past, the heat of what had been interrupted came flooding back through me. "I'm sorry we got interrupted the way we did," I said, letting my gaze drop to his groin, hoping he'd still have that hard-on going. Sadly, he didn't.

He chewed on the inside of his cheek, glanced at me. "What are you sorry for? Wasn't anything you could've done."

"No, I mean…it was shitty timing." I scraped my teeth over my lower lip. "I'm a firm believer that turnabout is fair play."

His gaze went heated. "That so?"

"Yeah, absolutely." I kept my eyes on him as he alternated between looking at me and at the road. "You made me feel…*really* fucking good, Errol. And I was looking forward to returning the favor."

He let out a tight, short breath. "Well, let's just keep one thing straight, Poppy—what I did, I did because I needed to touch you. Needed to know what you look like, sound like, feel like when you come." He held my gaze as long as he dared while driving. "Not because I was thinking about what you might do in return." A pause. "When I give you an orgasm, all I want you to do is sit back and focus on enjoying it. Nothing else. Once it's over, if you feel like there's something you want from me, you just feel free to go about getting it.

But don't ever do *anything* because you think you've got to because of what I did. Only greedy, selfish children bother with immature shit like keeping track."

I laughed. "You've got quite an opinion on that, huh?"

He smirked, chuckled. "Yeah, guess I do."

"Well, Errol, rest assured that I never do anything out of a sense of obligation. I'm a girl who knows what she wants, okay? And I'm not at all shy about taking what I want." I reached out and rested a hand on his thigh.

He held the wheel in both hands. "Glad we're on the same page, then."

"What's your last name?" I asked.

He quirked an eyebrow at the non sequitur. "Sylvain." He said it with a hint of a French accent—*Sylv-ANH*. "Errol Sylvain."

"Kiwi mum, French dad." He jutted his chin at me. "You? What's your last name?"

"Goode," I said. "Poppy Goode. G-O-O-D-E."

"Let's go one better. Full name." He flicked his sunglasses down onto his face—I think he'd actually slept in them, or he'd slipped them on the moment he woke up, I wasn't sure. "My full name is Errol Bastien Sylvain."

"Poppy Estelle Goode."

Silence. He glanced at me, and even though his

Wayfarers were too darkly tinted to let me see his eyes, I could feel them on my breasts. "How long have you had your nipples pierced?"

I glanced down at the objects in question—the piercings visible as dimples against the white cotton of the shirt. "Oh, not long, actually. Three months, maybe."

"What made you get them?"

I let my hand sidle upward on his thigh. "Well, it's kind of a story."

"You've heard plenty of mine. I'm keen for one of yours."

I sighed. "It's not really one with sad bits in it, but it goes something like this…once upon a time, I had a boyfriend, and things were super great. We dated for about six months, pretty low-key, nothing serious, but good times and what I thought was a standard unspoken agreement to fidelity, you know? Then, I had, in the words of Judith Viorst, a terrible, horrible, no good, very bad day. Some clumsy moron in the art department spilled paint all over a nearly finished painting, totally ruining three weeks of work. And then I tripped on my own feet and spilled my mocha all over myself, ruining my favorite white button-down *and* the white bra underneath, plus burning my neck and chest and arms all to hell. Then, on the way home to change, it started raining buckets, turning my brown-stained shirt totally see-through, and a taxi ran through a puddle and splashed me…and *then* as I was almost back to the shitty apartment I shared with two other girls, I dropped my cell phone and it went down a storm drain."

"Wow. That *is* a bad day."

"That was just the cake. Ready for the icing, and the cherry on top?" I stared straight ahead and tried to relate the event without letting myself feel the memory of it. "I walk into my apartment. Started ripping off my wet, ruined clothes, needing a hot shower and a glass of wine *so* fucking bad. By the time I get to my room, I'm down to my underwear and socks. Now, you need to understand one thing, first. I lived with my two best friends. We'd met day one at Columbia, at orientation. We all lived in university housing first semester and then moved out together and got an apartment, me and Shannyn and Yvonne. Shannyn was my real deal, best-best friend, and I was friends with Yvonne because she was childhood friends with Shannyn…anyway. Point is, we weren't just roommates."

Errol was already wincing. "No. You didn't. He wasn't."

"Oh yes, he was. Fucking *both* of them. In *my* bed. Not Shannyn's bed, not Yvonne's bed. *MY* motherfucking bed. I'll never forget that moment as long as I live, and fucking trust me; I've tried to forget it. Shannyn was riding him reverse cowgirl, and Yvonne was sitting on his face, and they were both making out while he ate out Yvonne and fucked Shannyn. It was like something out of a porno."

"No *way*. In your bed?"

"Yeah. My bed."

"Like, why, though? Just to twist the knife even more?"

"I guess, I don't know. I didn't stop to ask. I marched into my room, all but buck-ass naked. Shannyn and Yvonne scrambled off Reed and they all started stammering fucking stupid-ass excuses, like it's not what you think, blah-fucking blah. Reed sat up, and as soon as he was halfway vertical, I punched him in the nose as hard as I could. Broke that fucker's nose, too. Still naked, mind you, I punched both of my ex-friends, and then dressed, packed my shit, and walked to a friend's house. I got promptly shitfaced, and somehow we ended up at this piercing party in the Bronx. I was hammered, and it sounded like a good idea. Especially when the girl doing the piercing explained what it was like to have your nipples sucked on with piercings. So I got them pierced."

"Did it hurt?"

"Like a sonofabitch," I said, laughing, "and I was drunk at the time, and not really feeling much."

His eyes flicked to my boobs again. "And? What's it feel like to have them sucked on?"

My tongue compulsively traced the corner of my mouth, a nervous habit of mine. "I don't know," I muttered, my eyes on his, or where his would be if they weren't hidden behind sunglasses. "No one has sucked my nipples since I got them pierced."

He bit his lip. "What a fucking shame," Errol whispered. "Can I fucking *please* be the first?"

I swallowed hard. "If Farmer Jebediah hadn't shown up when he did, you'd be sucking on them right now." I reached out, leaned over, slid his sunglasses up onto his head so I could see those wild, hot, Aegean-blue eyes of his.

"Fuck," he growled under his breath. "I'm about ten seconds from pulling over and taking our chances of not getting got on the side of the road."

I was so damn horny in that moment that I nearly agreed. Only a narrow thread of caution, in the form of a memory of my sister Lexi having once gotten a ticket for public indecency for doing exactly what Errol was proposing, stopped me.

"I'd rather not risk an encounter with the police while naked," I said.

"Fuck. A side road, then?" His expression was tight, hard, jaw clenched and tensing, as if he was only just barely restraining himself from doing something inadvisable.

"We just left a side road so remote no one should

ever have found us," I pointed out. "I'm just as eager as you are, but I also know my sister got a public indecency ticket and said it really ruined the fun."

He growled. "Shit. No, being in the States on a temporary visa with only a New Zealand driving license, I really can't afford legal trouble."

He looked so unhappy, so forlorn, so irritated and turned on and frustrated. I just *had* to take pity on him, didn't I?

Of course I did.

Checking the road ahead and behind us—totally deserted, and we hadn't seen another car the entire ten almost fifteen minutes we'd been on the highway—I pressed the button to release my seat belt buckle. It caught on the bulge of my breast, slipped over the mound, and snapped back against the pillar. Errol's eyes cut to mine, raked down my body.

I only hesitated a moment, then my tongue did its nervous tic of flicking over the corner of my lip, back and forth, back and forth. His eyes caught the motion of my tongue, and he sucked in a deep breath, hissed it out. "Drives me nuts when you do that."

"In a good way, or a bad way?" I asked.

"In a way like I want to suck your tongue into my mouth."

"Oh." I gathered the lower edge of my tank top in my hands. "I like the sound of that."

"Poppy, my restraint is just about munted."

I grinned, slow, promising him with my eyes and my smile what I was about to do. "You just hold on to that steering wheel, Errol." I tugged the shirt down, flattening and stretching it against my boobs. "Keep us on the road. The sooner you get us to civilization and a motel room, the sooner you get your hands…and mouth…and…other parts, on me." I felt and heard the engine rev as he mashed the pedal down. "A speeding ticket won't help, though."

"Fucking hell," he snarled. "I'm losing my shit, here."

His eyes went to my chest, flicked to the road, back to me. "God, your tits are fucking fabulous."

I smirked at him, and I knew seduction was in my gaze. "What…these?" I tugged down until my tits popped out, and then drew one arm and then other out of the straps, and now I was topless, the shirt around my midsection.

"Jesus…*fuck*," he breathed. Slowed, foot coming all the way off the accelerator as he stared, open-mouthed. "How the fuck are you *real*?"

I played with them for him, squeezing, lifting and releasing with a jiggly bounce that set them swaying, flicking the bar through my nipples until they stood on end, aching, tight. Errol swallowed hard, and his breathing came in short huffs, and he was shifting in his seat in an attempt to adjust himself without touching himself, without letting go of the steering wheel.

"Looks like you're having an issue over there," I said, tongue licking my lower lip on its way to the corner of my mouth.

"Yeah, my issue is I've got a half-naked woman next to me, and she's the most beautiful human being I've ever seen in my life, and if I don't get to put my hands on those glorious fuckin' tits of yours I might just die right here."

I ran my fingertips in a light teasing touch over his bare arm from the sleeve of his muscle shirt over the outside of his bicep, over his forearm, to his wrist. Guided his hand to my breast. "I wouldn't want you to die. I mean, if you die, we crash and I die, and then we wouldn't get to have hot monkey sex later." I closed my eyes and groaned as his big strong rough hand closed over my breast, kneading the soft flesh and lifting the heavy weight of it, weighing it in his palm, brushing his thumb over the nipple, tweaking the piercing—which was a silver bar with fake pink diamonds capping the bar on either side. "So really, you touching my boobs is saving both our lives."

He laughed. "Fucking hell, Poppy, I *love* the way you think. Can I save our lives more often?"

"If you promise to play with my piercing like that every time...then I'd wouldn't just *let* you, I'd *make* you."

"Make me? I *beg* to be allowed to worship at the altar of your tits, Poppy. Consider me your acolyte, my goddess. Allow me the privilege of worshipping you."

I laughed, but the laugh turned to another groan, because he was *just* gentle enough as he flicked and tweaked, and also *just* rough enough.

I shifted to angle toward him, giving him access to the other one. "Righty wants some touches, too, you know."

He rasped a hoarse laugh, eyes soaking up my topless form as often and for as long as he dared while safely operating a moving vehicle. This was, perhaps, a little risky. But god, so worth it.

Finally, though the *issue* he was having inside his board shorts consumed my attention—namely, his cock was bent and angled inside the shorts in such a way that he couldn't entirely unfurl. I just...I *had* to help him.

I gently detached his hand and returned it to the wheel. Turned fully sideways in my seat, putting my feet in the open space between his seat and mine. He glanced at me, clearly not liking having my boobs taken away from his hand, wondering what my next play would be.

I unbuckled the latch, and he let it slide away to snap into place. Held his gaze as I found the laces of his shorts. My hair had come mostly loose from the braid at some point, and would get in the way, so I twisted it into a loose, sloppy bun at the top of my head and tied it in place with the extra hair tie I wore on my left wrist. His eyes, to his credit, ran over my face, taking in how I looked with my hair up.

"So…fucking…gorgeous," he breathed.

"Thank you," I whispered. "Now. Don't speed, and don't swerve."

"Don't speed, don't swerve. I'll do my best." He knew, I think, what I was about to do—it was fairly obvious—but he still seemed like he was holding his breath, not quite believing I really meant to do it.

I untied the laces, loosened them. "Butt up," I said, and he obeyed, lifting his butt off the seat, and I tugged the shorts down around his thighs.

His cock straightened instantly, slapping against his belly with a loud *thwap*.

My jaw dropped. His cock was…fucking incredible. I'd felt the outline of it earlier, but feeling the outline of it behind shorts does nothing compared to seeing it bare, and begging for attention.

Fat. Big, fat, plump cock. Pink, contrasting beautifully against his otherwise sun-golden skin. He was cut, and the head was a broad circle, weeping precum.

Trimmed black pubic hair, a buzzed thatch around the base, a few runaway hairs on his shaft. Long, straight—how long? Don't know, don't care. Long enough to put to shame anyone I'd ever hooked up with by a vast measure of inches, but shy of being *too* big. It was so damn *thick*, though. God, he would stretch me so tight.

He was breathing slowly, his stomach sucked in. Waiting.

Mustn't keep him waiting.

I reached out and took him in my fist. God, I couldn't make my fingers meet around his girth. It took both hands to span him—granted, I have ridiculously small hands for a girl built like me. I mean, I'm not short at five-seven and a half, and I've got huge tits, a lot of ass, thick thighs, a tight waist but still nothing close to being a size zero, or even single digits, not that I give a fuck about that, but still. I'm not a dainty thing. I once had a guy compliment on an IG post, "Damn girl, you THICCCCC!" Which I took as a compliment. That being said, I have tiny hands, and according to the female doctor at my last ob/gyn checkup, a very small hoo-ha.

I maneuvered myself so I could comfortably bend over him, between his chest and the steering wheel. One of his hands rested on my back, and then began making soft slow scratching circles, which was confusing, because who doesn't love a good back scratching, but while I was about to blow him? Confusing, somehow. I liked it, though. He drove with one hand and roamed my back, my shoulders, my neck, toyed with my ears, my arms, traced my cheekbone with the back of his fingers, reached as far down my back as he could, and then scratched and smoothed back up, making a circuit.

Affection. Intimate. My heart hammered, because he wasn't supposed to touch me like that. Grab my hair, maybe.

Kneeling over him, I glanced up at him. Stroked him in both fists. Grinned up at him. "I know I don't have to tell you this, but Errol, you have a magnificent penis."

He laughed. "A magnificent penis, huh?"

"Glorious."

"You know, the first real look I got at your tits, that was the word I had in my head—glorious."

I bit my lower lip. "Well. I've got glorious tits, you have a glorious cock…" I clenched my breasts together and lowered them onto his cock, feeding it between them and lifting and lowering until he started groaning.

"Holy fuck, Poppy," he grated through clenched teeth. "Holy…*fuck*."

I smirked at him before letting go of my tits and

taking his erection in my hand again. Stroked him, slow, twisting motions with my hand on the way down, thumb rubbing over the tip at the top. He began huffing, hips lifting, and my mouth was watering for him.

Once I had him in my mouth, though, it was my eyes that were watering—*so* fucking big, I couldn't get even barely half of him in. My jaws couldn't go that wide; my throat couldn't take that much. Didn't try, and wasn't about gagging myself. Not sexy, and if I was going to go down, I was going to do it in a way that *I* enjoyed too.

His flesh was hot, tasted salty, and the precum on my tongue was tangy, musky, a foretaste of what was to…come. Pun intended.

Stroked him, bobbing my head to take just enough of him. The head, and a few inches. Tongue slurping, swirling, flicking.

"Ohhh fuck, oh fuck," he snarled.

"Mmm."

His hand halted on my back, between my shoulder blades. Hovered, as if considering a move up to my hair, the back of my head. With one hand I guided his hand to my neck, the loose floppy bun of my hair, and then used both hands on him. He applied pressure, just enough to let me know how close he was, but not trying to force me to gag. How polite. It'd have been game over if he had, but no need to tell him that. I just focused on him, on the thickness of his cock in my mouth, the hot pulse of his flesh and veins against my taut lips, which stuttered over him as I raised and lowered.

"Poppy," he groaned, guttural. "Oh fuck. I'm about to go, Poppy."

"Mmm..." I moaned around him. "Mmmm-hmmm."

The vibrations are what did him in, I think. And the ragged, wordless groan he made as he held back, that was what did me in. My sex ached, and I let go of him with one hand. Hiked my skirt up over my ass and shoved my fingers between my thighs, to my clit. He watched that, and if he was holding back, he lost it when I started touching myself. I circled my clit and timed it to the rhythm of my bobbing head as I took his cock between my lips, and he matched the rhythms with his thrusts, and it took me sixty seconds at most to reach climax, already halfway to a second orgasm before we were caught earlier and now turned on AF by the feel of Errol and his sexy, ragged, broken, masculine groans of pleasure and his hand on my back and now on my head encouraging me with careful, polite pressure. I hummed my scream around him, had to let him out of my mouth to gasp for breath and bite down hard as the orgasm clashed and thrashed through me, and then I buried him in my mouth again and touched myself and stroked him and sucked him and licked him and swirled my tongue around the fat plump soft head of his gorgeous, throbbing magnificent cock.

My tongue was still swirling when he yanked on my hair twice, but the warning was too late, and one I wouldn't have heeded but appreciated all the same. He filled my mouth, shouting, and I heard the steering wheel creak under the crushing power of his grip, and he thrust, and filled my mouth even as I fought to swallow the first shot. Tangy, musky, almost sweet—cum I wouldn't mind tasting again. He gripped my bun as if for dear life, hips lifting, shoving his cock into my mouth hard enough that I backed away. I was jerking the base of his shaft with one hand, twisting and pumping as fast as I could, mouth bobbing rapidly, throat working to swallow and swallow as the man came and came and came, god, so fucking *virile*. The only word for it—monstrously virile. Months of pent-up cum, all blasting into my mouth in a hot, tangy, pulsing rush after rush.

Finally, my sex clenching with aftershocks, tits swaying, I awkwardly let go of him and lifted up onto my knees, hair drifting loose from the messy bun, a dribble of his cum on the corner of my mouth.

Smiled at him, somewhere between shy and proud. "Hi."

He couldn't catch his breath, and his expression as he looked at me, eventually, was one of shell-shocked, incredulous awe.

He'd stopped driving entirely, halted right in the middle of the lane, foot on the brake, one hand white-knuckle clutching the steering wheel, the other slack and listless on his bare thigh. His monster cock was still semi-hard, leaking post-drips of cum. I gathered him into my hand, slowly twisting my fist downward, bending over him to lick away the last drops, which made him shudder, groaning.

Finally, he was limp and draped in a comma to one side, and I moved up onto my seat. Smirked at him as I wiped at the corner of my mouth with my thumb, which came away glistening with that droplet—I popped my thumb into my mouth, my eyes on his.

He seemed incapable of words.

His mouth moved, working silently. He let out a harsh breath, head slamming back against the headrest. "Hi," he said, eventually, as if his search for words had come up empty.

EIGHT

Errol

BRAIN SHORT-CIRCUITED, I COULD ONLY STARE AT her—a goddess made flesh, a wild creature from some seductive mythology, a sexual siren. Perhaps a succubus…no, those were demons, I think, and she was more angel than demon.

She was still topless, her tank top around her midsection, and fuck me those bare tits were my undoing as a man. Words fail to capture their glory, but damn if I'm not keen to try.

With her arms resting naturally at her sides, palms on her lap, her breasts pressed outward against her biceps and were squished together, her cleavage where they met and began at her breastbone a gap so narrow barely a sheet of paper could fit between them. Teardrop shaped, they were wide and round at the bottom and draped nearly to her midriff, with long wide slopes upward from nipple centerline. Her areolae were wide, larger than an American silver dollar each, and a dark brown shade somewhere between caramel and milk chocolate. Her nipples were dead center in the middle of each breast, thick plump cylindrical nubs turned ever so slightly upward, as if looking up at me and begging me to kiss them. Each nipple was pierced horizontally through with a silver bar, each end capped with large pink diamonds—almost certainly cubic zirconium or glass, but a woman of Poppy's beauty, and breasts of her lush perfection absolutely deserved to have real pink diamonds.

I just stared, openmouthed, still fighting for breath, for composure, for words to express what I was thinking. I hadn't a clue what I was thinking or feeling, so I had nothing to say just yet. I just wanted to stare at her tits. Forever, if I could, but I'd settle for another minute or two.

"Um, Errol? You…gonna, like, drive?"

I shook my head. "Can't. You broke me. Error four-oh-four, page not found."

She laughed, a tinkle of music that set her tits to ever-so-subtly shaking. Keep her topless and I'll say and do anything to make her laugh, just to see what it does to those incredible, glorious, magnificent, perfect breasts.

"Fine. Switch, and I'll drive."

"Okay," I said, but didn't move, just sat, life drained clean out of me, mesmerized.

She tugged at my arm. "Errol." Snapped her fingers in front of me. "They're just tits. Wake up, dude." She was laughing, still amused, and also, unless I was mistaken, somewhat proud of how shell-shocked she'd left me.

I tugged my shorts up awkwardly, shoved the stick shift into neutral and set the parking brake, and then slid over toward the middle—Poppy moved out of the way into the space between the seats so I could take the passenger seat, and then she plopped into the driver's seat.

Still topless.

Maybe if I was quiet and a good boy, she'd leave her top off. That would be nice.

She glanced at me, smirking. "Okay, say goodbye to the boobies for now."

I shook my head. "Nope. Much better if we just…let them be. They need sunshine and fresh air."

Another of those amused tinkles of laughter. "Good try."

Alas, she slid her arms into the straps and tugged

the shirt into place, and behold, the sun lost its brightness.

I had to say something meaningful. "Poppy."

She pressed the brake, set the clutch, wiggled the stick, and pushed it up into third. "Yes?"

"Um. Number one, you're in third."

She bit her lip. "Oh." Down into second. "That one?"

I eyed her. "Do you know how to drive a manual?"

"Um. Sort of? I watched Dad a few times. Years ago."

"So, no."

"No, not really." A snicker of laughter. "I do have my license, though. I promise."

I frowned. "Why d'you make that sound like a lie?"

"I swear, I have my license. I just…haven't exactly driven in…a while."

"In how long?"

"Since I took the test?"

"And you can't drive a manual?"

She shrugged. "How hard can it be? I know the basics. Clutch on the left, and you use your left foot for that. Push it in while holding the brake, let it out and press the gas."

I checked our mirrors—it was just past six thirty in the morning, and the road was deserted. "Well, now's as good a time as any, and this is as good a place as any. Give it a go, then."

She hesitated. "Which gear is which?"

I laughed, tapped the top of the shifter knob. "It's written on there." I held her hand, helped her push it up into first. "First." Down. "Second." Up and to the right. "Third." Down. "Fourth." Back to far left, and up. "Reverse."

She nodded. "Okay, I think I've got it." She went through the gears on her own, naming them as she moved through them. "How do I know when to switch?"

I pointed at the tachy. "That gauge. See where it's red? Switch when the needle gets close. But really, you'll hear it in the motor, and feel it as well. It'll speed up and the motor will sound higher, and then it'll sort of go…sludgy and stop accelerating. That's when you kick off the gas, push in the clutch, switch gears, then hit the gas again."

"Oh. Makes sense."

"But all that's the easy part. Getting started is the hard part to learn. Once you figure out how to get into first, the rest'll be easy."

She glanced at me. "You, um, gonna tie up your shorts?"

I realized they were still only half on, and untied. "Oh. Yeah, right." I fixed it. "Why, was it a distraction?"

She shrugged, hiding a grin. "I mean, yeah. A non-erect penis has always been funny and fascinating to me." She ran her tongue over her teeth, smacking her mouth as if at a bad taste. "I need to brush my teeth."

I chuckled. "Need a rinse? I've got some mouthwash."

She smirked, quirked an eyebrow. "Yeah, that'd be good. I've got this…musky aftertaste. Must be from something I swallowed recently."

I clambered into the back, found my toiletries and my bottle of mouth rinse. Brought it forward to her, and she made as if to pour it into the cap rather than sip from the bottle.

"No need to be weird about germs at this point, yeah? Considering where your mouth just was, it's not gonna bother me if you go right from the bottle."

She gave me a sideways glance and a grin as she swigged from the bottle, capped it, handed it back. Swished it around for a good half-minute, then rolled down the window and spat it out.

"Considering where my mouth just was, huh?" She realized the parking brake was still engaged, and released it—good thing, too, because I'd forgotten. "You were going to say something, before the driving lesson thing."

I grinned. "Yeah, well, I'm still working out what to say. All that comes to mind at the moment is…dear *god*, woman. And close second to that, thank you. Maybe thank you is first. My blood is still making its way into my brain, I think, so sorting out normal operations might take a minute or two, or five. Because Poppy, you sucked the smart right out of me."

She blew on her fingernails, buffed them on her shirt front. "Well, you know what they say, right? Men think with their dicks, which means I just *blew…your…mind.*" She mimed her brain exploding, both hands bursting from closed fist to open beside each temple.

I laughed. "I've not actually heard that one."

"No? Where do you get your memes, bro?"

"I'm either traveling or off-grid eighty percent of my life. Haven't got time for memes."

"Oh, well I guess that's a reasonable excuse." She put the shifter into first, let out a breath. "Here we go."

"Gently. Let out the accelerator, and when it starts to get close to almost all the way out, start pressing the gas pedal so you sort of meet in the middle. Give it a go; you'll see what I mean. And you will stall out first few times, so don't worry about it."

She gave it a shot, and the motor revved, we

lurched forward, and then abruptly and jerkily halted. "Wow. Okay. That was rough."

"Nah, she'll be right. Try again. Gas sooner, clutch out more slowly at the end."

She tried again, with better success, but we still stalled out after ten feet. A third and fourth try, and then the gear caught and we were rolling.

"You got it!" I said. "Good job!"

She pumped a fist. "Working the stick, baby!"

I snorted. "Yeah nah, that was what you did a few minutes ago, babe."

That got a laugh from her, but then the motor started to protest as the RPMs grew. "So I should switch now?"

"Too right—let off the gas, push in the clutch, pull the shifter straight back to second, let out the clutch, and go on the gas again."

We lurched and the gears crunched painfully, and then she hit the gas a little too hard and we bolted forward, the speedo needle climbing rapidly until she regained control.

She socked my arm. "You said that would be easy!"

"It was easier than learning to start, though, wasn't it?"

"I mean, a little? It still sounded like I was breaking the transmission, though."

"A bit more practice and you'll have it. No worries." I gave a somewhat meaningless gesture, pointing at the road ahead of us. "Why don't you stop and try going into first again."

She did, and it took another few tries to get going, but fewer than the first time. Up into second for a ways, and then she stopped, started, and had a go at first again. Within twenty minutes of taking the wheel, she had it down, if not smoothly, but there was no gear grinding or dangerous lurching.

"I'm a bit envious of how fast you picked that up," I said, once we were cruising, windows down, at a steady fifty-five. "Took me most of a day."

She looked pleased. "Well, you're a good teacher."

"Yeah nah. Don't really matter how you teach it, it's more about whether you just...*get* it or not. Some people can, some can't. You're clearly one of the sort who gets it. Not much to do with me."

She smiled. "Well, I still think you're a good teacher, and thank you for letting me learn on your van." She eyed me. "If you've regained full use of your faculties, you can take over if you want."

I shrugged. "I mean, if you don't like driving, I will. But otherwise, keep after it. No worries on my end." I grinned at her. "But, yeah. I think I've mostly recovered. I'm still not entirely certain I didn't actually die and go to heaven, and then get sent back to earth."

"They say if you get sent back, it's because you've still got work to do." A hot smirk, cocoa eyes mischievous, lascivious. "And buddy, I've got some pretty solid ideas as to the work you were sent back to do."

I played along. "Oh yeah? What's that?"

She tugged her skirt up, bared her upper thigh, her sex—dark fuzz, trimmed into a narrow line leading down to her slit; she obviously tended to keep it trimmed that way regularly, but hadn't shaved recently. Meaning she hadn't anticipated this encounter and hadn't been planning anything with anyone. Why that made me feel a bizarre rush of...not gratitude, not pride, but...pleased-ness, that it was me? Something like that. Plump outer lips, taut and narrow slit, a keyhole of darker flesh where her clit was. Begging to be licked. Kissed. Touched, played with. Worshipped, teased...used roughly till she screamed herself hoarse and begged for a break.

"You," she murmured to me, sliding a fingertip up and down her seam. "Here."

"Jesus," I growled. "Pull over and I'll eat you out till you forget your own fuckin' name."

She bit her lip, slouching low in the seat. "Errol..."

"You want to know what the single sexiest thing I've ever seen in my life is?"

She slid her finger up and down, up and down, circling, up and down, up and down, circling. "What?"

"You, touching yourself while going down on me."

"You thought that was sexy?"

"Fuck yeah. Why wouldn't I?"

"Not everyone does. Had someone tell me it was selfish."

I snorted. "What a fuckwad he was, then. As far as I'm concerned, if you're doing *that,* I *want* you to make yourself feel good at the same time. If I could have reached, I'd have done it for you. Alas, in my experience sixty-nine is more awkward than it is sexy."

She bit her lip, huffing a laugh. "Same."

Her hips flexed, pumped, and I couldn't take it anymore. "Hands on the wheel, Poppy."

She grabbed the wheel in both hands, slid her thighs apart, one foot on the gas pedal. I leaned over, found her slit with two fingers, and she moaned. Leaned back, slouched low, head against the headrest, gripping the steering wheel in clenched fists, eyes darting from the road to my fingers to the road. Took my time, this time—teased her. Slow. A fingertip up, down. In, swirl and slide, out. Gathered her sweet juices—I pulled my fingers out of her and slipped them into my mouth, licked every last bit off while she watched, biting her lower lip, groaning. Smeared her essence all over her clit, swirled soft slow delicate barely-touching circles until she started bucking in her seat, against the seat belt.

"Fuck...Errol, I'm so close," she murmured. Louder, then: "Fuck it. I can't take it anymore. I need your mouth on me." She saw a dirt road ahead on our right, and jammed the brakes and yanked the wheel around, sending us into a sharp, tire-squealing, leaning turn, hitting dirt too fast so the back end skidded around, and then brought us to a jolting stop. Yanked her seat belt off, pivoted in her seat.

Mine was already off and it was my turn to kneel in the cramped space between seats, reaching for her. I yanked her ass toward me so she slouched backward, sliding lower, sideways in the seat so her head thunked hard against the glass.

"Ow," she laughed, rubbing her head.

And then I had her thighs hooked over my shoulders, soft as silk against my ears and cheeks, strong and thick and solid, and her sex was lush and wet and salty and tangy on my tongue. No more teasing, now—I devoured her, hungry, ravenous, eager. Tongue needling her clit, then flattening to lap at her, two fingers and then three slicking in, squelching out through her arousal. She flew over the edge almost instantly, screaming loud, one hand knotting in her hair as she arched up off the seat, thighs levering onto my shoulders, squeezing my head until I thought it might pop like a watermelon in a hydraulic press. Flexing, thrashing, driving, grinding, her other hand clutching at my head, fingers tangling in my hair, holding me hard against her slick wet slit, moving with my rhythm as I licked and lapped and swirled my tongue on her.

"Fuck oh fuck oh fuck, Errol, fuck, Errol fuck, Errol, oh god oh fuck oh god, Errol…" Her breath caught, her voice broke, and then I felt her coming, felt her channel squeeze impossibly hard around my fingers, and her voice lifted in a scream, which broke into a hoarse whimper as I tongued her through her climax, past it, not slowing, fingers driving, tongue lashing, demanding another. "Again? Oh shit, oh fuck, Errol, god yes…please, god, please don't stop—*again*, Errol make me come again—"

I got hard all over again at the way she talked through her orgasm, the dirty, wild things she said.

"Eat me, Errol," she growled, as the second orgasm built up in her. "Eat me so fucking good, Errol… yeah, just like that—ohmyfucking*GOD*!" That last syllable was a shrill scream as the orgasm broke over her, and she was just wordlessly screaming, clutching my hair with both hands, riding my face like a cowboy breaking a bronc.

Whoooop-WHOOOP! The warning burble of a siren behind us.

"Shit!" Poppy shouted, yanking away. "Sit up, sit up."

Thinking fast, she shoved her hand into her purse, came up with her phone, and tossed it into the footwell, far forward near her feet, under the pedals, righting her skirt at the same time.

"Wipe your face," she hissed.

"Why," I said, grinning. "Have I got something on my beard?"

She choked back laughter, reaching out to wipe at my mouth with her palm. "Let me do the talking."

A uniformed officer bent over at the driver's side window. Poppy rolled it down. "Good morning, Officer."

He was young, stern-looking, clean-shaven. "Good morning, ma'am. Sir. There a problem here?" He was wearing mirrored aviators, but it was obvious he was searching the interior. "Funny spot to stop, this early. Seems I saw some…unusual movement in here as I passed."

"No, no problems," Poppy said. "I just dropped my phone, and pulled over to try to grab it."

"That why neither of you are seat belted?"

"Yeah," Poppy said. "I actually dropped it over here between the seats, so he went to grab it, then it slid under my feet, so I figured I'd better pull over to get it." She leaned forward, angled to extend her reach, made a face of concentration as she hunted by feel, and straightened with her phone in hand. "There. See?"

I wondered if he'd say something about the beads of sweat still dotting her forehead and upper lip, or the way she was still short of breath—she was disguising it well, though.

He obviously wasn't entirely sure he believed her. But, without anything else to go on, he just frowned. "Well. This road here is a dead end onto private property, so I'd keep a move on." He tipped his hat. "Ya'll have a nice day. Drive safe."

"Thank you, Officer. You too."

A moment later, tires crunched behind us, a motor revved, and the patrol car pulled around and drove away—thankfully in the opposite direction we were headed.

"Some quick thinking there," I said. "Good on ya."

She grinned. "I think maybe we'd better put the sexual hijinks on pause till we're somewhere... private."

"Yeah, maybe we had better," I agreed. "Much as I'd rather put you on your back and give you a couple more screamers."

She laughed, low and hoarse. "I think we've both been to heaven this morning."

"Well, I got heaven two ways, because you taste as good coming on my mouth as you make me feel with yours."

She closed her eyes, slowed her breath. Opened them, smiled at me, bright, eager, calm. "So. Nearest hotel?"

"Hotel, motel, Holiday Inn…" I quipped, quoting a tune I'd heard on the radio a while back.

She snickered. "Oh man, old school." She plugged her phone into the auxiliary jack, hunting through her music app. "I've got a playlist for that!"

And so we hit the highway again, for real this time, jamming to old school American hip-hop, funk, and soul. Hours passed as easily as the miles, and our conversation flowed as freely as the day before.

You'd think what with the—as she'd so humorously and aptly put it—sexual hijinks of the morning, that the sexual tension would have eased between us.

Yeah nah. Not even. Worse, matter of fact.

Every time our hands brushed, sparks flew. Her eyes roamed my face, my body, mouth, hands, the fly of my shorts. And mine did as well.

Neither of us dared to outright touch each other, out of an unspoken mutual agreement—any touch, however innocent, would set us off, and after the close encounter with the police this morning, neither of us fancied a ticket or a further temptation of fate.

No, best wait till we got somewhere like civilization, and a motel, where we could lock a door behind us and do things proper-like.

As in, get her lush body totally naked, so I could explore the many fine curves, feel her skin and taste her again and fucking finally get myself inside that sweet tight slit of hers.

Never in my life have I wanted anything so bad. Feeling her under my fingers, tasting her, having been so close but so far only made my need to be inside her worse than anything.

And judging by the way her eyes kept flicking to my shorts, to the outline of my cock behind them, she was feeling the same.

So, when I say the hours and miles passed easily, that's a bit of a lie. They crept. It seemed we were prowling through the wops for hours on end before we started to see evidence of humanity instead of just forest and cows and hay and corn and wheat. I'd no idea where we were except heading north, and I didn't rightly care. Neither did she—she just kept blasting us fifty-five miles per hour north, ever north, through one-light town after one-light town, where there was little but a single gas station and maybe a small dairy, a used car lot, or a home and farm store.

Nothing like a decent place to stop until well past noon. We paused to refuel at a junction, got shitty coffee, and I fixed us snacks for the next leg of our trip.

An hour or so later we passed signs for Moline and Davenport, and I'd no clue which state they were in, or which we were in—little two-lane roads like this don't get big signs advertising the state line. I learned, if they're there, they're old and worn and if you blink you miss them. It was only early afternoon then, so we blew through them despite our growling stomachs. What was pushing us on, I wasn't sure. The playlists we listened to were endless and varied, first from her phone, then mine.

We switched when we stopped to fuel up a second time, and I let Poppy pick a playlist from my phone. She perused for a minute, scrolling through the ones we'd already listened to, until she got near the bottom of the list.

"What's this one?" she asked.

I glanced without really seeing—the sun was low and bright, and I refocused on the road. "What one?"

"It doesn't have a title." Shit, no, not that one; she tapped before I could say anything, though. "The songs are all…what is this? Gaelic?"

I shifted. "Uh, yeah. Irish Gaelic. It's just…some old stuff. Reels and jigs, and the like."

Just old stuff. Good one, mate.

She shrugged. "I'm down for some Irish reels," she said as she tapped the phone.

Fuck.

Instantly, my toe tapped. Drowsy Maggie, Dad's favorite tune to fiddle. Close my eyes and I could see Dad beside me, leading the way on old Moll, the fiddle passed down from his great-grandfather. Fucking deluge of memories, all hitting like a load of bricks, all within half a measure.

She didn't miss a trick, though, Poppy didn't.

"You okay?"

I shrugged. "Sure."

She frowned. "Okay, well, bullshit. But that's your business." She paused the song, found a playlist of my favorite hard rock songs, a mix of American, New Zealand, and Australian bands.

She eyed me a few times, but even half of that recording of Drowsy Maggie was more than I could manage and remain on an even keel.

"That was, uh. My dad's band." I slammed old cold coffee, just for something to do.

"Oh." She loaded that with a wealth of meaning. "The sad bits."

"Yeah."

"I thought your dad was French?"

I laughed. "Yeah. It's…well, not all that complicated, actually. He was born in France, moved to

Newfoundland as a young man. His father, grandfather, and great-grandfather all played the fiddle, more for fun and entertainment than anything, and my granddad taught Dad. Then, when Dad moved to Canada, he picked up the Cape Breton style of fiddling, ended up in a band that moved him to Dublin, joined a different band, this one proper Irish music, and that one blew up in Europe and the UK, parts of Canada, Australia, New Zealand. Never really got picked up here, though, for whatever reason. He met my mum after a gig in Christchurch, and…the rest is history."

She hummed. "There's a lot covered in that phrase, 'the rest is history,' I think."

"Yeah, sure." I tried for easy breezy. "We've all got that shit, though, yeah? No sense digging into it all. Just a bloody bunch of sad stuff that doesn't make for good storytelling."

"Meaning, off-limits."

"I dunno about off-limits, exactly, just…don't see the point in talking about it."

She just nodded and didn't push it. Conversation lapsed for a while after that.

"I didn't mean to bring up painful memories, Errol. I'm sorry."

I rolled my shoulder, left hand out the window, diving and rising in the air current. "Couldn't have known."

We stopped for food in Davenport, but it was still too early to stop for the day, and something about that weird issue with the music had chilled the fervor of our chemical combustibility. We drove, and drove. Signs for Dubuque, which I felt was maybe in Iowa.

Late evening. Sunset over cornfields.

"Hey, Errol?"

"Yeah?"

She pointed at a dirt track through a cornfield as we passed it, the sunset perfectly aligned with the road, a spreading umbrella of oak and cottonwood interrupting the corn. "I want to go shoot that."

"All right," I said. "Sounds good to me."

I brought us to a halt and reversed down the shoulder, pulled onto the dirt road.

When I halted and shut off the engine, we both ducked in back to sort through our photography gear; I just needed my Nikon, she needed a handful of rolls of film, which she shoved into the pocket of her skirt; I hadn't realized her skirt even had pockets.

We spent a quiet several minutes each wandering the road, snapping shots. I went into the corn rows a ways, knelt to capture a solar flare through the nodding heads while Poppy focused more on the dirt road and the sunset with the stand of trees as a frame and focal point.

After a while, I joined her on the road. "Hey, I've got an idea."

"Okay?" She eyed me, and I had a feeling she was expecting some kind of a sexual game, but things were still a bit odd, strained—memories tend to linger, for me, and leave a stain of bitter pain, and I think my reaction set something off in her.

I wasn't sure what, and I didn't like it, and I wished she'd have just picked another playlist so we could have carried on in mere sexual tension rather than bizarre emotional tautness and confusion.

I handed her my Nikon. "Switch?"

She grinned. "Hell, yeah. I've always wanted an opportunity to play with one of these. I had a Canon Rebel when I first moved to New York, but it got stolen on the subway and I never got around to saving up to replace it, and I'm too stubborn to ask Mom."

"Rebels are a decent starter kit," I said. "And really, a professional can get a good shot no matter the camera. The photographer makes the camera, not the other way around."

She glanced at the shot counter on her Minolta. "Hold on, I've got three shots left on this roll, and then you can have a fresh roll to work on."

She looked around for something to shoot, saw me, smirked. Lifted the camera and snapped one of me before I could react. Backed up a step, two, tilted the camera sideways and bent to get all of me in the frame. I stood for it, letting my Nikon dangle loosely at my side, sunglasses up on my head. She closed in again, got a close-up of my face to finish the roll. Pulled the used roll out.

I reached for it. "Been a while since I've run a roll into a manual. Let me. It'll be fun." I took the camera from her and a new roll of black and white, fed the end of the celluloid in, settled the canister in place, closed the back. "My first camera was a cheapo Mom got me thirdhand when I was...oh god, eight? Nine? I used that till I was fourteen, and that's when Dad got me my first good one. A vintage Leica. I still have that one, actually, carry it around in my gear, but I think the shutter is stuck and haven't gotten around to getting it fixed."

"What was your first digital camera?" she asked, playing with the Nikon to familiarize herself with it.

"That one," I answered. "My portfolio was all black and white from actual film, but when Jerry got me this job, I used my entire savings to buy that D6 and a handful of lenses. I didn't get my first pro-quality telephoto zoom lens till after my first paycheck, though, because those cost a mint."

I watched her for a few minutes, fascinated by the way she chose her subjects. A lot of her work was fairly close up, which gave me an idea. I shouldered her Minolta and jogged back to the van, came back with my macro lens.

"Here. Ever shoot macro?"

She smiled, nodded, but it was bittersweet. "I had a bunch of lenses for my Canon. Zoom, a macro lens as well as macro filters, a portrait prime. I fell asleep on the train with the camera bag under my feet, and when I woke up, it was gone."

"People suck," I answered.

A shrug. "Yeah, but there's as many good people in the world as there are shitty ones. You just gotta focus on looking for the good."

She switched my prime for the macro and immediately knelt in the dirt to get a series of shots of a big fluffy caterpillar inching along the side of the road. I returned to the corn rows after watching her for another minute or two, worked the solar flare angle again in black and white, and then tried some avant-garde, almost abstract views of the stalks and rows as geometric patterns of vertical lines and shadows.

We spent more than an hour before we'd gotten everything we wanted. The sun had fully set by that time, and the chilly awkwardness between Poppy and me seemed to have gone.

"You want to get to Dubuque and find somewhere to crash for the night?" I asked.

She nodded, and her eyes betrayed renewed lust. "Yeah," she murmured. "Sounds good."

It was another hour into Dubuque itself, and it took us twenty minutes to find a decent motel. We parked outside the office and went in together. The clerk behind the low counter was reading an Agatha Christie paperback, smoking a cigarette despite the "no smoking" placard above his head, feet propped on the desk, half-moon readers low on his nose. He was older, bald with a long gray beard, thin but with a round belly.

"Single king is seventy-five," he said, without looking up from his book. "Pay now. Check out at noon or stop in to extend a night."

I glanced at Poppy. "Uh."

She smirked, snorted. "Don't get weird on me now, Errol. One room."

I shrugged. "Didn't want to presume."

She snorted again. "Well, I can't say I don't appreciate the sentiment, because I do, but I think at this point one room and one bed is a foregone conclusion."

The clerk wasn't amused by our banter. "Seventy-nine-fifty."

I handed him my card, and he took it, swiped it, handed me the receipt to sign, took it, shoved it into a slot in the cash register drawer, handed me the customer copy…all one-handed, without even looking up from his book. He reached over his head, glanced up, pulled down an actual key on a ring attached to a large white plastic card with a red number 12 on it, tossed it onto the counter. Went back to his book. "Room twelve. Halfway down on the left."

"Thanks," I said, stuffing my card back into my wallet.

He just grunted, and ignored us.

Bemused, I led the way back out the van. Twelve was nearer the end than the middle, so I moved the van in front of the room. Poppy had the key, so she unlocked it and went in, immediately turned on the ancient air-con unit while I grabbed my suitcase and toiletries. Poppy grabbed her bag and went back into the room.

It was small, with fake wood beadboard paneling, popcorn ceiling, a ten-year-old TV with a cable box beside it, a single king bed covered in a scratchy-looking white comforter with four thin pillows. A decent bathroom with a bathtub and a showerhead I'd have to bend backward to fit under, a pedestal sink, and a rust-pitted mirror.

I saw Poppy glancing at the shower as she sat down on the bed and began unlacing her boots. "Go ahead and take the first shower," I said.

"That would be amazing," she said, sounding breathlessly grateful. "I smell awful. Haven't had a shower in a few days."

I smirked at her. "I didn't notice any smell."

She grinned, snorting. "You weren't licking my armpits."

"Yeah nah, not my kink, but if that's what you like, I'll give it a go." I leaned into her, touched my nose to her arm near her armpit, and gave a sniff. "But, I will say, a shower wouldn't go amiss first."

She cackled, shoving me away. "Ew. Jerk."

I just laughed. "I'm gonna get all the expensive stuff out of the caravan. It's got locks, but they're not the best and I'd rather not take any chances of my kit being nicked while we're sleeping."

"Is that your polite way of giving me privacy to get in the shower?"

I shrugged. "If you want it to be."

She held my gaze. "I mean, I won't be using the bathroom in front of you, but I'm not going to be weird about modesty at this point."

"Right, because once you've had your mouth on someone, privacy seems a bit silly."

She hesitated. "About earlier…"

"No worries, really." I stood up, headed for the door. "Take your time in the shower. I'll just be uploading today's shots from my camera."

She just nodded and began rummaging in her bag. "Okay.

When I got back to the room with my various bags of photography gear—my many lenses, spare cameras, SD cards, my iPad, power adapters, card reader adapter for the iPad and the camera connection adapter, cell phone and charger, Poppy was already in the shower. She'd left the door partly opened, enough that I could see the tub with the shower curtain drawn closed, and steaming escaping in coiling banks and swirls. She was singing quietly in a smooth and pretty alto, an old Taylor Swift song, by the sound of it.

I connected my camera to the iPad, waited for Photos to load and synch today's shots. I got some good ones, some crap ones, and a couple gold star ones that I moved to a different folder to edit and add to the ongoing project file. Then I got to Poppy's section, particularly the macro stuff, and my brain about exploded. Fucking spectacular. And she claimed photography wasn't even her main bag? I'd give just about my left arm to see her canvas work, if that's the case.

One shot in particular of the caterpillar was just wicked good. She'd caught it mid-arch, with a flare of sunspots behind it, casting its own shadow in the golden hour light. It was in perfect clarity, filling the frame, caught with a sense of motion, as if at any moment the photo could become a video. Without even thinking about it, I transferred the shot to Lightroom and started touching it up, brightening the light, punching up the colors, smoothing out the edges. Nothing noticeable, until you saw the final version next to the original.

I heard the shower shut off, the curtain rings rattle as she tugged the towel down, and the rings scrape against metal as she dragged the curtain back. I couldn't help but glance up, and my breath snagged in my throat. Dripping wet, hair was pasted to her cheeks and slicked back against her head and around her shoulders, fabulously long. Droplets of water dribbled down her forehead, dotted her upper lip, beaded on her shoulders…slid down her cleavage where she had the white bath towel wrapped around her torso over her breasts. It was a small towel, and barely covered her ass, leaving all of her thick golden-tanned thighs bared.

I swallowed hard. Had absolutely no ability to look away.

Had I ever seen such beauty? Never. She was fucking perfect—female beauty at its nadir, feminine allure crystallized and refined and shaped into the body and person of Poppy Goode.

She caught me staring. "What? Never seen a girl just out of the shower?"

"Seen the sunrise from Mount Fuji, sunset in the Gobi, seen the midnight sun in the Arctic Circle, seen glaciers crack off and slide down mountainsides, seen ice calve off the shelf into bergs the size of cities. I've seen flocks of birds so thick the sun goes dark, seen a lioness give birth in the wild, seen the bottom of the ocean and the top of the world. Seen some of the most beautiful women from just about every country on the globe, seen 'em anywhere from totally nude to garbed in the full panoply of state." I couldn't, didn't try to look away from her, from the way the water caught the light and the way the towel both hid and revealed her curves all at once. "Never in my life have I seen anything so beautiful and breathtaking as you, right now, just like that."

She huffed, shaking her head. "Jesus, dude. What the hell do I say to something like that?"

I shrugged. "Don't have to say anything." I forced myself to swallow, to breathe, to look away. "Just the truth, as I see it."

A brief but taut silence. "Errol?"

I looked up. "Yeah?"

She shrugged, embarrassed or awkward or… something. "Thank you."

I smiled. "Just the truth, Poppy. You're so fuckin' beautiful it's hard to look at you for too long, sometimes."

"People have told me all my life that I'm beautiful. But when you say it, especially like that?" Another shrug, her voice quieter now. "I guess I…*feel* it. Feel beautiful, in a way that I don't always feel."

She was within touching distance, and I had to touch her. I swiped a fingertip down the outside of her arm, through water droplets that still trickled over her skin, here and there.

"You ought to feel beautiful always," I whispered. "You ought to feel like the queen of the world. Like…like Venus, or Diana, or Aphrodite."

I wanted to touch her, to pull that towel off, to lick every last droplet off her flesh. But now she was clean and I wasn't.

"I'm…I'm gonna rinse off, too," I said.

She nodded. Glanced down at my lap, at the iPad. "Whatcha got there?"

"Oh, this." I turned it to show her.

She tucked the edge of the towel in tighter between her breasts, and then took the iPad. "Wow."

"It's yours. I edited it."

She stared at it for a long time. "I…wow. It's actually…not bad."

"Not bad? Pop, it's fuckin' brilliant."

She smirked at me, bemused, or amused, or both. "Pop?"

I shrugged. "I dunno. Sorry."

"No, it's fine. It's just..." She turned away, but not before I caught something.

"What?"

A shake of her head. "Like you with that playlist. That nickname is just a...a thing. I haven't heard it in a long time."

"Sorry, then. Won't say it again, if it bothers you."

A hesitation. "I don't know if it does, actually. It's been a long, long time. Since I was little." She turned back to me, smiling, and it only seemed a little forced. "Maybe try it again sometime, and see how I feel about it."

I wanted to know, but considering how I'd avoided discussing my shit, it wouldn't be fair to press her on hers. I pushed off the bed, headed for the bathroom, peeling my shirt off as I went. She was watching me, and I felt her gaze as sharp and intense as mine had been when she got out of the shower. I paused just inside the bathroom, contemplating shutting the door. Instead, I reached in and turned on the water to heat up. Glanced at Poppy, and then shucked my board shorts. Stood naked, facing the shower but looking at Poppy.

She was motionless, eyes roaming me. Standing near the bed, iPad in one hand. Eyes wide, mouth slightly open. "Is this one of those moments where you're trying to make the ice cream last longer?" she asked, after a moment.

"Actually, this time, I think it's more about getting clean so I can get dirty again. You're all clean, wouldn't want to get my grime on all that nice clean skin."

"Oh." That answer seemed to appease her.

I stepped into the shower and drew the curtain closed.

As I showered, I kept wondering if I'd hear the rasp of the curtain rings, feel her step in with me.

I never did, and it only made me hungrier for her.

NINE

Poppy

I DIDN'T WANT TO GET DRESSED. I WANTED TO STAY NAKED, catch him fresh out of the shower, dripping wet and steaming.

I found excuse after excuse to not get dressed, to stay wrapped in my towel, even when the air conditioner's icy blast made me shiver.

Eventually, the water shut off—and by eventually, I mean half the time I was in the shower, and probably because I'd already used most of the hot water. He tossed the curtain aside and stepped out. He had forgotten or not bothered to bring a towel closer than from the rack over the toilet, and with the layout of the bathroom, that meant he had to either get one from inside the other end of the tub, or get out and reach over the toilet—which is what he did.

Naked, water sluicing off of him.

At the sight of a naked Errol, my nipples tightened, hardened to points, aching with intense and immediate need, and my center pulsed with damp arousal. He was a god. Every inch of him was lean and hard and corded with ropy muscle. He wasn't… how should I put it? Neither Instagram fitness model shredded nor Mr. Olympia bulky. He was a whole different kind of fit—he was lean and hard from a life lived doing hard things. His arms would stretch a T-shirt sleeve, and his abs were cheese-grater defined, his hips angular, his chest flat and hard. His thighs spoke of an ability to hike miles on end carrying all his gear. His hair, wet and flat, hung to just past his shoulders—it would curl up and shrink as it dried into wavy locks just shorter than shoulder length.

He grabbed a towel, let it drop from his hands to open it up, patted his face dry, his beard, and then dragged it over his head, grabbing the ends to shimmy it over his back, his buttocks—and holy moly, that ass was *tight*, so hard, so round, I just wanted to bite into it like a fucking apple. He whipped the towel around front, scrubbed off his abs and palmed his junk with it. And the way he handled his manhood was with rough familiarity, obviously, but I felt he should have been more reverent with such beauty. It was so gorgeous, his cock. It needed to be carved out of marble and displayed as the paragon of male glory—*this is what a real man is hung with*. Just my opinion, obviously, and no man is less of a man because of what he may or may not be packing between his legs. I've had as much fun with a small dick as a big one, but…it is true that size matters. It's just a matter of subjective opinion, woman to woman, what that perfect size is.

Errol was perfect, for me.

So perfect. I wanted to hold it in my hands, pet it. Kiss it. He had such a pretty penis that I just wanted to snuggle it. Even slack, it was beautiful, which was quite a marvelous trick, since most limp dicks were nothing short of comical. His was just…pretty. This morning's activities rampaged through my mind as I watched him finish toweling off.

His fingers between my thighs, under my skirt this morning. His cock in my hand, filling my mouth until my jaws ached to take all of his thick, turgid, salty inches. His mouth on my pussy, the way he made me come, as if he was greedy for my orgasms.

I knew I was for his—I wanted to feel him come again. And again. I wanted to make him shout the way he had, out of control, riled and wild. I wanted to do such dirty things to him, and all of them were in my mind, all at once.

The towel held in front of him, draped from chest to dangle tantalizingly in front of his sex, he swaggered into the bedroom. Blueblueblue eyes on me.

"You're looking at me funny, Poppy." His voice was low, rough.

I nodded, distracted by my thoughts and by the ravaging need I felt to yank that stupid towel out of his hands so I could resume ogling his body, which was, in short, a work of art along the caliber of Michelangelo's David. In fact, now that I think of it, Errol was a living embodiment of that sculpture… just with a way bigger cock and his own unique facial features and hair. But the body? That was Errol.

"What are you thinking, Pop?"

That nickname.

It didn't hurt. Just…twinged a little. But in a good way. It'd been so long since I'd heard it that it was just…interesting. And the way Errol said it? It made me shiver. That fucking accent. Jeez, until him, I hadn't known just a voice, the timbre and the accent, could make me tingle with desire.

But that intimate tone, just then? *Whaddya-thinkin', Pawp?* It set my skin to pebbling.

I met his eyes. I was sitting on the edge of the bed, still in my towel. Cold, and now shivering from desire as much as chill. Nipples so hard you could cut diamonds with them, the metal making them tingle until a single breath on them would have made me quiver with near-climax.

"What am I thinking?" I repeated.

He stood in front of me, towel still held casually in front of him. "Yeah. You know, penny for your thoughts kind of thing."

I gazed up at him. "I'm thinking…you don't need this." I yanked the towel away. Tossed aside. Immediately, his cock began hardening. At face level, too. Yum. "I'm thinking…well, a lot of things. None of them…wholesome."

He lifted his chin to stare down at me with arousal and ego and curiosity and heat all stampeding in his expression. "Is that so? Do share, then, please."

"Details?"

"Every last one." The roughness of his voice, like a file across stone, caressed my skin, made my core feel hot and taut and heavy with need.

"I'm thinking of all the things I want to do with you." I let my eyes linger on his cock as it unfurled, lengthening and thickening to a full and glorious erection before my eyes. "*To* you, to be more accurate."

"I wonder if we're thinkin' of the same things," he growled.

"I'm thinking about shoving you onto the floor right where you're standing and riding you until your cock hurts. I'm thinking about bending over this bed and begging you to pound me from behind."

"Ohhh you dirty girl, you," he snarled, his grin sinfully eager. "That last one you mentioned has my interest."

I stood up. "Does it, now?"

"Sure does." He stepped close. His hands slid around to my backside, lifted the towel to palm my ass cheeks, one in each hand. "I've got this image, see, of you bent over that bed so I can see those big tits of yours hanging and swaying, and doing exactly as you said—pounding into you from behind."

"How would you do it, Errol? Slow and gentle, or hard and fast?"

"Bit of both, I'd say." His grip tightened. "What I've been picturing is going in nice and slow at first, just so you can get used to me, you know? Then a bit faster, a bit harder. Then I'd pound you until that thick, juicy ass of yours starts shaking."

I laughed. "Thick *and* juicy?"

"Please, take it for the compliment I meant it as, yeah?"

"You make my ass sound like a steak."

"Well, I can't think of anything I'd rather eat than a nice, thick, juicy steak. So, yeah. Your ass is exactly like a steak, in a complimentary sort of way."

I laughed. "I'm complimented, don't worry."

He gnawed at his lower lip, and I wanted to take that lip from his teeth and soothe it with my tongue. "One problem, though, Pop, and I just thought of it this second."

"What problem?"

"I don't have any frenchies with me."

I cackled. "You don't have any what-now?"

"Frenchies. Frangers. Jimmy hats." He laughed. "Y'know. Condoms."

"Frenchies, though?"

He shrugged, laughing harder. "Yeah, a bit weird, I guess."

I frowned at him. "You don't have any?"

He tilted his head, thinking. "Well, I might. In a bag I carry my extra stuff in. The random shit I might need but don't bring into the hotel with me all the time." He shrugged. "I'll go look."

I glanced at him. "I'm more dressed than you are."

"You're in a towel."

"And you're naked."

"You're all but."

"What's the bag look like, and where is it?"

"Back of the caravan, behind the seat. A red backpack. Old one. One strap is almost off."

"I'll get it." He just nodded. "I'm not sure there are any in there. It's, um, been a while, if you know what I mean. And, ah, the last time I needed one, I didn't provide it."

I just smiled. "It's okay. We're both adults, no need to be weird about it. I haven't needed them myself, either, so I'm certainly not carrying any with me."

I tightened the towel, opened the door and set the latch bar so it wouldn't lock behind me, headed for the van. It was a hot, sticky, humid night, the air thick and moist and close. Bugs fluttered around the parking lot lighting, and a shred of grayish clouds floated lazily past a quarter moon. The parking lot was empty but for our car and one other near the office—the night clerk. The clerk himself was outside, on a cell phone, a cigarette in his mouth. He eyed me without curiosity, and turned away, walking back inside, tossing his butt aside with a spray of orange sparks.

I opened the rear hatch, where Errol's other nonessential gear was stowed. A middling-sized black duffel bag, half-open, showing a dirty pair of running shoes and a pair of rubber rain boots. A small bag that contained some kind of headphones, by the look of it. The red backpack, which I shouldered.

And a violin case. Fiddle case, rather. Black. *Old*. The silver clasps were tarnished with age. Scratches, rends, stains. A tag attached to the handle, newer leather, with a name scrawled inside—*B. Sylvain.* Under that, in smaller, neater letters—*E. Sylvain*.

Weird.

I flipped up the latch, feeling like I was prying, digging into secrets. Opened the lid. Within was, well, I'd call it a violin. A fiddle. It was dark cherry, glossy and warm with age, yellower streaks here and there. Soft strings, exquisitely carved head. God, the thing was *old*. You knew just by looking at it. I touched a string, the largest one, and the sound that emerged was honey and sunlight.

The bow was nestled in the lid, held in place with a swiveling knob. Aged, fraying horsehair, radiating elegance and art.

"That's sort of a private thing, there, Poppy." Errol's voice behind me. Tight, upset.

I jumped a foot in the air, letting the lid close with a soft *thump*. "I'm sorry. I know, I just…" I turned. "I'm sorry. I didn't mean to pry."

"It was my dad's."

"It has your name on it," I couldn't help pointing out.

A pause. "It's a family heirloom. All I've got of him."

I ducked my head. There was way, way more to the story, I could tell. He was wearing a pair of gym shorts, but tiny ones, almost booty shorts. The kind of shorts track and distance runners wear. Red, with a white stripe.

Nothing under them.

Bare-chested.

"I apologize, Errol. I shouldn't have opened it."

He shook his head. Reached past me to fasten the latch, pushed it further back. Took the red bag from me, and made to close the hatch. "No worries, Pop. Just…one of those things, you know?"

The sad bits, he meant, the hard sharp things I saw fleeting in the back of his eyes, buried deep, behind the jovial, easy-going, New Zealander laid-back attitude. The pain, the bitter, tight, shadowy things.

The things he didn't talk about.

Like me and Dad.

I got it, and I didn't care to have those particular bags of bones exhumed from their closets, so I didn't push it.

We went into the room, and he rifled through the bag, came up from the very bottom with a small box of condoms.

But there was that chill in the air between us again. Unspoken, which neither of us dared breach.

I sat on the bed, wanting to ask, knowing I wouldn't, knowing I won't. We're not like that. Shit, there's no "we" to be like that. We're strangers whose paths have crossed for a short while. There's chemistry, sure, and attraction. But sharing the deep, painful things that form the shadows and edges in our souls? It's not that. Can't be, won't be that.

He knows it, I know it.

"I was just curious, Errol. I'm sorry."

"I'm not pissed off."

"But the moment's gone," I said, sounding plaintive.

"Oh, I don't know. Give it a minute, eh? We can make a new moment."

The most awkward silence we'd experienced yet enveloped the room.

I didn't know how to get the moment back. And I wasn't sure I wanted to. If we got the moment back, we'd have crazy hot sex, and if we had crazy hot sex, I wasn't sure my stupid heart—which remained stubbornly and firmly romantic despite my best efforts to squelch it—wouldn't get involved somehow.

He was flipping the box in his hand, not quite looking at me, staring at me, but definitely aware of me. Waiting for a signal as to how to proceed.

"I'm…I'm tired," I said. Lame excuse.

I mean, I *was* tired. Sleeping on the ground hadn't exactly been restful, and after a night on the bare hard ground, and then hours in the car, had me feeling sore all over, physically exhausted.

But wanting him, needing his touch, needing to filled by him, to taste him…that existed outside the realm of mere tiredness.

But the weight of the emotional baggage we were both carrying around and refusing to touch… was a stumble in the careful steps of our sexual waltz, where we took what we wanted from each other without giving away anything.

I mean, maybe it was just me.

His expression seemed to tighten with anger or disappointment, but then was quickly masked. "Yeah, no worries. Been a long couple days, eh?"

I groaned at the hurt in his voice. "Errol…"

He shook his head, turned away, tossing the box back into the open top of his backpack. "I get it, Poppy."

I stood up, moved around in front of him. "You do, huh? What is it you get? Because I admit I'm a bit confused about what exactly is going on? Which one of us is upset here?"

He blinked down at me. "I don't know that *I'm* upset, exactly. I have a weird attachment to that fiddle, yeah, but it's over three hundred years old and a family heirloom and the only thing I own that connects me to my father and that whole side of my family. So I'm a bit possessive of it, and maybe I overreacted to seeing you handling it."

I shook my head. "Errol, you have every right to that. I shouldn't have been snooping through your stuff. I was curious, especially after that whole thing with the playlist. You didn't overreact. So I'm not upset either."

He laughed, pawed his fingers through his hair. "Then what the hell is going on with us?"

I laughed, too. "I don't fucking know, honestly."

He let out a slow breath. "How about we just scrap the whole last few minutes? Let's just lay down and turn on the TV and not have any expectations of each other or ourselves or the situation."

I felt a small smile cross my lips. "I think that sounds good, actually. I just need to, um, get something on."

He smirked. "I mean, don't get dressed on my account."

I swallowed hard. Because those tiny shorts he was wearing wasn't helping my libido. His bare chest was a hard plane of masculine muscle and sharp angles, and I wanted to run my hands over it, over the furrowed ridges of his abs, wanted to trace the hard V-cut where torso met abs met hips met cock.

Trace, taste, with hands, tongue.

"You can't look at me like that, Poppy. Not and think this is going to stay platonic."

"Look at you like what?" I asked. "And what makes you think I want anything to stay platonic?"

"Maybe I was mistaken, but in my experience, when a woman says 'I'm tired,' that's generally code for 'piss off, mate, it's not fuckin' happenin'.'"

I laughed. "Yeah, that's pretty accurate, generally."

"So that's what made me think you want this to stay platonic."

"Maybe I don't know what I want."

His lip curled in amusement. "You talk dirty like you can't wait to fuck, and then you go through my personal effects, and then you say you're tired, and then you look at me like I'm something to eat and you're fucking starved. Yeah, Poppy, I'd say you're a smidge unsure of what you want."

A silence, breathing and coiling and hissing between us like a rattlesnake, taut with tension. Did I dare go down that road with Errol?

How could I not, though? That was the real question. After the way he'd made me come? Fast, and hard, and numerously, just with his tongue and fingers? Could I—and more to the point, *would* I—let slip an opportunity to experience what promised to be the hottest sex of my life?

Yeah, probably not.

I was working out what to say, how to push us past this silence, when Errol did it for us.

"Fuck it," he breathed, his voice a low, guttural

snarl. "Not gonna stand here waiting for you to figure yourself out, Pop." His fingers closed on the edges of my towel, applying enough tension to begin loosening the knot at my chest, but giving me ample opportunity to demure. "You figure out you *don't* want it, now's the chance to say so. Otherwise, I'm taking what I want from you."

I held my breath. "What you want?" I echoed.

"What's the matter, Poppy? Cat got your tongue?"

"That's such a stupid saying. What does it even mean?" I reached out, rested my hands on his hard waist, touching firm warm skin and angular bone.

"Dunno," he murmured. "Don't rightly care, either." He was still holding the edges of my towel, still threatening to rip it off. "Last chance."

I tucked my fingers inside the waistband of his short shorts. "Or what, Errol?"

"Or I'll have you facedown on this bed with my cock inside your tight little pussy before you've blinked twice."

I stared up at him, eyes wide. Blinked once. Twice. Bold, daring him to follow through. "Weird. Didn't work."

He growled a laugh, yanked sharply on the towel. The rough, cheap white terrycloth fluttered to the floor, leaving me nude.

Oh, shit. He was *not* playing. His fingers hooked into me, driving into my slit, two of them filling me and scissoring, his thumb pressing against my clit. Tugged me closer.

Heat billowed within me, abrupt and tumultuous and fervent. My knees buckled at the sudden assault, but I was held up by his touch, his two middle fingers scissoring and twirling inside me, his thumb scraping and pressing and circling, and it was all at once, and not gentle, just rough enough to feel *so* good.

All he needed was the one hand, apparently. The other just dangled at his side, and he took me from unsure to orgasm in sixty seconds flat, had me quivering and shaking, had my knees buckling yet again so I was forced to cling to him and be held up by those same digits pierced inside me.

As I came, gasping, whimpering, needing to fall, laughing in disbelief at how fast he could bring me to climax, he just watched, a slow grin on his face, lips smirking, eyes wild.

His fingers slowed as my orgasm blossomed to full flower, leaving my face buried in his chest, my arms around his neck, hips driving against his fingers.

"Fucking hell, Errol," I gasped. "How do you do that?"

He growled a gruff laugh, his fingers slicking out of me and releasing me unexpectedly, so my knees gave out. He let me fall, pushing me backward onto the bed. I hit the mattress, and he was on me by the time I'd bounced once. Lips locked around my left nipple, tonguing my piercing until I screamed, another climax shearing through me—or the precursor to one. My hips bucked and I snarled my fingers into his hair, and he did not let up, one hand cupping my breast and shoving it into his mouth, his other hand around my other breast, fingers tweaking the bar and flicking my nipple.

"Oh *fuck*," I groaned, arching up to press my tits against him. "Yes, fuck, yes, please, Errol."

He laughed, pulling away from my tit just long enough to let the sound grumble out, and then he was at me again, plying my peaked nipple with his lips and tongue and teeth; switched to the other one, and now I ached deep inside. A thrum of need pulsed low, and there was stimulation to my clit to push me over the edge. His mouth on one nipple and his fingers at the other with equal stimulatory skill, I felt myself rising, rising. Back and forth, from one breast to the other, sucking and flicking, biting and licking, tweaking and twisting, he slowly and unhurriedly brought me closer and closer to climax from nipple play alone.

I'd always had sensitive breasts, and after the piercings they were even more so, and I'd long wondered if I could come from nipple stimulation alone but had never been able to get myself there, and neither had anyone else.

Errol did.

I scoured his back with one hand and knotted my fingers in his hair with the other, hips thrusting against his thigh and hip as he moved from breast to breast, hands never idle, his rhythm one of insatiable need. And I was aching, pulsating with heat, and the more he slathered his tongue over my nipples and flicked the bar with his tongue and twisted it with his fingers, the more the rollicking pushing thundering *need* inside me built and built to a crashing crescendo, and he did not hurry, even when the thrusting of my hips and the quavering plea in my whispered chant of his name begged for more, for him, he didn't alter or falter.

I was taut with need, an orgasm that wouldn't break coruscating and burgeoning inside me. Thighs splayed wide around his hips, his waist. Hands on him, everywhere.

Digging into the waistband to clutch at his firm ass, rounding his hard shoulders, his angular waist, the furrows of his abs. Seeking *him*.

He didn't hurry.

Licked.

Tongue flicked and circled left nipple. Right. Lingered on the right side for a while, and then his fingers replaced his tongue, which moved left.

"Errol…please," I whispered.

I needed to come.

I was building to a painful pressure, and this nipple play alone wouldn't get me there, wouldn't take me past the climax into screaming orgasm.

And then, as he suckled my entire nipple, piercing and all, into his mouth and flicked and twisted the piercing with his tongue and his fingers pinched my nipple around the metal bar,

I came.

I came so hard it fucking *hurt*.

I coiled into myself, clit throbbing in desperation for stimulation, slit clenching on nothing, breasts full and nipples hard, he was there. Above me. Surrounding me.

I clawed at him, hands raking his sides. Elastic caught in my finger and he moved, wiggled, and I was still coming and I felt hard warm skin under my hand. Need guided me, my hands blindly seeking as I came and came, wave after wave of bliss crashing hard and fast, a new kind of pleasure heretofore unknown—tighter, hotter, higher, an orgasm from nipple stimulation alone was clearly its own unique beast and it showed me its teeth as it ravaged me for what felt like long minutes.

When I returned to my senses, I was slicked with sweat and Errol was kneeling between my knees, naked. Hard abs narrowed down to his cock, which was standing erect and begging for me, pink and thick and veiny, the bulbous head shiny, straining. Balls heavy, taut against him. Belly pulled in, eyes wild. Muscles hard with restraint.

He had the condom box in his hands, fumbling with it. I yanked it out of his grasp, stuck the corner in my teeth and tore at it like a lion ripping flesh from fresh prey. Black foil packets within—these were upscale condoms, I noticed. I yanked the string free of the box, ripped one packet away, tossed the box and the rest of the string aside. Somewhere, I didn't care where it went. With my teeth again, I made quick work of opening the condom.

I gripped the enormous shaft of his cock and rolled the condom onto him—this I did slowly, caressing him with the act.

It was an oddly still, quiet, slow moment. His pulse was pounding in his throat—I could see it beating and wanted to kiss that spot on his neck. My own was hammering like a war drum. Sweat cooling on my skin, nipples aching, slit begging to be plundered, filled, used.

And yet, despite our wild need, we both held utterly still, eyes locked as I slowly, slowly rolled the condom down his cock, one little brush of my fist at a time, each stroke starting at the top. When the ring of latex was fully seated at his base, I cupped his balls in both hands, caressed them, squeezed, kneaded. He let me, eyes on me.

And then he pulled from my hold, pulled away. Knelt over me, on all fours above me. Dipped, and his mouth brushed mine, lips gently nuzzling mine. A touch, only. His tongue licked over my upper lip, my lower. I moved to kiss him back, but he pulled away. Lifted upright, slowly.

I reached for him, but he imprisoned my hand. The other. Pressed them up over my head. A momentary vignette, then. Me, stretched out, nipples peaked and need piqued, aching, breasts sagging to either side and upward, on my back, hands over my head; him, up on his knees over me, cock straining and sheathed in white latex, the tip extending, waiting to be filled with his cum, balls heavy and thighs bunched and muscles heavy and hard, eyes bright and Aegean blue and roving my flesh and my curves.

His hands pinioned my wrists.

Gripped.

A slow smile curved his lips.

"May have taken longer than two blinks," he

murmured. "But I said I'd have you facedown on the bed with my cock buried inside you."

"But, I'm not—" I began.

The third word had barely left my lips when he roughly flipped me, kept my hands pinned up beyond my head. Hands gripped my hips and yanked my ass backward, toward him, lifting. Ass down, face up. I groaned as his palms caressed my spread ass cheeks, and then he plied them apart, and I felt his tongue slip against my clit, licking downward, tickling and wet and unexpected and gentle, his lips then, more of a kiss than anything.

And then I felt him.

The broad round head nuzzling against my entrance. Breached me, slowly, gently, carefully.

I gasped at the size of him, a shrill, breathless whimper. "Oh *fuck*," I hissed. "Errol, oh *fuck,* Errol, you're…oh fuck, your cock…god, oh god, so fucking big."

Barely an inch. Maybe less, and then he pulled back. "Poppy, Jesus you're tight." His voice was wild and low and desperate. "Can you take me? Tell me you can take me, Pop."

"Give me more and I'll tell you," I murmured. "Give me more of that big fat fucking cock, and I'll let you know*OHFUCKYES*—yes, fuck, yes, fuck, yes."

He had my ass in his hands, fistfuls of flesh gripped

in rough, clawed hands. And then he let go and caressed sweetly, delicately. Pushed, just a little, and that tiny pulse of his hips gave me another huge penetrating inch, and god, thank *fuck* he wasn't any longer, wasn't any thicker, or I couldn't have taken him and enjoyed it. He was just barely too big for me, more cock than I'd ever taken and so fucking good, stretching me so it hurt so deliciously, filling me until I was unable to breathe, gasping for air at the shock of him inside me.

He was so gentle, so careful, despite his otherwise rough use of my body. I gasped as he fed another inch into my clenching slit, and then paused. Leaned forward so his belly was pressed against my back, and his long arm slid under me and his big roughened gentle palm cupped my breast and his other wedged low against my hipbone, reaching between my thighs to where we were joined, and then he was pressing two fingers against my clit and circling, and I gasped, and the gasp became a whimper and the whimper a shriek because *how the fuck* did he know I needed that extra stimulation, when I didn't even know myself until he did it?

I was already on edge, and that little touch pushed me over, and I came with his thick cock only partially inside me, his hands cupping my tit and swirling around my clit and making me come and the orgasm sent a rush of heat through me, wet and slick.

He slithered a thrust, a gentle one, no deeper yet than maybe half his length, out and in, and I felt his veins stuttering against my sex through the now-wet latex of his condom and I needed more. I needed all of him.

"Pop?" he growled, voice low and feral.

"Yeah?" I breathed.

"Can you take me?"

I swiveled my hips in answer, writhing to get him deeper.

"Need your words, Poppy."

"Yes," I gasped. "Yes, I can take you. Give it to me, Errol. Give it all."

His forehead touched my spine and his breath huffed hot, and he growled in animal relief as he pressed his hips forward until they kissed my ass cheeks, and he was fully within me.

I could not breathe for the aching stretching enormity of Errol inside me, fully filling me. I was split open, glutted around him.

"Fuck, oh *fuck*," he snarled. "Holy fuck, Poppy. Holy fuck."

I gripped the bedspread in my fists and pushed myself backward, and he pushed harder against me and somehow there was more of him to fill me, and then his hands were gripping my ass and now, now he was pulling back and I ached for the emptiness within where he just was. I cried out, needing him to fill me, stunned at the wondrous ache of absence.

His grip on the crease of my hip and curve of my ass was rough, harsh, wild. I gloried in it. In the fingerprints he'd leave. Slowly, once again carefully and gently, he thrust all the way into me, and now our moans were synched. One groan, two throats.

"Poppy," he breathed.

"Harder," I sighed.

"Oh thank fuck," he whispered, and withdrew.

Fucked into me, and *now* it was real, now it was on. He shoved his huge slick hard hot cock into me and his hips slapped against my ass and he held the cheeks apart to get deeper and I pushed against him with his next thrust, pulled forward when he pulled back and rolled my ass back into him when he next thrust in.

Again, and again, his cock drilling in, my thrusts meeting his.

"Poppy," he moaned, and there was a question in his voice.

"Huh?" An answering wordless moan was all I could manage.

"You feel too fucking good," he growled. "I want it to last forever, but you feel too fucking good."

He pushed deep, thrusting hard, and I felt his balls tap against me. I curled backward into myself, reached between my thighs. Felt his shaft like a piston sliding into me, and then I felt his sac fill my hand, and I squeezed. He snarled, leonine and guttural, so his next thrust I did it again.

"Want you to come," I gasped, voice tremoring as his thrust shook me, as he fucked into me hard. "Come for me, Errol."

"Don't wanna come yet. Want to fuck you forever." He lost his voice as I caressed his balls on his next pounding thrust. "Fuck, when you do that, Poppy? Makes me insane. Feels so fucking good. Too fucking good. Can't last much longer, you make me feel too fucking good…"

I had to grip the pillow and writhe against the mattress and scream into the bedspread as he drilled into me, thrust after thrust, and each one I caught at his balls and squeezed and kneaded. Until his thrusts faltered, and I heard his breathing go hoarse and heard him whimper, a low masculine sound of desperation, of abandonment.

"I can't—" he whispered, voice breaking. "Can't…can't stop it."

Pushed into me, and now his thrusts were deeper without pulling out, and I had his balls in both my hands, cupping and squeezing, and his groan became one of agonized disbelief as I clenched around his balls and kept him from coming as he let go. He was pulsing against me, gripping my ass and spreading me apart and pushing deeper, and now he was shouting as I clenched hard, holding on to him a beat longer.

And then released him, my grip now soft and caressing, squeezing his delicate pulsating sac in time with the rhythm of the vein I felt behind his balls.

He shouted, a loud hoarse broken male scream of release. "POPPY!" A wordless, guttural roar as another quaking wave wrenched him, and he jerked out of my grip and pulled back to fuck me, twice, three times, fucking me hard through his release, and then another wave crushed him in its grip and I had his balls in my palms again, kneading now, swift and gently as he feathered small helpless thrusts deeper and deeper and deeper.

His face was slack against my spine, his breath hot and damp, and he was limp.

He let me go, and I fell forward, and he went with me, covering me, lying on top of me.

"Holy shit," he murmured.

"No kidding," I breathed.

I was aching.

Crushed by him, but not minding.

"Poppy." A question in the form of a flat statement. "You didn't come again."

"No, but I came three times before you did, so—"

I never got the rest out, and he was sliding down my body, gathering himself slowly as if summoning the strength to even move, lips stuttering over my spine, and now his lips kissed the swell of my right ass cheek and then he was pushing me over onto my back and curling down between my thighs.

He kissed me.

He kissed my sex, lips slathering over my clit, worshipping slow and soft.

This was not just to make me come so we were "even," oh no, this was something else.

Thanks for the way I'd made him come, as if he owed me thanks for the fuck of a lifetime.

I could die right now and die happy, knowing I'd been well and truly fucked.

But yet, he wasn't satisfied.

He used his fingers to pry open my slit and bare my clit for his mouth, and this was all about making me come, but…the speed, the gentility, the silky slither of his tongue and the soft press of his lips, it was about giving me…something.

What, I couldn't name.

But something.

"Errol?" A gasp, as I flew out of my depth.

"Just take it," he whispered, the words huffing against my taut nether lip and swollen clit. "Take it, and say my name when you come."

I took it from him, and I didn't just say his name when I finally came again, for the fourth time in I had no clue how much time—I screamed it.

I screamed his name until my voice broke and the sound of his name on my tongue lost meaning—semantic satiation, a professor had called that phenomenon.

I think I actually passed out.

When I returned to awareness, I was on my belly still, and my sex was aching and pulsing and tingling, and I was awash with post-orgasmic blissed-out glow. I heard a faucet running, managed to pivot my head until I could see into the bathroom. Errol was standing naked in front of the toilet, in the act of peeling the condom off, careful not to spill, wrapped it in a folded wad of toilet paper, which he then used to wipe himself with, and then discarded the whole in the trash. Washed his hands. Dried them. Returned to me, dick swinging long and limp.

Fierce blue eyes, going soft with affection as he saw me.

He tugged the blanket out from under me, covered me with it. Lay down under the blankets beside me. We were both unsure of what was next.

I wasn't a cuddler after sex, and I felt like he wasn't normally, either.

I twisted my head the other way; still unable

and unwilling to move any more than was necessary. Stared at him.

Words failed us both.

My eyes fluttered. He was within reach; close enough I felt his body heat warming us under the blanket. On his back, next to me, head to one side.

I was a stomach sleeper, and so I let myself float.

My eyes flickered open, briefly, partially, and he had one hand across his chest, the other down his side, near mine.

Another floating drifting in the warm darkness of near-sleep. Another flutter of my eyes, but this time I saw nothing. Too dark. But I felt him.

I felt his hand in mine.

I didn't withdraw mine. His hand in mine was a strange comfort in this drowsing dark of unfamiliar comfort, this blissful sleep of absolute safety and absolute satiety.

I've never, ever, not once, finished sex and felt utterly sated. I always felt like there was something missing. Like I hadn't come all the way. Or not enough. Or, that I hadn't gotten enough of him, or that there wasn't enough of him to fill me, to complete me.

I was so used to that feeling that this, this satiated existential physical wonder…it was too much.

Unfamiliar.

Frightening.

But only frightening—and indeed, more truly termed terrifying—because now I would never feel sated again.

Sex would never be the same.

Fucking would never be the same.

Orgasms, touch, kisses, none of it would ever be the same, now that I knew what this felt like.

TEN

Errol

I WOKE TO NEAR DARKNESS.

Aware of her.

Aware that I was aching with renewed and intensified need for her.

On my side, facing her, hearing her slumber, soft girlish snores.

She was still on her stomach, and I didn't think she'd moved.

I drowsed back under.

Woke again, later. Achingly hard.

Dull reddish-orange light streaming like a knife

through the darkness from between an inch-wide crack in the curtains. Felt her against my body. Couldn't help but hold. Reached, filled my hands with soft curves.

She murmured in her sleep.

Wiggled, rolled to face away, pressed deeper against me.

This was spooning?

God, now I got it.

Now, with this glorious creature of womanly perfection nestled in my arms, feeling her soft curves pressed all against me, I got it.

Drowsed again, and this time it was to fall more fully asleep than before.

The next time consciousness returned, it was slowly, and disorienting. All was dark in my world.

I ached.

Yet something began to soothe the ache. Something caressed the ache with unhurried affection. I heard a sound, and I think it was me, and I was moaning my appreciation of the soothing caress of my ache.

Darkness receded, and the soothing caress intensified. Became more than merely soothing.

And that was when I awoke more fully. Eyes flickered, shuttered, opened. Full daylight streaming white-yellow through the crack in the curtains.

Blankets were gone. I was on my back. A shape was above me. Curled, curved over me. I felt hair tickling my thighs and belly, obscuring her face. She was sitting on my thighs, hair splayed in a curtain around her and over me. I felt her small strong hands around my cock and her tight wet mouth was on me.

"Ohhhhh*ffffuuuuck*," I growled, my voice sleep-rough. "Poppy?"

No answer. She just continued her ministrations.

I pulled her hair into my hands and held it, curled it around my fist, and now I could watch in the dim light as she went down on me. Slow, unhurried. Fists pumping and twisting around my base and shaft, mouth suctioned around the head.

Her eyes met mine in the near dark, and a smile lit up her eyes.

I wanted her.

This, yes, always.

But *her*.

I tried to pull her up, but she shook her head. Paused, let me fall out of her mouth. "Just take it, Errol," she murmured, echoing my words from the night before. "Take it and enjoy it." A hot grin, her lips curving against my cock, and then her tongue slid up my erection. "Take it and say my name when you come."

And then her mouth went over the top of my

cock and down, her lips stretched around me, and her fists pumped twisted. She backed away and caressed my length, and then put her mouth on me and took as much of me as she could, or wanted to—I didn't care which, I only knew that it felt incredible.

Again, and again. Mouth down my shaft, sucking. Tongue flicking and licking as I slid out of her mouth. Pump, twist, caress, lick the tip, lick the seeping, weeping droplets of precum. I groaned as the first shudders started in me, low in my gut, in my bones, my balls boiling, cock hardening further, swelling as she gulped around me, spat me out and kissed the head.

Then, as I began to grind, began to thrust helplessly, she just gripped me at the root and held me away from my belly and went down, bobbing, tongue working.

My hands gripped and knotted in her hair. I fought for air, for words. "Poppy…I'm…*oh fuck.*" Words eluded me.

I knew there something I was supposed to do, let her know I couldn't hold out, couldn't wait. But I was gone, brain melted, my whole body arched up off the bed and she was sucking me higher and higher to an ever more elevated state of existential ecstasy, and I was not *me*, not a man, not even a person, just a being of pure sexuality, pure pleasure, and purely at her mercy.

"Pop—Poppy…" I gasped, her name a whisper, a breathless benediction. "*Poppy…*"

I exploded, and she moaned a sound of surprise, gulped, and somehow went deeper, took more of me, pumped me hard and fast and I exploded again, a sound rasping out of me, something like her name but a hoarse whimper of her name, and only my heels and shoulders were touching the mattress, the rest of me bent upward nearly to breaking and she still did not relent but sucked the very life out of me, a sensual succubus; I groaned in disbelief, and still she sucked until I broke, until I could not come any more, and even then she suckled and licked and kissed as I descended helplessly back under the frothing churning surface of wakefulness.

I felt her cheek against my belly. Her hand petting my cock as if it was a favorite pet.

I moaned, murmured, tried to rouse myself, because now I needed, wanted, was ravenous for her pleasure, for her to scream, but I was utterly spent and couldn't even stir a finger.

"Ssshhh." She wiggled up my body, cheek sliding against my belly, diaphragm, and then resting on my chest. Thumb on my lips, then grazing gently over my eyelids like a battlefield priest closing the eyes of a deceased warrior. "Shush, Errol. Back to sleep."

I had no fight. I slept, and it was with her in my arms, and it felt like, for the first and only time in my life, the whole of the universe was finally oriented correctly, as if something had clicked into place.

The last time I woke, she was asleep beside me, on her stomach once more, hand curled up against her cheek. Plump buttocks bare, blanket rucked at the backs of her knees.

Hair a spray of inky black around her tanned shoulders and wisping around her lips, her back a sexy curve, a delicate sinuous line from shoulder to ass, one thigh drawn up, the other stretched out.

My stomach rumbled, and my entire being demanded coffee, so I dressed silently in my stubbies and a tank top and thongs, headed out for the Maccas I'd seen back down the other way a kilometer or two. Hit the drive-thru, got four large black coffees and four different breakfast orders of various items that sounded good to me. Brought it all back and tiptoed in, juggling the bags and the key and trying to quietly close the door.

She stirred as I set the food down on the small table near the window, rolling to her back, bringing one foot up under her other knee, arm across her face, the other splayed across the bed. Breasts draped to one side as she was tilted slightly. Unaroused, her nipples were fat flat buttons of pink. Belly button was a tiny dimple between the lush expanse of tan flesh between her breasts and sex.

Her sex was a pink rosebud, partially opened with the way her thighs were splayed, thigh bent up ninety degrees, calf and foot angled down under the opposite thigh. I brought one coffee over to her side of the bed, removed the top so it would cool. Crawled onto the bed, and she stirred, head swiveling to the other side, making a soft smacking sound with her lips.

Bracing my hands on either side of her hips, I bent over her sex. Huffed a hot breath on it. She mewled quietly, hips flexing. Oh, she was ready for it. I licked up her slit, ending with a pressing swirl over the nub of her prominent clit. She flexed her hips again, mewled more loudly, shifted, wiggled. I let her settle, and then went to pleasuring her with slow precise licks—up and down, side to side, circles; up and down, side to side, circles; again and again, and now her huffing breath and mewling voice were louder, more insistent, and her hips began to move to match my tongue, lifting and circling, flexing and swaying. I held her lips apart and shoved my tongue inside her, and she gasped, and I think that was the first moment she began to surface toward wakefulness.

"Errol…" she whimpered, soft, sleepy—not sleepy, asleep. Dreaming.

"Come for me, Poppy," I murmured.

"Mmmm…" she breathed. "More…more."

I gave her more. She seemed to like being fingered while I ate her out, so I gave her two fingers curling up and in, and she responded by gasping aloud, but a glance told me she was still dreaming, thinking this was a dream.

Let her dream of being pleasured, then. As long as I got to feel her come, hear her scream, taste her pleasure.

It didn't take long. I had her bucking within a few minutes, and I felt her hands reaching for me, so I helped her find my head, my hair, and I grunted as she tangled her fingers into my hair with knotting strength, jerking me hard against her slick wet hot sex.

And then, as I fingered her the way she liked it, licked her the way she needed it, she came.

And as she came, her eyes flew open, wild and confused and desperate and bliss-fraught. "Errol?"

"Say my name, Poppy," I growled, pausing only briefly. "Come for me, and say my name."

"Errol! Fuck, *Errol*!"

She came, and I tasted her pleasure as it washed through her, and she writhed against me, held me against her and rode my mouth and screamed a deafening scream.

Finally, the orgasm left her, and she wilted.

She pulled at me, and I crawled up. Sat beside her. She clung to me, rested her head on my thigh. I reached over and carefully grabbed the hot coffee. Blew across the top, toward her.

She mewled. Shook her head. "Sleepy."

"So sleep."

"But…coffee."

"And pancakes, and hash browns, and McGriddles, and sausage, egg, and biscuit sandwiches, and…something else, I've forgot what."

She huffed. "Fine," she growled, as if I'd insisted she rouse herself.

And sat up, tugged the blanket up to her waist, but otherwise stayed naked from the waist up, which I thoroughly appreciated, especially when she shifted and wiggled to get her pillows behind her just so and the blanket this way, making her tits jiggle and shimmy delightfully.

I handed her the coffee, and she took it, closed her eyes and inhaled the steam, and then took a slow, careful, slurping sip.

Handed it to me, watched me with every bit as much lustful intensity as I'd watched her.

We shared the coffee without talking.

Ate all the food, sharing the various options.

More coffee.

All without talking much… at all.

Fucked again, slowly.

Wordlessly. Missionary.

Her eyes on mine, an aching tumult of unspoken things weltering and billowing between us as our bodies met and joined and crashed.

She bit my chest and clawed welting lines into my shoulders, and I left fingerprint bruises on her hips from jerking her into me to get deeper, harder, because for as hard as I fucked, as deep as I got, she begged breathlessly for harder, deeper.

I kissed the bruises, and she licked my welts.

Still, we spoke of nothing real, or meaningful.

Noon came, after a nap and we finished the last, cold coffee.

Finally, out of food and out of coffee, we both showered and dressed in clean clothes. Me, in convertible shorts that looked like normal dressy golf-ish shorts, but were made of quick-dry togs material, and a clean tank top; her, in cutoff denim shorts that only just barely covered the juicy globes of her taut round ass, so that the underswells were visible for a tantalizing moment at each step, and a seafoam green V-neck T-shirt. I had the unique and breathtaking pleasure of watching her dress, which was nearly as erotic to me as if I'd gotten to watch her strip.

She wore a blue thong under her shorts, a minuscule string around her waist with a triangle of shimmery, stretchy fabric cupping her sex and another string stretched between her ass cheeks. Her bra matched, and was equally provocative, a pushup style which added extra size and lift to already massive and tight tits, so the lush weight of her breasts filled and overfilled and spilled out of the half-moon cups, leaving her nipples mostly covered and the upper half of each areola bared. Then she had the audacity to cover the artwork that was her body with stupid clothes, which somehow only made her all the more beautiful, in a different way.

She watched me watch her dress and gave an extra shimmy as she wedged herself into the shorts, a teasing grin on her face which told me she knew exactly what she was doing to me with that little wiggle.

We packed our things.

There was a heated, volatile tension crackling between us. Sexual chemistry sparking, waiting to be ignited by a look, a word, a touch.

But there was something else. Something darker. Heavier. Sadder.

A sense of ending.

Once our bags were packed and all that was left was to leave, we stood facing each other at the foot of the bed. Her hands were shoved into the back pockets of her shorts, her hair done in twin braids hanging down to her shoulder blades. Eying me, a million things percolating in those cocoa eyes.

We'd spoken maybe half a dozen words each since last night, as if beginning a conversation would hasten the end we both knew had arrived.

"So…" I swallowed. "You're headed toward Alaska?"

She nodded. "Yep. Figured I'd see some of Canada."

"I was thinking I'd make my way to the west coast, and then make a big loop down into those big states with the four corners that all touch. Can't remember all of them."

Silence.

"So, you're heading west, and I'm heading north from here," Poppy said, and her expression showed a hint of sadness, regret. "I guess this is it, then, huh?"

Something within me wanted to argue. To say or do something. *Go west with me. We can go north from California. I don't need to be anywhere specific.*

Instead, I just nodded. "Guess it is."

She just waited. Gazed up at me, a soft glow to her eyes. "Thank you, Errol."

"For what?" I asked.

A shrug. "A good time. Good conversation. Taking photos together." She glanced at the bed, smirked. "And…that."

I shook my head, huffing a laugh. "*You're* thanking *me*?" I shook my head again. "I'm the one who should thank you, Poppy. That was…fucking unreal. Especially the way you woke me up."

She blushed, ducking her head. "I mean, I'm a practical sort of gal. Not gonna let a good erection go to waste, you know?" a hot, lusty grin. "Besides, you more than paid me back."

I groaned. "We have to get off this topic."

Poppy snickered. "*Get off* the topic, huh?"

"Bloody hell, Pop," I laughed, "You're such a hard case."

She blinked in confusion. "Hard case?"

"Funny. A comedian."

"Oh. In American slang, a hard case is, like, a tough guy." Her gaze went back to the bed. "I just showered, brushed my teeth, and dressed, or I'd suggest another go for old time's sake."

I let my eyes communicate how I felt about that. "Probably for the best we don't," I said, in contradiction to what I wanted, what I felt, what I thought. "We did, we'd spend another day here, in that bed."

"What's stopping us?" Poppy asked, eyes wide.

"Nothing."

A moment, a tableau, in which we both considered the outcome of another day spent fucking, eating, talking.

It was the talking that had me shutting down. Talking would lead to questions neither of us was brave enough to answer. And I saw Poppy come to the same conclusion.

"You go first," she said.

I swallowed. "I don't like just leaving you here."

She smiled, bright and brave. "I walked from Manhattan to where you found me, Errol. I'm good."

"I know. It's not about what I think you're capable of, it's...how I feel about it. Doesn't seem right to just drive away and leave you on foot."

Something crossed her face, then, fleeting but intense. "I know," she said, cheerful and peppy. "But I chose to go on foot. And I'll get a ride at some point. It's fine, Errol. I've got this." A pause. She swallowed, and I wondered how much acting she was doing. "I'm good. Promise."

I scraped my damp hair back from my face.

Shoved my sunnies higher on my head. "Yeah… yeah, you're good." I sighed. "Okay, then. I…it's a weird goodbye, isn't it?"

She nodded and shrugged. "Yeah, it kind of is."

"So…goodbye." Wrong, wrong, wrong. "Bye, Poppy. It was…it was amazing to have to known you."

"To have known me biblically, you mean?" she said, smirking.

I groaned. "You gotta stop with the suggestive jokes or they'll stop being suggestive." I met her smirk with my own. "But yes, Poppy Goode, it was *incredible* to have had the privilege of knowing you biblically."

She closed her eyes, briefly. Opened them again, and it seemed to me she forced the smile. "Goodbye, Errol."

I shouldered my bags, opened the door. Stood on the threshold, looked back at her. "See ya."

Turned, tossed my stuff in the campervan, drove away. Poppy was in the doorway, hands still in her back pockets, leaning against the doorpost, watching. Waved once, as I backed out of the parking space.

Drove away, then. Hit the junction and went west.

Alone once more, I should have been excited about the next leg of my journey. Instead, the van just felt…empty.

A mile, two. Radio off, window down.

It was a beautiful day, sunny, warm, clear blue skies. I even found an amazing highway-side ghost town, the diner empty as if waiting for cars and customers and cooks and waitresses, a mechanic shop with roll-down doors like sad eyes, a gas station with twin petrol pumps like aged sentinels. There was even a newspaper rolling listlessly down the street, blown by a lazy stream of wind.

I spent forty-five minutes there, and got a couple hundred wonderful shots.

It wasn't the same.

I drove on, west, and the farther I went, the more my gut ached.

Finally, an hour and a half west of Dubuque, I found myself pulling off onto the shoulder. Outside my van, watching a lone cow idly browsing among a patch of clover.

Wondering what was wrong with me.

Why didn't I enjoy the open road, now? The quiet, the solitude. The endless possibility.

The answer was obvious.

Her.

She made everything seem…more alive. Better. Brighter. Possibilities seemed…shinier.

The open road held potential, with her in the van. Now it just seemed like an endless journey to no purpose.

Why had we separated? I could have gone north with her.

Could have, or should have?

Was it just the sex that was appealing? Sure, it had been, by several orders of magnitude, the best sex of my life, and not because she'd woken me up with her mouth on my cock. The way we'd fucked had been… intense. Not just erotic, but…

Dammit.

Meaningful.

The answer to everything hit me like a lorry going 120 km/hr.

We'd separated because to stay together would have meant opening up the old wounds. We'd fucked a couple times, but to go beyond that, to remain together, traveling, meaningless, idle conversation would run out—*had* run out already. We'd butted up against the sad bits, as I'd called them. My own and hers.

I hated talking about Mom, about Dad. Hated sounding all poor-me. Hated bringing any of it up. Hated the pity, the compassion, the sorrow. Hated the discussions of how it had affected me. Hated all of it. Wanted to just...bury it all behind miles of highway, behind stories, behind professional achievements, behind *life*.

And getting close to a woman meant opening all that up. Trust me, I'd tried. I once spent six months in one place, and it had not turned out well. Perth, two years ago. I'd done all short-hop assignments and stayed local to Perth, and I'd gotten friendly and then more than friendly with a surfer/bartender named Leslie. Blond hair in a chic, easy-maintenance bob, green eyes, small tits and a sizable ass that looked great in a wet suit; she'd had a penchant for cowgirl, and was prone to gushy sentiment afterward. She would claim, outside the heat of the moment and afterglow, that she wasn't looking for love, but during? She always wanted an emotional availability from me that I just wasn't capable of. Hadn't been capable of then, and wasn't now.

She'd always been after me to talk about things. About my tragedies, about how they'd shaped me. She shared hers without reservation, and god was she brave about it—dad never in the picture, mum with a slew of shitty boyfriends, one of whom had abused her mum physically and Leslie sexually, but she'd chosen to not let it make her hard and broken and chose to trust men, as long as they earned and kept her trust.

Inspiring, beautiful. She was a great woman, Leslie.

But she'd confronted me one night. Late, after a double-round of sex. She'd stood naked in her bedroom and demanded that I either open up or fuck off. She wanted a partner for life, not just sex. Someone who trusted her with himself, with his heart.

So I'd fucked off. Told her I wasn't ready for that, maybe never would be, and I was sorry. Packed my things that night and hopped a red-eye for Thailand, where Jerry had been after me to go for a piece on jungle temples.

Standing on the side of the road, I realized that now, finally, twenty-four years of buried shit was bubbling up, and that I'd finally come to a point where I had to find someone I trusted to hear it, to understand it, and me.

And I had.

She hadn't pushed me for it. If anything, she'd been only too eager to avoid talking about mine for fear of having to talk about hers.

I'd made the wrong choice.

I should have gone north.

Should have taken that moment, there in that motel room in Dubuque, when we'd been faced with the choice to either jump in or run, and we'd chosen to run.

I'd been running all my life.

Time to stop running, I think.

I had no idea what I would do. What it would look like, feel like, where it would lead me. But I had to do something different, this time. This empty feeling, this...*missing* her was different. I've never missed anyone, before. Never let anyone in far enough that my emotions got involved to the point of suddenly missing them...needing them.

All I knew was that something was drawing me not west, but back to her. Maybe she'd tell me I was barking up the wrong tree. Maybe she wouldn't be ready to open up her past to me. Shit, I had no idea where to start, or how to open up. Closing off was a familiar instinct. Staying aloof, staying cool. Keep the past in the past. The present is now, and the future is yet to be written, so what's the point in rummaging through old pain?

Why do it at all? Where would it go? Our paths had crossed for, what, forty-eight, sixty-some hours? Two days, not quite three. Some sex, some conversation.

Say we open up—say I do, she does. We share our pasts and have the whole talk about everything, the thing we'd both been avoiding. Then what?

She comes with me on all my travels? That's not her life. And mine isn't in Alaska, that's for fucking certain. So, then what?

Fuck if I knew.

I just knew I'd regret it for the rest of my life if I didn't go find her, and at least try.

Took close to two hours to get back to the motel. Well past noon by then. The day clerk was a woman, grandmother age and friendly.

"Oh, the lovely young dear in room twelve?" she mused, upon me asking. "She left hours ago, I'm afraid. Just after my shift started. On foot, bless her heart. Headed for the junction, I think. There's a gas station there at the corner, you might ask Darnell if he saw her."

Darnell was a black man with a shaved head and a neat goatee and wire-frame glasses. "Yeah, I saw her," he said, glancing up at me as he counted out the cash in the till drawer. "White girl with li'l bitty booty shorts, an' a big ol' backpack. Came in…oh, three, almost four hours ago. She bought…let's see." He glanced away, thinking. "Beef jerky, and filled one of those plastic hiking bottles with water from the drinkin' fountain over there. What else she buy? Oh, I know…candy—M&Ms, Skittles, and…some of them gummy fish in the yellow and blue bags. Swedish fish."

"Which way did she go after she left here?" I asked, though I knew the answer.

I felt her path, felt the pull northward.

Darnell gestured at the northward spur. "Thataway." He eyed me, then. "Let a keeper get away, did you?"

I laughed at his insight. "Yeah, mate, I sure did."

He patted a handful of cash into a neat stack. "Well, good luck to you, son. Hope you find her."

"Me, too."

Northward, then. Slow, watching the shoulders. Watching side roads, dirt roads, tracks that led off into nothing.

Afternoon sun faded into orange, and the hours found me having made the trip from the junction where US-61 crossed the river east before breaking off into US-151 and US-61, going east and north and west and north, respectively, all the way to Sparta, where WI-27 met I-90. Almost two and a half hours, 117 miles. It seemed impossible that she'd have made it that far, but if she'd found a ride anything was possible. Finding her was impossible.

Had we exchanged numbers? I went through my phone, and discovered we hadn't.

What if she'd found a ride and was now miles beyond Sparta? I'd been going slow, watching for her on foot, assuming she'd have stuck to this northward route. But what if she'd found an alternative route? Found somewhere to take photos and I just passed her? I couldn't explore every sidetrack and dirt road between Dubuque and Sparta.

Fuck.

I'd let her get away.

I couldn't let her stay gone. Couldn't.

So, I refueled and went back the way I'd come. Another two hours plus back to where I'd started—no sign of her. Tried another sequence of spurs north and west—WI-35 following the Mississippi River until it rejoined the 27.

Woods, fields, farms.

Dirt roads and silos. Semis and pickups, blink-and-you-miss-them towns. Afternoon turned into evening, exploring offshoots, pausing in gas stations to ask if anyone had seen the most beautiful girl in the world recently, wearing cutoff jean shorts and a green shirt.

Evening into night. Where was I? I'd lost track of myself. North of Sparta? Way off the beaten track, full night. Nowhere.

Resignation rattled in me. I pulled into a truck stop outside Black River Falls—an oasis of light in the midnight darkness, piers of pumps crowded with idling semis, passengers cars on the other side with roof racks piled high, drivers and passengers stretching and yawning and all of us caught in the weird midnight friendliness of strangers crossing paths in this little island in a sea of nowhere nothingness.

There was a diner, windows facing the lorry side of the truck stop. I got coffee and a cheeseburger, sat alone at the window and ate slowly. Listlessly.

Watched the huge trucks pull in, refuel, and leave.

Finished, I sipped a fifth cup of coffee and wondered what I'd do next.

A semi roared to a stop at a pump. Driver's door opened, as did the passenger's door.

Out of the driver's side descended a round middle-aged man in baggy jean shorts and a dirty white wife-beater, wearing battered sneakers and an out-of-place cowboy hat.

From the passenger side?

A long tan leg, wearing laced-up hiking boots. Body blocked by the door, all I could see for a moment was legs, the boots, the calves, backs of knees as she reached in.

Even so, I knew her. I knew those sensual, elegant legs.

Then she hopped down from the high cab, slamming the door.

She had a black hoodie on, backpack on one shoulder. Those little stubbies left her legs bare and her ass highlighted.

She rounded the front of the lorry, and the driver gave her a paternal hug, waved at her, pointed as if giving advice—*ya'll be safe now, hear?* A smile. A wave.

And then she angled for the diner entrance, rather than the gas station.

Paused, though. She stood outside, back to the window, without looking in.

Leaned against my window, centimeters away from me, without seeing me.

Brought her cell phone to her ear, and spent twenty minutes on the phone, and I waited.

Unable to breathe, because she was *here*.

After a day spent searching, *she'd* found *me*. Or… fate had brought her to me.

She shut the phone off and shoved it into her backpack and let out a breath.

That's when I knocked on the window.

She bolted upright, jumping in fright.

Spun, hand to her chest, gasping.

When she saw me sitting there, she just blinked. Disbelieving.

Errol? she mouthed.

I just smiled.

Patted the seat beside me.

Another moment, and then she headed for the door, and my table.

ELEVEN

Poppy

My heart was hammering as I sat down in the booth across from Errol. The shock of the fright had passed; now, it was a complex amalgam of emotions clashing my heart like a medieval battlefield, chemical reactions in my body combusting, a starburst of conflicting thoughts in my brain.

A momentary, incendiary silence.

"Hungry?" he asked, voice pitched low as if confiding a secret.

I could only nod. "Famished."

He twisted on the bench, half rising, flagging the waitress; she came over, chomping gum, pad and pen ready. "She'll have a double cheeseburger with fries," he said, glancing at me for confirmation; I nodded.

"And a chocolate milkshake," I added.

She left to ring in the order, came back in a matter of minutes with my shake, and then we were alone.

"You're here," I said. "North. Way north."

He swallowed hard, swirled coffee dregs at the bottom of his mug. "Yeah. I, uh, I got about two hours away and realized I'd fucked things up."

My heart clenched, hope and fear competing. "How so?"

He didn't answer immediately. Took a sip of his coffee but grimaced and set the mug down. "Ugh, it's gone cold." He was restless, shifting in the booth, tracing rapid swirling patterns on the chipped Formica tabletop. "With you."

"How—" my voice broke; I cleared my throat. "How did you fuck things up with me, Errol?"

"I should've gone north." A significant pause, his eyes meeting mine. "With you."

"Errol—" I started, broke off when the waitress dropped off my food.

"Eat first." He sat back, arm slung across the booth back.

But when I was done eating, we still hadn't

started talking. I was loathe to open up this Pandora's box. Why had he come back? Fucked what up? We'd agreed to go our separate ways, mutually.

He paid for both our meals, and then we just sat in the booth, staring at each other. "Poppy, I…" he blew out a breath, scrubbed his face, pawed his hair backward. "You want to get out of here? With me, I mean. Drive a bit further together. We'll go north."

"Sure." I hesitated, though. "But I'm confused as hell."

"Me too."

"You came back. Sort of." I blinked at him. "Wait…how the hell did you know where I'd be stopping?"

He barked a laugh. "I didn't. Spent the whole fuckin' day looking for you, Pop. All up and down the area—Twenty-seven, Thirty-five, One-fifty-one, Sixty-one…all over. Dirt roads and side roads and two tracks and deer paths. Gave up, and here you are."

"But did you come back…for me?"

He nodded. "I came back for you."

"Why?"

He looked like he was wrestling with deep emotions, which was odd for him, to let me see the turmoil. "Let's drive a bit first. I need a minute to figure out where to start."

"You've been looking for me all day, but now that we're back together, *now* you have to figure out where to start?"

He laughed. "Yeah, well…I've started the conversation in my head about a million different ways, but now I'm sat across from you, it's all gone out of my head."

It had only been part of a day. Twelve hours, even less. But it had felt like a lifetime without him.

I was pitifully glad to see him.

So glad it terrified me.

The hope I was feeling terrified me. Because… hope for what?

What did I hope was happening here?

We went to his van, and I made for the passenger seat.

"Actually," Errol said, stopping me between the headlights. "Would you mind driving?"

"No," I murmured. "Not at all."

Behind the wheel, I pointed our headlights north, and he turned to stare out the window, lost in thought. I didn't rush him. I had my window cracked, and the radio was off. The only sound was the wind through the window and the hum of our tires.

The small analog clock in the dashboard read well past two, almost three in the morning, and I found myself yawning.

"Need to stop soon, Errol. Been a hell of a long day." I glanced at him.

Asleep? I laughed. Fine. I'd figure it out myself.

I saw a sign for Lake Eau Claire County Park; a few turns, a dead end, some slow crunching rolling down remote back roads and bumping over rutted two-tracks, and I found a spot on the lake where it was highly unlikely we'd be discovered. I wasn't sure if it was illegal or whatever, since we weren't technically an RV and we weren't camping, just parking to sleep.

I pulled around so the passenger side sliding door was facing the lake, and shut off the engine. Sat with the silence sudden and thick, except Errol's soft breathing. I wasn't tired, suddenly. Or, rather, exhausted to a degree that simply falling asleep wouldn't be possible.

Unbuckled. Pivoted to put my feet between the seats and unlaced my boots, kicked them off, laid my socks over them.

Errol snorted, stirred, woke up. "Poppy?" Disoriented. "Where're we?"

"Parked on the shores of Lake Eau Claire, Wisconsin."

He sat up, looked around. "Nice spot."

"Glad you approve."

"How long was I out?"

"An hour, maybe an hour and a half."

"Sorry. Didn't mean to nod off. I had, like, a pot of coffee, so I'm not sure how I even managed it, honestly."

I shrugged. "It's fine. But now I'm wired and tired at the same time."

He laughed. "Yeah, I know the feeling. Let's get out and stretch our legs."

A quick look around the area revealed that this was a spot that saw fairly regular use—cigarette butts, a fire ring near the shoreline, a garbage bin with a metal lid chained to it, a picnic table. Errol pointed at the fire ring. "You fancy a fire?"

"Sure. Will we get in trouble?"

He shrugged. "Nah. Keep it small, I doubt anyone will notice."

I lifted my palms up, slapped them against my thighs. "I hope you know how to make one, because I don't."

His laugh was somewhere between derisive and sarcastic. "Yeah, Pop, I can make a fire."

And he did, quickly, efficiently. He gathered an armload of sticks and branches of varying sizes, used a stick to dig a small hole in the ashes within the ring and set a bunch of the smallest sticks in a pyramid shape, points steepled together. Shredded some bark and broke up other sticks even smaller, piling it all under the steeple of sticks, and then tossed a lit match onto the whole. Some gentle blowing, and the flames caught. After another few minutes, the flames were bigger and yellow and bright, and he gradually built it up to a merry little blaze that gave off decent heat in the cool of the summer night.

We sat side by side, watching the fire flicker.

He glanced at me, long and slow and meaningful, thinking, letting me see the emotions in him. "Poppy, I…" he trailed off. "You know, I think I know a better place to start than talking."

I laughed. "Well color me intrigued, Errol."

He pounced up onto his feet, went to the back of the van, returned with the fiddle case. Sat down with it on his lap. Turned the tag to face me. Pointed at the bottom name, E. Sylvain. "Me, Errol Sylvain." The one above it, B. Sylvain. "My dad, Bastien Sylvain." He withdrew the card, gently, flipped it over and showed me the other side—there were another four names, in increasingly smudged and faded ink, going from the most recent on top to the oldest on bottom; he pointed to each in turn as he named them. "My grandfather, Jean-Paul; great-grandfather, Marc; great-great-grandfather, Emil; and my three-times great-grandfather, Henri Sylvain."

"So when you say this is a family heirloom…" I said, somewhat awestruck.

"I mean exactly that." He traced the middle curve of the instrument with a reverent finger. "It's not worth much, like, it's not a Stradivarius or anything of the sort, but it's priceless because it's old as hell. Henri Sylvain was born in the mid-seventeen hundreds."

"Wow." I watched him touch the strings, the bow. "So cool that you have it."

He eyed me, then his attention returned to the instrument. He sighed. "Yes, it is cool to own such an old thing, something that ties me to my ancestors." He lifted the fiddle out of the red velvet case with exquisite care. Held it by the neck with familiarity, resting the other end on his knee as he deftly removed the bow. Let out a slow, sad breath. Rose to his feet. Turned away to face the lake, campfire at his back, the orange glow sending his shadow dancing in long twisting flat gyrations on the placid surface. Fiddle held at his side, bow pointing to the earth.

He...played?

If he could play the fiddle as well, I was going to be mightily annoyed that any one person could contain so much talent.

Moving slowly, as if drawing on something only half remembered, he lifted the fiddle to his shoulder, tucked his chin against it, adjusted the position of fiddle and chin, bow still held slack against his thigh. Spine straight, shoulders back. I couldn't see his face, but I had a feeling his eyes were closed. Seeing some past memory.

The bow seemed to float up, up, as if under its own power. Rested on the strings with a soft *zzzzhring-gggg*. He drew the bow along the largest string, twisted the tuning knob; the next, and the next and the next, and back to the first, sawing a couple short notes each time as he tuned, and then all went silent again.

I just watched, silent.

This was a different Errol I was seeing, and this one spoke to my heart, not just my loins.

A deep breath, broad hard shoulders lifting, settling as he sighed. And then the bow lifted once more and this time, he struck the strings with sudden force, a jarring clangor of double notes that he somehow drew out into a long, plaintive wail, the bow sawing smoothly back and forth. A three-count, a four-count, and then, without missing a beat, he tilted the bow across the strings and his fingers began to dance across the strings at the neck, near the headstock.

A jig, a reel—I didn't know the difference. A quick, lively, merry tune.

In fact…

It was the tune that I'd heard a few snatches of when I'd started that mysterious playlist of "just some old stuff." I also recognized the tune as the song they dance to in the lower decks in the film *Titanic*.

My jaw dropped as he played, because he was… it was magical. The notes flew from his fingers, from the bow, from the fiddle, radiating across the lake in echoing waves, and there was nothing but him and the moon and the stars and this little campfire and me and the music, and he just played and played, tune after tune, as if he'd broken open a wellspring somewhere deep inside and the music just had to flow, flow, flow.

His toes tapped, and then his shoulders began to move, and then his knees began to dip with the notes and the rise and the fall of the melodies, and then, impossibly, this tall aloof laid-back surfer photographer was dancing in the sand, barefoot, sawing at a three-hundred-year-old fiddle with a virtuosic talent I'd had no clue he possessed.

It was seared into my very soul, the sight of Errol wheeling and spinning with his feet in the sand and splashing in the rippling moon silver-lit lake, fiddling a jig that would make the stars themselves dance.

How long did he play? I didn't know, didn't care. But after a timeless time of dancing and playing, he came to rest once more, near me, facing me, eyes on me. The jig slowed and became a ballad, a slow sad song; mournful, as hesitant as he'd begun.

Then, with a sigh, the fiddle dropped from his shoulder and the bow drooped to point at the dirt once more.

Silence reigned.

He sat, nestled the fiddle back into the case, the bow as well, and left the lid open, firelight glinting off the aged red wood.

"What…the…fuck, Errol?"

He smiled at me. "I haven't played in a long, long time."

"Well, you wouldn't know."

He snorted. "I messed up several times."

"Errol."

He sighed. "My dad was gone a lot when I was a kid. Gone more than he was home. But when he was home, he taught me to play. Insisted on it, said the Sylvain men had played the fiddle for three hundred years and I was no exception. Mom made sure I kept up practicing. The best days of my childhood were when Dad came home from a tour in Europe and would want to know what I'd been playing. It was the first thing, always. 'Play for me, Errol,' he'd say. 'Let me hear what you have learned.'" He said it in a French accent, echoing his father's voice. "And I'd play for him. I was always so desperate for him to approve, you know? So I'd…I'd practice my ass off all year for the moment he'd come home and ask me that question."

He breathed out, slow, harsh.

"Of course, then, this was his fiddle. I had a

cheap one mom had bought thirdhand. Always out of tune, a real piece of shit. But I played my heart out for Dad, year after year." Another pause. "I was alone a lot as a kid. Mom was an artist; I think I told you that. She had been a photographer, but when she had me she'd retired from photography and focused on painting. Abstracts and still lifes, mostly. She had this studio out back of our little house, and she'd be in there for hours...sometimes for days at a time. Lost in the art, she called it. She sold them at this gallery owned by a friend of hers, and later, sometimes, online. Enough to keep us afloat, with a bit of cash Dad would send every month."

He twiddled a finger in the dirt, not looking at me.

"I learned to be self-sufficient by the time I was, what, six? Seven? Mom would make a bunch of food all at once and put it in the fridge and freezer, but other than that, she'd be in her studio. And, it's not that I wasn't allowed in—I was. She just...wouldn't even notice me. Didn't see me, or hear me, even if I stood beside her and shouted. Just...lost. I'd sit in there with her until I got bored, just watching her paint. Then I'd go play. I'd get myself ready for school in the morning, make my own lunch, do my homework, play, watch the telly. Put myself to bed.

"Once she'd finished a piece, though...she was all

mine, for at least a week, sometimes two. She'd keep me out of school and we'd take drives all over New Zealand, sleep in the car, or on the ground watching the stars. Swim on the beach and go on hikes, and she'd tease me and tickle me and tell me stories, and it almost, *almost* made up for days and weeks of pure neglect. More than made up for it, I felt, in the moments I had her to myself, and nowhere near made up for it when she was painting. Then, randomly, Dad would appear and he'd stay for a month, and I'd have this...this little taste of what it was to be part of a normal family." Sad, his voice. So sad, bitter, lost to me, lost in the memory. "We'd go for ice cream together, or go round the dairy together and shop for dinner, and we'd all cook together, and Mum and Dad would sing and dance in the kitchen and kiss each other right in front of me."

Long hard pause.

"And then he'd leave again. Kiss me on the head, tell me to keep my chin up and take care of Mum, and keep practicing on the fiddle. He'd promise to call and write, but he never did. And Mum would do his washing and she'd find things in his pockets. Notes, and phone numbers, and addresses, and leftovers from smoking dope and packets of coke. Frenchie wrappers." He shrugged. "Never said shit to him about it, and I never knew her to see anyone else. They never argued. He never raised his voice, and he was always kind to me, always my dad, playing and wrestling about. And Mum was…just Mum. She'd stop painting when he came home, and that always steamed me off, that. She'd never stop for me, not for nothing. But Dad came home and she'd quit her painting for a solid month. I loved those times as much as I hated them, because they always ended."

"Fucking hell, Errol. What a childhood."

His laugh was a bitter bark. "Just getting warmed up, Pop." He stood, paced away; I snapped a stick into pieces and fed them to the fire. "That was life, until I was twelve."

"What—" I didn't want to ask. Didn't want to know—it was a weight I didn't want. The intimate knowledge of his pain was a burden I'd been avoiding. "What happened when you were twelve?"

"Mum got sick."

My throat closed, my heart skipped a beat, dropped out of my chest. "Oh, Errol."

He stood with his hands in his hair, elbows facing out, head tipped back to watch the stars in their slow wheeling dance. "I found her in her studio one afternoon, after school. On the floor, paint all over the place, in a pool of vomit. She'd been going to chemo while I was at school. For fuckin' *months*. She'd been dying for fucking months, Poppy. And she never fucking told me. Until it got too bad, until the chemo was killing her as fast as the cancer was."

Hot lump in my throat, burning eyes. "God."

"He wasn't in it," he muttered in response to my epithet. Bitter. Furious. Aching with old pain. "She hadn't told Dad either. Made me promise not to tell him."

"Why?"

A shrug. "Fuck if I know. Some weird thing they had, I guess. Same reason she ignored the…finer details…of his life on the road. She loved him, he loved her, and they both loved me. But it was…just fucked up, I guess." He sucked in a breath through his teeth, summoning the courage to tell more. "I took care of her. She'd lost weight and I'd got bigger, so I could and did carry her around. Couch to bed. Bed to bathroom. Helped her bathe. Helped her onto the toilet. Fed her. I used to brush her hair. She loved that. She'd make me brush her hair till my arm hurt.

"Then the money started to run out, and…and she was out of it by then. Out of it from the pain. She'd stopped chemo, refused treatment. I never got up the sac to ask what kind of cancer it was, and don't care to know, now. Aggressive, killing cancer is all I know. She was going to die and she knew it, fought it for a while to try and keep things in some semblance of the shitty normal I knew, but then it just became obvious death was…the only possible outcome, and soon. So, when she started to pass out from the pain, when money to buy food and all ran out, I had to call Dad. I never even—I never even knew she had a way to call him. Figured he just showed up when he felt like it, and they never talked during his tour. Turns out, they had a system in place. He'd send her postcards with his next location, and a hotel phone number, in case of emergencies."

"She never called him?" I asked.

"Not in front of me, no." He walked into the water, knee-deep; I waded in after him, and the bottom was squishy, muddy, soft, cool, and the water was blood-warm.

"Did he come back?"

"Yes."

"How long?"

He glanced at me, and the moon was the only light but for the dull orange flicker of the low fire behind us. The moon's silvering shine was brighter, though, washing the lake and our skin and his hair till everything seemed to bloom silver, the color of melted mirrors.

"How long what?" he asked.

"How long did she…last?"

"Six months." He swallowed, ducked his head. I didn't dare look at him for fear of seeing tears, seeing pain too deep to put into human expression; another weight I was reticent to pick up. "Six months from finding her on the floor of her studio to the moment I watched her breathe her last."

"When did your dad show up?"

"Two months before. I took care of her alone for four months."

"Fucking god, Errol. You were *twelve*."

"She was my mom," he whispered, voice hoarse. "I would sit on the bed next to her and read to her. Her favorite was Nora Roberts. I read so many books to her. Books a twelve-year-old boy had no business reading, but she was too weak to even hold the book at that point."

"You dropped out of school?"

He nodded. "It didn't seem to matter, and she needed me. People would come by asking about me not going to school, but I always managed to talk them around to buggering off and leaving us be. Mom just wanted to die in peace, and I wasn't about to leave her alone for something so stupid as fucking *school*."

"Then your dad showed up."

"Yeah. Dad." He kicked at the water gently, sending circling ripples skimming across the glassy lake. "He was fucking useless. Didn't know how to understand her dying. He paid bills. Took care of her…estate, I guess you call it. Sold off her paint stuff, put the house up for sale, whatever other stuff a kid my age had no understanding of. Stayed gone, couldn't help her to the bathroom. He'd sit with her late at night, in the mornings. Talk to her, play for her. The fiddle was his instrument, but he played guitar and sang too, and he'd sing her these old French folk songs."

Crickets chirped, a frog croaked; a night bird sang.

"We both knew the end was close. She was passed out most of the time, thankfully. When she was awake, she was in…just…just unutterable fucking agony. Unbearable to watch, not a damn thing we could do. She refused to go to the hospital. They'd drug her up and for some reason she wanted to…to *know* when the end came. She made Dad leave. He threw a fit, but he left. She told me to find what was beautiful in the world." He swallowed. "'Find what's beautiful in this world, Errol. Make art out of the beautiful. Be the beautiful. There's beauty out there, Errol. Find it. Play it as music, paint it, photograph it, write about it, dance about it, whatever it is. You have art inside you, Errol. I see it in you.'" He quoted her words with a soft, quiet inflection to his voice. "'Just don't let it consume you like it did me.'"

"What did that mean?" I asked.

I could feel the weight of his pain gathering in me, felt myself taking it up.

"Wondered that a long time myself. Best I can figure, she drowned herself in painting because it was the only way she could deal with…with whatever her deal was with Dad." A shrug. "I took it to heart. I never let art consume me. I take time off. I read books. I go for drinks. I watch sunsets." A harsh laugh. "I think she meant something else, though."

"Like?"

He ducked his head again, bent and scooped the lake bottom muck in his hands, splatted it from palm to palm. "Like…" a pause. "Like love. Like…not letting art push away…people. Relationships."

"Oh."

"Art didn't push people away." Another harsh laugh. "Life did that."

"Life. Meaning loss. Tragedy. Pain." I felt my voice drop to a whisper. "I know a little something about that myself." Louder, then. "So…after."

"He sold the house." Bent again, scrubbed his hands clean in the water. "Let me pick a few things as keepsakes, which he then put in storage, except a few photos and little knickknacks. Put his stuff in storage, got rid of a lot. Basically, cut ties with Christchurch except a storage unit which I think he meant for me, for…eventually."

"And you still have that?"

A nod. "Yeah, but I haven't been back in years.

Been considering just cutting it loose, having some-one sell it all off. Everything that matters to me is there," he said, pointing at the van. "Once ends were tied up, we left. I got on a plane for the first time, and that was the beginning of my life with Dad, on the road. That was when I got into photography. We'd tour for three or four months, and then the band would unplug in London or Dublin or Glasgow or thereabouts, and they'd all scatter for a bit, then come together and write new songs and practice, and Dad would hire a tutor for me, so I could get my basic education finished. But schooling was irrelevant."

"What'd you do?"

"I played with them. Father and son dueling fiddles? It was gold. Turns out I had a talent, and getting to play on stage sort of lit me up. Plus, staying up late, skipping school, nicking a pint or a glass of whiskey when Dad was playing? What kid wouldn't want that life? I grew up in a hurry, or rather, finished the growing up that Mum's dying hadn't done. The usual suspects applied to a teenage boy living with a touring band of single men—drinking, drugs, women. They kept their tour tightly spaced, so each date was close in terms of kilometers to the next, so we'd drive part of the day and have time free. I had Mum's camera and with nothing better to do while Dad and Jonesey and the others did their adult stuff—pubs and chasing fanny—I would go exploring wherever we were, with the camera. It was just something to do, something that connected me to Mum. When I was with her, and Dad was gone, the fiddle was my connection to him. With Mum gone, living with Dad, the camera was my connection to her. As the years went on, I got more passionate about the photography, and playing in the band with Dad was just…part of life. Something I did because…just because it was what I did."

"You were part of a touring band at twelve?"

"Oh, yeah. Played all over Europe. Not huge crowds—they weren't a great big famous draw, but they could pack out pubs and kept booking shows for decades." He shrugged. "That was life, touring and playing and photography. And then…" a ragged, bitter sigh. "And then."

"Fuck."

"Yeah." Hand through his hair. "That playlist you turned on. It was in a pub in Dublin. Recorded live. My first-time solo opening with the band. Dad was so fucking proud."

"That was you? On that song?"

He nodded slowly. "Yeah." Pause. "I was sixteen. Packed-out pub, spilling out onto the footpath. It was some holiday or other. We played for six hours nonstop, just went through our whole song list over and over, and then just started jamming. Dad and me dueled, he'd play this amazing riff on the fiddle and I'd try to match it, you know? It was kind of a joke, obviously, because Dad wasn't just talented naturally, he was a consummate professional. He'd been playing professionally every day of his life since he was my age, and I was just this kid with raw talent and zero real experience. But they loved it, and I loved it."

I swallowed hard, feeling the weight of what was coming. "It's amazing that you had that."

He nodded, a jerky movement, his chin coming to rest on his chest. "It was. It really was amazing. Best day of my life, in some ways. Next day, we slept in as we'd played till some ungodly hour. Came time to load up and make for the next stop, and nobody could find Dad. We checked the hotel, hospitals, checked with the police, asked the barman if he'd seen Dad leave with anyone."

He chewed on the silence, teeth grinding, breathing harshly.

I couldn't breathe.

"I found him. He was in the van. We had a big old caravan, a proper one, with a kitchen and a bathroom and all, and we lived in it. If our stop didn't have decent accommodations, we'd stay in the caravan, but once in a while we'd treat ourselves and stay in a proper hotel. That night, we'd stayed in a hotel. I figured I'd check the caravan, because sometimes

Dad would get restless, reclusive, sort of. Need to be alone. Missing Mum, I always thought, but he'd never say as much to me. So, yeah. I checked the caravan. He was in the dinette booth. Facedown on the table in a pool of bloody vomit. Bag of coke open nearby."

"God, Errol."

"He'd overdosed. Police later tested the coke he'd been taking and turns out it was laced with something. Not just impure coke, but something awful, something poisonous. All I remember was a big long compound name, don't remember what, doesn't matter."

"No. God, no."

He swallowed hard. "His eyes were open." A whisper, raspy, hoarse. "I couldn't get up. I'd fallen down, sitting on the step up in to the camper van, and I couldn't get up. Just sat there staring at my dad. Eventually Jonesey, Murray, O'Brien, and Connor found me."

"Orphaned at sixteen, Errol. God, I'm so sorry."

"The band nearly broke up. I stayed with Jonesey, who was always closest to Dad. Jonesey plays the penny whistle, flute, Uilleann pipes. He took me off to the coast, and we camped out on the beach in the freezing cold, and he got me drunker than I've ever been, before or since. Just absolutely pissed. Let me cry and yell and all that. Then we went back to Dublin and the rest of the guys convinced me to carry on with them. So, I took Dad's place. Sixteen, and I was the fiddler for a touring band. I wasn't as good as Dad, but I could keep up, and I learned." He stared out over the darkened lake, the glow of the fire behind us dying. "That was when I properly got into what I do now. I had nothing to live for. Playing in the band was…it reminded me of Dad, and part of me hated it. But I had nowhere to go, and the mates from the band were the only thing like family I had left. I needed Mum more than ever, and her camera was the best thing I had to feel her. But I needed…I needed a rush. So I'd climb up to the top of skyscrapers and hang over the edge and take ridiculous photos. Or jump onto a moving freight train and take one from the top as it went under a tunnel. Hang off bridges over big ravines. Crazy stuff, just to make my heart pound, to feel like I was alive. Then, it wasn't about the art, it was about the rush. But gradually, I started to really appreciate the art of it. The guys from the band were pissed off at me more often than not, because I'd be impossible to find, off taking photos and climbing the sides of old castles and banging about ruins."

"You said that was how you ended up working for *National Geographic*."

He nodded. "Eventually. Not before the guys

got fed up with my bullshit. We broke up. And, honestly, it was my fault. The fiddle, the band, it wasn't my future. It made me miss Dad more than anything, and I was this angry, angsty, lonely, confused boy with no family, no clue who the fuck I was, or what I wanted. We broke up in Prague. They all went their separate ways, except Jonesey. He stayed with me a week or two, but eventually I pushed even him away. I was eighteen. I spent the next year, maybe two, just sort of…floating around. I'd saved money, and Dad had saved a lot too, so I was able to live off that as long as I was frugal. And I was. I barely ate, walked everywhere or took a train. Just sort of wandered Europe on my own. I took…god, hundreds of thousands of photos during that time, and that's when I really discovered a passion for it. For myself, not just to connect me back to Mum.

"And yeah, I'd run into Jerry in a hotel bar not long before the band broke up, and he'd said I needed more experience, a broader portfolio, and gave me his card. I knocked about Europe basically just getting distance from Dad dying, and started focusing on really learning to take artistic level photos. Finally, I felt I had something to show him, and we met up in London, and that's when what I told you earlier happened. He pulled strings and got a barely educated kid, not even twenty, on the staff of

National Geographic as an adventure photographer. Out of duty to Mom, yes, but I think also because he saw himself in me. He'd lost his own parents young, and had gotten his own break in photojournalism as a war correspondent in Vietnam. So yeah, I think he saw me as a chance to sort of pay back the breaks he'd gotten as a young man. Take care of someone he saw as a lot like himself. More's the luck for me."

"And the rest is history?"

He nodded. "And now you know. I've never talked about any of that, not since it happened. Jerry was at Mom's funeral, of course, but it was only the band at Dad's. I've never talked about Mum dying, about taking care of her. Dad, the overdose, none of it."

"Never?"

He shook his head. "Who would I talk to about it? I work alone, mostly. I send in the photos and Jerry takes care of putting an article to it. Sometimes I'll work with a writer to create a specific piece, but usually it's just me. I've never had any close mates. I call Jonesey once in a while, check in with him. He's married, now, living on a sheep farm in the English countryside. Women? Never saw the point in sharing that shit with them. Women have always just been…for fun. For a bit of companionship. Except Leslie, but even she couldn't get me to share that shit."

"Who's Leslie?"

He laughed. "Closest thing I've ever allowed to..." He pivoted, waved between him and me. "To whatever the fuck this is." A shake of his head, disbelief and amazement and confusion and pain conflicting his expression. "I lived with her for six months in Perth. I was doing a long-term piece on Aborigine life, so I'd take day trips, weekend trips, sometimes a week or two at a time out into the bush researching and shooting. Leslie was...comforting. And comfortable. But she wanted me to share, to open up, to be all..."

"Gushy?" I suggested.

"Yeah. You get it."

"Oh boy, do I get it."

"I just couldn't. I cared about her, but I just...I couldn't bring myself to talk about it."

"It feels selfish, in a way," I said. "To put that kind of burden on someone."

He nodded, sighing in relief. "Exactly. It's too much for most people."

"Especially if they've never lost anyone. That kind of pain is very lonely."

"She was steady and stable, sweet, kind, affectionate, totally vanilla. Worst thing she'd ever experienced was some secondary school bullying about her weight."

"Not the same."

"Not making light of it, because I guess it was pretty bad. She struggled with it, even when I was with her, years out of school. She'd lost a lot of weight but still had trouble seeing herself as beautiful. Which she was, very. So, I'm not saying her pain was less than mine. But it's just..."

"Not the same."

"No." He went back to the fire, added a couple larger sticks to brighten it back up.

I sat in the sand beside him. "Errol..." I fought with myself over how to ask the question. "Why? Why me? Why now? Why go back for me, why look for me? Why tell me all this?"

He poked at the fire, adjusting the sticks. "I don't know, Poppy. Truly I don't. I just know I got about two hours away from the hotel and realized..." He swallowed hard. "Realized it just...it wasn't the same."

"What wasn't?" I asked, my voice not quite a whisper.

"Driving. Being in the van. The road." A long, boiling pause. "Me."

I'd been ignoring my emotions all day. Fighting them. Focusing on my feet taking one step after another, and wishing I had something strong to drink. Then I'd been in the semi with Marty and he was a nonstop font of rambling conversation about everything from politics to raising his daughters to the crazy shit he'd seen as a trucker, and he'd made it easy to push things away.

"You, how?"

He shook his head. "Pop, I…"

"Errol, you can't hunt me down and throw your life story at me and open up my own fucking bullshit wounds, and not tell me why."

"I don't fucking know!" He shot to his feet, paced away. "Okay? I don't fucking *know* why. I just couldn't go another mile. The van was fucking empty. Music was pointless. Even when I stopped and got these great shots of a ghost town, it wasn't the same." He pivoted to stand staring down at me—glaring, more accurately. Seething. "It wasn't the fucking same without you, Poppy. I can't explain it beyond that. I just know that that moment in the hotel room, before we went separate directions. It was a moment where we could have…done something different than we're both used to doing. I run, you run. We're runners, Poppy. Someone threatens to get close, to get inside, to get under our walls, threatens to understand our pain, and we run. I'd rather jump out of a fucking airplane than talk about Mum dying, about watching her die, about…about how she'd cry in her sleep…" He turned away, wiping his face. "How I'd hold her and beg her to stop crying. How do you fucking talk about that? Why bother in the first place? So the other person can feel sorry for me? Fuck no. No thanks, and piss off. And yet with you, there's something else."

He turned back. Crouched in front of me, eyes damp. "I threw my life story at you, yes. I shared my shit with you. Shared the sad bits. Because...because I don't have a choice. I had to find you, had to...to figure what this connection is, between us. What it means. Because it's real, Poppy. What it is, I don't fucking know. But it's there and I know you know it."

"You want mine, don't you." It was a question, but came out as a statement.

"Yes." Flat, declarative, no room for mistaking anything. "I want yours."

"I didn't want yours, Errol. I'm sorry, but I just didn't."

"You think I wanted this?" He flopped down on his butt in the sand. Took my hands. "I didn't. I don't. This is scarier than skydiving, scarier than a plane crash. Scarier than war. Scarier than being kidnapped by Somalian pirates."

I snickered. "Bullshit."

"Spent two and a half weeks in the hold of a ship, surrounded by drugs they were smuggling. They thought I was a spy for some government. Eventually, they realized I really was just a photographer in the wrong place at the wrong time. They smashed my camera—fortunately it was a safe I'd been using and not my good one—and left me just off the coast of Madagascar. Literally, put me in a little rubber Zodiac and set me adrift. I had to hitch a ride on an oil tanker back up the coast to where I'd been taken, where my stuff was. A lot of it had been stolen, and I had to hunt it all down and buy it back."

I laughed, shaking my head. "You oughta write a book."

"Nobody would believe any of it." He went serious. "I didn't want this, Poppy. But here it is."

"You just want me to blow you again." Maybe I could joke my way out of it, and barring that, fuck, suck, and jerk my way out of it.

He didn't take the bait. "I'm not going to lie, Pop—yes, the sex with you is a major reason I'm drawn to you. It's like nothing I've ever experienced, and I find myself wanting more. Not just because… how do I put it? It was hot, it was unforgettable. But it was…" He let out a sharp breath. "It was…*deep*."

"Yeah, you got *real* deep, all right," I said, snickering.

"Quit joking, Poppy. You know exactly what the hell I mean." He sounded angry, and I didn't dare meet his gaze.

I ducked my head, his chastisement hitting like a spear to the heart. "Yes, Errol. I do know. I don't want to, but I do."

"You can't pretend this isn't happening, Poppy. You can't act like a blowjob is going to distract me from what this is. You want to suck me off? Go ahead, I'll enjoy the shit out of it. But it's not going to change the deeper shit happening, here. You want to get on your hands and knees? I'll fuck you silly. But when we're done, this will still be here."

I felt my heart cracking. Felt the calcified shell around it spiderwebbing. "Stop, Errol."

"Why? So you can go back to acting like this thing with us is just about sex and photos?" He strode to the van. Yanked open the driver's side door, got in, started the motor. "You want to run? Take it. Take the van. I can hike out with my shit on my back. Wouldn't be the first time, won't be the last. So go, Pop. Take it and go, if that's what you want."

"I'm not taking your van, Errol," I snapped.

"Fine. I'll take you to the nearest highway. You can keep walking. Go back to hitching rides from fat old lorry drivers."

"Hey, that's not fair. Marty was nice."

"Good on him," he snarled back. "Not the fucking point."

"Then what *is* your point?" I shouted, leaping to my feet and shoving my face up into his. "What the *fuck* is your point? What do you *want* from me?"

"What I want from you is *you*."

I felt tears jump into my eyes. "Me."

"You."

I choked on my breath. On my tears. "What does that mean? You want to know about me? You want my sad bits? Fine. My dad gave up on us. He got fat and he got obsessed with work and with money, and he stopped being a dad to me and my sisters, and he stopped being a husband to my mom. He gave the fuck up. He didn't leave us. That would have been better. I went from being his little girl, his baby, and the youngest, to no one and nothing. I was...I was the apple of his motherfucking eye, and he gave up, and I don't know why. I'll never understand what I did wrong. Was he cheating? Did he have another family? I don't know! I don't think so, but I'll never know. My sisters and I...we're all fucking disasters, and all it's his fucking fault. He abandoned us without ever leaving. Quite a trick, actually."

I sobbed, batted his comforting hand away.

"No," I snapped. "You wanted it, well...here it is, asshole."

I tried to quit, to stop talking, but like Errol opening the floodgates of music and his own pain, once mine was a trickle, it became a torrent.

"Mom was busy with work, with Lexie and Charlie. Charlie was a dancer and Lexie took music lessons, and Mom's time was devoted to them, their lessons, their lives. She had a little she-shed built out back for me, and bought me all the paints and brushes and canvasses I wanted, and left me alone. I didn't get lessons. I taught myself. I didn't have friends, I didn't go to summer camp or to the mall. I painted. Charlie had boyfriends and Lexie was…well, problematic, especially later on, but that's a different story and one I'm not sure I have all of. Torie was… just Torie. Reclusive. Interior. And I had no one. Dad died and we all turned inward. Mom especially. She lost her husband and a significant portion of income, and had to figure out life and figure out how to take care of five girls, so I guess I don't really blame her, but…I guess maybe I do blame her even though I intellectually understand. It's Dad I'm angry at. He had a stroke or a heart attack or something. Just… gone. Bam, alive one day, gone the next. And I think he didn't care, he knew he was unhealthy. We had family meetings about healthy choices so we could all help Dad. But he wouldn't help himself. Didn't care. Kept hitting fast-food drive-thru's and bringing home donuts and drinking all the time. And I'll never know what his issue was. What was his pain, Errol? What demons was he fighting? What could have been eating him up so bad that Mom and the five of us girls weren't enough love for him?"

I had to stand up to bear up under the burden of it, the weight of everything I'd been burying and ignoring and suppressing and running from. I bent at the waist, arms around my middle, as if to hold my guts in, as if they'd spill out with my words.

"Why wasn't I enough? How did I go from his baby girl to fucking...nothing? Not enough to be worth living for? Why didn't Mom *see* me? Didn't she see that I needed her? I've never been enough. Or too much. I want attention, Errol. Everything is about that. I know that. Acting out, the men I've dated." I snorted. "Dated. Kind of a strong word for it. They give me attention, but it's never enough. And then they either leave or want what I don't know how to give. And I run."

"So you learn to leave first and not offer even a hint of anything more than hooking up."

I sighed bitterly. "I'm not a slut."

"No judgment here, Pop. That accusation could be made of me, and it would probably stick."

"Lexie just flat out owns it. I'm not that brave, not that fearless. She gives zero fucks. But I also feel like there are parts of her that no one sees, no one knows. We all had secret lives, I think. Except Charlie. Her life was all about Ivy League universities and top-dollar jobs. Cassie lived only for dance, and that was taken away from her by a car accident. Another whole thing. So I guess it was just me and Lexie with secret lives."

"What was your secret life?"

"That I was hooking up with guys regularly by sophomore year. My whole life was that paint studio in the backyard, and hooking up. And everyone knew it. It was one of those unspoken secrets of the school community, that Poppy Goode was an easy girl."

"Poppy—"

I waved him quiet. "No, don't. It's just true. I wanted validation. I wanted fulfillment. I wanted to be the center of someone's attention. It's called I have serious daddy issues, Errol. Look it up—abnormal psychology one-oh-one."

"Not sure how abnormal that is, though."

"And then I met Reed O'Reilly, and I thought he was the one. I thought he would fall in love with me. I thought he could make me feel whole. I thought I could pour all I was into him and somehow, there'd be this magic moment when I'd get it all back. Where he'd—" My voice broke. "Where he'd love me back."

"Instead, you caught him fucking your best friend and roommate."

"In my bed."

"And you realized no one would ever fulfill you,

no amount of sex or alcohol or drugs would ever fill that hole."

"So fucking stereotypical, right?"

"When I was knocking about Europe after the band broke up, I was drunk most of the time. That's my dirty little secret. I would make myself wait until evening, but I'd buy a bottle and drink the whole thing until I was so pissed I didn't know who I was. Which was the point, after all, right?"

"Do you still drink?" I asked.

He shrugged. "Nah, not much. I got to a point where I realized I'd end up like Dad, just twenty years younger, and went cold turkey for a few years. Now I can have a drink or two, even get a bit pissed, but I don't let myself go down that hole anymore. It's dark down there, Poppy. Dark and lonely."

"Yeah, it is," I agreed.

"I just compensated in other ways."

I forced my eyes to his. "Sex."

He nodded. "Yeah. You can't OD on sex, can't get cirrhosis of the liver from it. It's never the same twice, even with the same girl. And I realized I get as much fulfillment, if not more, from what I can make my partner feel as what she can do for me. Get by giving, I guess you might call it."

I bit my lip. "I noticed."

He laughed. "Poppy, you and me? We just barely

scratched the surface of how things could be." His eyes were serious as the laugh faded. "And I think you know it as well as I do."

Dawn was breaking gray on the far eastern horizon.

Errol and I stared at each for a long time, silent now, many things yet unsaid, but so much out there for each of us to chew on.

"Let's go to bed," he said, eventually. "In the van. And, just for tonight…just sleep."

I nodded. "Okay."

He put out the fire, put up the camper top and made a bed out of his sleeping bag and the blanket, and we climbed in, both fully dressed.

Apart, at first.

But then, as we began to drift off to sleep, he turned to face me. Eyes sleepy.

"Pop?"

"Mmm?"

He hesitated. "Come here." Arm extended, up over my head.

"I'm scared, too."

"Why?"

I had to keep my eyes closed and let the truth come out in a whisper he must have had to strain to hear, even mere inches away. "I'm afraid to let you close and then…and then lose you."

His palms cradled my face. "Poppy."

I shook my head, hating the tears, hating even more the awful vulnerability. "You can tell me you won't. You can say all the right things. You're a storyteller, Errol. But that doesn't change how afraid I am of really letting you in. I can tell you my story and I can pick up the weight of yours, we can share pain and fuck like champions, but…the real stuff? The deep stuff? It's fucking terrifying."

"I know," he whispered. "Just…try? This little step, one little step. Just let me hold you."

"I don't know how to let you hold me."

He laughed. "Well, that works out because I've got no clue how to hold you. I'm not a cuddler."

I snorted, a distinctly undignified splutter. "Well, we've got that in common, if nothing else."

He slid his arm under my neck, and I went stiff as a board all over. He drew me in, brought me closer. Body to body, and he was as stiff and awkward as I was. But my head was on his chest, and I could hear his heartbeat.

"Just…breathe with me, Pop," he said. "Breathe in…"

We dragged in deep, slow, noisy breaths together.

"And out…"

Exhaled together. I felt myself softening.

"I'll be here with you when you wake up, Poppy. No expectations of anything. We just wake up together."

I felt my heart yearning for him. For what he was offering. For the shelter. The safe harbor of his arms.

"You can't take this away from me, Errol," I whispered, the words wet with tears. "You can't give this to me and then take it away."

"I won't."

"How can you promise that?"

"I can promise it because I...because I need it from you just as badly, Poppy. I'm just as scared as you are."

I nuzzled closer. Burrowed into his hold, my nose against his chest, his heartbeat under my ear. His arms encircled me, strong bands of iron holding me together when everything else inside was threatening to burst open, to fall apart.

He smelled like comfort. Wood smoke and skin, male scent. His breathing was soft and deep and slow.

I didn't have to *do* anything.

Be anything, or anyone.

I didn't have to perform.

I didn't have to talk, or share, or give or take.

Just...be.

Letting Errol Sylvain hold me was like coming home.

TWELVE

Errol

I WOKE SLOWLY, AND THEN ALL AT ONCE I WAS AWAKE.

Poppy was still in my arms, facing me, nuzzled into me. Her arm was thrown over my ribcage, her thigh over mine, mine over hers, her other arm curled up against my chest, her fingers under my chin.

Soft. Warm. Comfortable.

I never wanted to leave this moment.

I felt her stir. "Errol."

"I'm here," I murmured. I squeezed her gently. "Right here."

"Don't leave?" she whispered, and it was such a small, vulnerable couplet of words that my heart threatened to crumble, break open like a dropped egg.

My lips touched her forehead, kissed as delicately as I could. “I won’t.”

She clung to me. Nuzzled closer. Sighed. “Errol?”

“Yeah.”

“Can I go back to sleep?”

“Yes. I’ll be here holding you.”

A silence, her breathing, closeness, fulfillment.

“Errol?”

I sniffed a laugh. “Yeah, Pop?”

“Would you understand if I said I didn’t want to…to do anything, just for right now?” A fearful pause. “I just want to know what it’s like to just…be held. And nothing else.”

I kissed her forehead again, her temple. “Just relax, Poppy. I’m not letting go. I’m not going anywhere. I don’t want anything but this.”

She sighed, reassured. Contented.

I felt her drift back into sleep, and after a while, I did too.

When I woke next, it was late in the day, and I didn’t care. Poppy hadn’t moved, was still sleeping. I had to pee like nothing else, but held it. I was hungry. I needed coffee.

But nothing came close to needing this, holding Poppy.

Eventually, she stirred, groaning softly. "Mmm."

I looked down at her, rolling to my back and bringing her closer, more on top of me. "Hi."

Her eyes flickered up, melted milk chocolate and full of warmth and contentment. "Hi," she whispered, a small smile on her lips.

"Sleep all right?" I asked.

She just brightened her smile. "So good." She clung closer, her arm clutching at my neck, burying her nose in the side of my throat. "Thank you."

"For what?"

"Holding me," she whispered. "For making me feel...understood."

"I should thank you for the same," I said.

She gazed at me. Her hand rubbed over my chest. Her grin went crooked, and I knew what she was thinking.

I caught at her hand. "Poppy?"

She frowned. "Yeah?"

"This can just be...this. It doesn't have to be anything else."

She blinked at me. Fearful, worried. Conflicted. "I want you more than ever, Errol."

"I know. Me too." I pressed my palm to hers. Threaded my fingers into hers. "That will be there, later. For now? Let's just…enjoy this for what it is."

Her eyes slid closed, and a sigh escaped. Relief. Gratitude. "I was worried you wouldn't understand."

"Poppy. Maybe you're not understanding *me*." I held her hand and palmed her cheek with the other. "I'm saying *I* want it this way, for now. For me. Not just for you."

Her forehead pressed against my breastbone. "I feel like you actually…see me. See *me*."

"Because I do."

A peaceful silence, full of warmth and understanding. "Errol, I…I really don't want to move, but I've got to pee *so* bad."

I groaned as I let her go. "Oh thank fuck. I've had to pee for at least an hour."

She laughed as I slid out of the bed and out of the van, stretching in the afternoon light. This wasn't really a campsite, more of a picnic spot on the backside of a day park, which meant there wasn't anything like a loo, so I just went behind a tree and cut loose. When I came back Poppy was looking around, dancing.

"Um?"

"Not really anywhere to go but behind a tree, unfortunately," I said. "But, I do have…this." I dug in a cabinet in the caravan, came back with a roll of TP and a small folding camp shovel. "You ever pee in the woods?"

She shook her head. "No."

"Well, um. You have to dig a hole and squat over it."

"Why dig a hole? Won't the pee just soak into the ground?"

I couldn't help a snicker. "Sure, but um, the hole is so you don't splatter pee on yourself."

She bit her lip and blushed. "Oh. Right." A louder laugh. "Good thing you know this stuff." She trotted toward a nearby large tree.

"Poppy?" I called after her. "From what I've been told, you might have the best luck just taking everything off from the waist down."

She didn't stop moving, just gave me a thumbs-up as she vanished behind the tree. I saw the spade moving, a pause, and then a long groan of relief. A few minutes later she returned with the spade and the toilet paper and a disgusted expression.

"Not my favorite thing ever," she muttered. "I appreciate toilets a lot more, now."

I laughed. "Wait till the first time you have to do the other. Be glad I keep toilet paper on hand."

She shuddered. "Can we talk about something else?"

I just laughed harder. "It's just nature, baby."

She shook her head. "A little too much nature for this city girl."

"It wasn't that bad, was it?"

She went red. "Let's just say next time, I'll have to remember to make the hole deeper."

I chortled. "Yeah, well, that's how you learn. My first time taking the long drop out in the wops, there wasn't a long drop and I didn't know you had to dig a hole."

She cackled. "Long drop?"

"Outhouse, but I'm using it as a polite euphemism for taking a shit."

She shook her head and covered her ears with her hands and closed her eyes. "YUCK! Can we reserve a *little* bit of mystery, please?"

I set out the camp stove and a carton of eggs, put on a pan of scrambled eggs and some bacon. Except for the fact that it was well past noon, it was a nice pleasant morning. We ate and I made coffee and we didn't talk about anything heavy.

I was about to suggest we head out when her phone rang from somewhere deep in her bag. By the time she found it and dug it out, the caller had given up.

"My sister," she said, by way of explanation to me. "I'm gonna call her back."

I shrugged. "All right. I've got no plans."

She just laughed, and called her sister. It rang a couple times and then was answered.

"Hi, Lex." She listened. "Actually, I'm sure Mom told you already, but I'm not in New York anymore. Uh, Wisconsin, I think." Another minute or so of listening. "Lex, girl, I love you, but you suck at small talk. What do you want?"

A pause.

"You are motherfucking shitting me." She tugged on her braid. "Lex—Alexandra, don't bullshit me. You? *You* are getting married." Another pause as she listened. "After that video, I figured you guys were pretty serious, but getting *married*?"

Pause, listening.

"Wow. Okay. You really love this guy, huh? Not just because he's a hot, famous superstar?" A laugh. "Okay, okay. You do. You love this dude. I never would have thought it, but okay. As long as he makes you happy. So, big question is when is the wedding?" She coughed in surprise. "You're fucking kidding me. Less than two weeks? What the hell is the rush? Okay, okay, whatever, your business. Well, I guess it's a good thing I'm like halfway there." She glanced at me. Meaningful, but I couldn't fathom the look. "I, um…no, I'm not exactly alone. I mean, we're still sort of…figuring things out, you could say. Lex, don't, okay?" A pause. "Is he coming to Alaska with me? Like, for the wedding?"

Ah, that was the meaning. I grinned at her. "Yes, I am."

She didn't grin. It was a deep, serious look. "You can't make a big deal out of it, Lex, but yes, he's coming to Alaska with me." Another stretch of her listening. "All of us together again, at last. It'll be fun. Okay, yeah, I gotta go too. Okay, love you, Lex. And congratulations. See you soon. Bye." She hung up the phone and set it aside.

I moved to sit beside her in the open sliding doorway. "What's up?"

"My sister Lexie is getting married to Myles North. In Ketchikan, in two weeks." She huffed, wiped her face. "So my leisurely time frame just got shortened. I can't believe it—my sister is getting married. In *two* weeks. I didn't even realize they were that serious."

"What else? Something is bugging you."

"Not bugging, just..." Her eyes lifted to mine. "You and me. This. It's not even new yet, and now you're coming to Alaska with me, to meet my whole family? Including all four of my sisters' boyfriends whom I've never met, and my mother's new boyfriend whom I've also never met. I just...are you sure?"

I felt...uncomfortable, I had to admit. "I...I think two weeks to get from Wisconsin to Alaska is plenty of time. We'll take it slow and we'll figure things out on the way." I took her hand. "Because yes, Poppy, I'm sure. I don't know what the hell this is or what we're doing, I just know I'm going wherever you're going, and if that's to meet your whole family, great. You're amazing, so I'm sure your family will be, too."

She shook her head. "They're all in serious relationships." A shrug. "Well, except Torie. From what I can tell, at least, but no one's ever sure what's going with her."

"So?"

She held my gaze. "Errol…"

"No expectations, Poppy. No pressure. We figure it out, one step at a time. Whatever it is, whatever it looks like. We're just two people who like to be together. You get me, I get you. That's all it is."

She shook her head, but not in disagreement, I didn't think. A long silence, and then she looked at me again. "I had a thought, just now. Not sure how you're gonna feel about it."

"Okay. Hit me with it."

"Have you ever had a relationship with a girl that wasn't based on sex?"

I outright laughed at that. "Yeah…nah."

She smirked. "Me either."

I followed where she was leading. "You're suggesting we take time without a physical, sexual component."

She nodded. "I know it sounds crazy, but I—"

"It's not," I cut in. "It makes total sense."

"It does?" She didn't expect my reaction.

"Poppy, I know I'm a guy and therefore expected to think solely with my dick, but…I have got a heart and a soul and a brain. And yeah, it makes sense. Neither of us have ever had a relationship, period, let alone anything like one that wasn't entirely predicated on sex."

"Was it sexual for you with Leslie?"

I nodded. "Sure. Met her at a bar, hooked up with her, kept seeing her, and it just sort of became…something. Sort of. Not really. It was mostly sex, and that's why it ended, because she wanted it to turn into something not just sexual, and I wasn't having any of it." I jutted my chin at her. "You and Reed?"

"Same. He was in one of my classes. He was cute and funny. The sex was good, and it seemed like he was into me. Never had a clue otherwise until I walked in on him cheating on me."

"So, we're agreed. I think it makes sense for us to try it. I'm not saying I'm excited about it, but I think it's smart. It's something I've never done, never even thought about. Would never even consider, normally. Like, no sex? What's the point in anything, then, yeah? But with you…there's a point."

She chewed on something silently, started to speak, but stopped.

"Out with it," I said. "Whatever it is, just say it."

She looked away from me. "I guess I'm worried, though."

"About?"

"If we cut out sex, what if..." She ducked her head. "You're gonna say I'm dumb, but just hear me out. I've been told my whole life that I'm beautiful, okay? By everyone. So this isn't...it's not exactly a self-esteem thing." A sad laugh. "Maybe it is. I just... since I became sexually active, the only attention I've ever gotten from men has been sexual. I've been proposed to by strangers. Asked by random men on subways if I'll star in their pornos. I was in Starbucks one time and this obviously super-rich guy asked I wanted to be his wife and move to...some country in the Middle East. Saudi Arabia, I think it was, and be his, and I quote, lead wife."

"Damn."

"Yeah. And guys I connect with, it's sex. Professors have offered me the easy A if I sleep with them. I can't have male friends because they always end up trying to hit on me. If a guy finds out I've slept with someone he knows, he assumes I'll bang him too. It's always all about sex. So...I guess part of me wonders..."

"If it's possible for me to feel anything for you, enjoy being around you, without sex being a part of it?"

"Right," she said, in a quiet whisper.

I held her hand. "Nothing I say is going to matter, not in this." I touched her chin, brought her eyes to mine. "I'll just have to show you."

She swallowed. "Why would you want to?"

"Because I told you about Mom and Dad." I dropped my gaze. "Because...you mean something to me. You matter to me. Because I want...I want something to matter, something that's not sex, too, Poppy. A lot of what you just said is true of me, too. And I want something more from this."

"How long?" she asked, searching me; the meaning of her question was obvious.

"Hell if I know." I stood up, paced away. "Until we know. Until..." I laughed. "I honestly don't know. How about we say at least through your sister's wedding?"

She bit her lip. "That's a long time."

I snorted. "Yeah, it is."

"We could always change our minds."

"Or we could stick to it and see what grows out of it."

She nodded, eyes dropping. "Until after the wedding, then."

"Pop?"

She just laughed, standing up and pacing away. "It just sounds impossible. As much as I feel like it's the only way you and I can make any sense of this crazy thing, it just seems impossible. I fucking *want* you, Errol. Right now. All the time."

"With you all the way across all points," I said. "Do we need, like, rules of engagement?"

She rolled her eyes at me. "We're adults. We're choosing this."

"So if we get to a point where it stops making sense, we just...go with it?"

She bored a stare into me. "We have to be careful with logic like that."

I laughed. "Because one or the other of us could easily talk us out of it."

Poppy laughed with me. "Exactly."

I moved to stand behind her; she twisted to look at me, and then leaned back against me. I held her, non-sexually, my arms around her shoulders and middle. "You know what's weird, Poppy?"

"What's that?"

"It's been less than three days since we met."

She huffed a laugh. "That *is* weird. Feels like a lifetime has passed since then, somehow."

"That's what made me turn around. Feeling like I was missing someone who'd always been there, in that seat next to me. I've never felt that way about anyone. Not like this—this hard, this much, this fast."

"Me either," she whispered. A laugh, then. "Three days? How is it possible to go from not knowing someone to needing them in three days?"

"I was hoping you could tell me."

"I always thought it was storybook romance bullshit. Like, a trope to sell books and movies."

"Me too."

"Joke's on us, huh?" She sniffed, not quite a laugh.

Silence.

"So." I squeezed her. "Ketchikan, Alaska. Two weeks. You and me, alone in that caravan, no sex. Just us and our thoughts and ideas and our emotions."

She faked a shudder. "I'm gonna start regretting it, you put it like that."

"Me too." I laughed, then sobered. "Look at it this way—how we fell asleep, and woke up? Together like that? We have that. As much as we want, all night, every night."

Her head twisted to press a kiss to my jawline, just under my ear. "I like that," she whispered.

I melted, the way she whispered, the way she kissed me. Turned her in my arms and slashed my lips across hers, slow and hot and deep. She was the first to pull away.

"No fair," she murmured. "Instigator."

I laughed. "Sorry. You whisper to me like that, kiss me on the jaw like that, and it just…does something."

"You mentioned rules of engagement, like how to avoid ending up fucking."

"Yes?"

"What about nonsexual touching?" She put herself back in my arms, leaning against my chest, gazing up at me. Traced a finger through my hair, over my ear. A thumb over my lip. "Like this?"

I choked. Blinked hard. Felt my heart skipping beats, trying to grow three sizes that day, all at once. "I like it."

She smiled up at me. "You do?"

I closed my eyes, afraid she'd think me less sexy and less masculine if she saw the emotion I was feeling.

"Errol?"

"Mum—" My voice broke. I cleared my throat, tried again. "Mum used to do that. What you just did, with my hair. She used to brush it over my ear. Ruffle it. I hated it, back then. I was a big boy, didn't want my mum playing with my hair like I was some dumb baby, you know? Silly macho boy stuff."

"I don't know if that means I should do it again or not." I couldn't open my eyes. She touched my closed eyelids with her thumb. "Errol. It's okay."

I shook my head. "Dunno why I'm—it's stupid."

"It's not."

I heaved a breath, tried to compose myself. "I still miss her."

Everything burned. Eyes, chest. Lungs.

I felt something warm and soft and wet touch my eyelids: she was kissing them, one and then the other.

"It's *okay*, Errol." Her arms went around me.

"It's stupid."

She laughed. "I know. Big tough guys like you aren't allowed strong emotions."

"Don't mock."

"I'm not." A laugh. "Okay, maybe I am. But it's teasing, not mocking."

"I just…I don't know how to…"

She ran her hands through my hair. Brushed it back. Palmed my cheeks, thumbs grazing over my eyes, and I knew her thumbs would come away damp. Into my hair again, soothing. Caressing, again and again.

"When I tell you it's okay," she whispered, "what I mean is that it's okay to let me see what you're feeling. I won't think less of you. I'll still be attracted to you."

"Not what we're taught, as men."

"So unlearn it." She kept stroking my hair, and each touch of fingers soothed the ache in my heart. "I'll still want to suck your cock even if I've seen you cry, Errol."

I broke out laughing, even as I felt things break open inside. "Is that so?"

"It is so," she insisted. "I could show you, right now."

"Don't tease, Pop." I shook my head. Forced my eyes open, to meet hers.

"Who's teasing?" Her gaze was serious, hot, open, frank.

"We just made an agreement about no sex until after your sister's wedding."

She bit her lip. "That could start after."

"You do that, I'll want to give you an orgasm or three, and then we'll spend the rest of the day doing dirty and delightful things to each other."

She moaned, rested her head against my chest. Sighed. "Dammit."

"You started it."

"I was trying to reassure you."

I clutched her close, feeling her torso expand with each breath. "You did. More than you'll ever know."

She gripped my shirt in her fists, pushed away from me. "Let's get out of here before I change my mind."

"Next stop, Ketchikan."

She snickered. "You may have a bit to learn about North American geography if you think that, Errol."

"Figure of speech, you hard case."

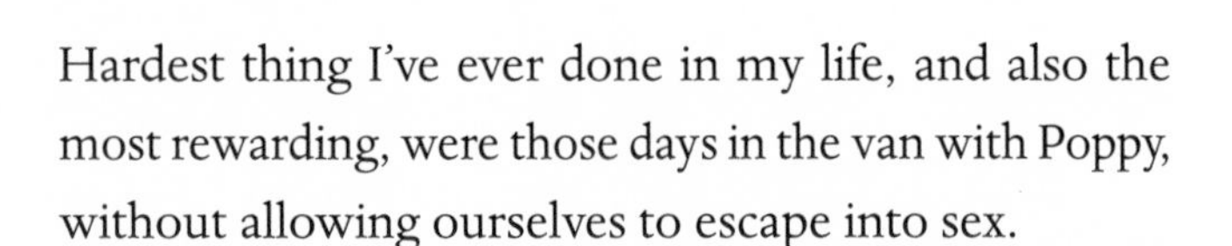

Hardest thing I've ever done in my life, and also the most rewarding, were those days in the van with Poppy, without allowing ourselves to escape into sex.

It was always there, just under the surface. Threatening to boil over, or like a room full of explosives just waiting for a spark of ignition.

We slept together, and just slept. Curled around each other in the back of the van, under the camper, under the stars. Every few days we'd take a room so we could shower and we'd restock supplies, and sleep in a real bed. And we'd wake up together, and it seemed the most natural thing in the world.

Also the most natural thing in the world was to wake up with her body against mine, to feel want surging through me, and she, half asleep, would respond with a sultry shimmy of her ass against my desire, and more than once we nearly forgot our own plan. One of us would always remember, though.

With difficulty, I admit, and I know she felt the same way, too.

We had to create boundaries. I couldn't let myself watch her strip for the shower, or when she got out and dried off and dressed. It was too hard to resist her, so when it was her turn to shower, I'd leave the room and go find food or bring back ice we didn't need, or just stand outside wondering why I was doing this to myself. She did the same. Or went out to call one of her sisters, or her mom.

We talked almost every waking hour. About everything. Embarrassing childhood stories, bullies, victories, crushes. Hookup disasters, language misunderstandings, hated movies and times a movie moved us.

There was always something to talk about.

Even sex. We talked about sex a *lot*, actually, perhaps strangely. Since we weren't having it, it was less weird to share things from our pasts. Things past lovers had done that drove us nuts in good or bad ways. Favorite positions—reverse cowgirl for her, and doggy style for me; and least favorite—sixty-nine for both of us. We talked about close calls with condoms going missing or coming off. We even, late one night while sharing a bottle of wine in a hotel room in Saskatchewan, tried to tally numbers of partners. That had been uncomfortable for both of us.

But it drew us closer.

She asked me things I'd never have told anyone else, like what my darkest desire was, and I answered.

It was as we were passing beyond Prince George, nearing the last leg of the journey.

Out of the blue, too. Listening to music, windows down, watching the scenery.

She just looked at me, chewed on a fingernail. "Darkest desire."

I arched an eyebrow. "Like, fetish, or fantasy, or what?"

A shrug. "However you want to answer it."

I hesitated over that one, for a long while. "God, not an easy one."

She just gazed levelly at me. "Nope."

I turned my eyes back to the road. "I guess it might be kind of boring. I'm not into, like, rough stuff or choking or tying anyone up."

"Errol, just tell me. I hope by this point you know you can trust me."

"Yeah." I sighed. "It's just one of those things I've never trusted anyone enough to bring up."

"And it is…?"

"Anal."

She snorted. "Not all that dark, you're right."

I shrugged. "You asked."

She held my gaze. "Interestingly, that's my answer to that same question."

"Don't make things up, Pop."

She told me everything I needed to know with a single look. "I'm not."

"I guess for me, it's partly that I know I'm not…

small. And I figure it requires a lot of trust, which I've always been short on."

"I've always been too scared of it to even consider it. Yvonne, my former friend and roommate, she used to tell me all the time that I didn't know what I was missing. She said the key was to ease into it. 'You can't go full anal the first time,' she'd say. 'You gotta take baby steps. But once you're there? Hold on, honey.'" She mimicked her friend, using a mocking nasally voice.

I laughed. "Can't go full anal, huh?"

"Apparently not."

"I wonder how she found that out."

She snorted. "Probably the hard way, knowing her." Her eyes met mine, and we both laughed, somewhere between amused and aroused. "Someday?"

I growled a sigh. "Maybe we'd better get back to having regular sex first, before we discuss that."

She rolled a shoulder. "Maybe." Another sultry look. "Any other dark desires you want to share with me?"

"I...um. Not really. That's it." I glanced at her. "You?"

"I've always had this fantasy of a guy I totally trusted tying me to the bed and just...using me as he wished, for as long as he wanted." A significant stare.

"Obviously, I've never trusted anyone anywhere near enough to even think about going there."

I let out my breath, eyes closing briefly. "You know, I've got some climbing rope back there somewhere. Quite a lot of it."

She shifted in her seat. "No teasing, Errol."

"Who's teasing?" I growled. "How well do you trust me?"

She clutched at the seat belt where it passed through the deep valley between the mountains of her breasts. "Enough to know that after this wedding, you and me, Errol? We're gonna need a cabin in the woods and a week alone."

"Why a cabin in the woods?" I asked.

"Because I have a feeling you're going to make me scream. A lot. Loudly. And I wouldn't want to disturb anyone."

"Oh." I throttled the steering wheel until my knuckle joints ached. "Yeah, you're right about that. A *lot* of screaming."

The longest, most interminable part of the trip into Ketchikan was the ferry. God, so bugger-all interminable, it felt like. Nothing to do but sit and talk, watch the waves. Out of sheer boredom, I got out my fiddle and played.

Except for Poppy, I'd not played for anyone in years—I had the instrument with me all the time, but I only ever played alone, to feel some sort of connection to Dad, and usually only when I was in a certain mood.

Of course, as it tended to, playing the fiddle drew a crowd. And the gathered crowd included a towering old fella with a twelve-string guitar and a knowledge of Irish music, and so he and I jammed for a while, keeping toes tapping. He even sang a few, in a rough but tuneful voice, words and verses to tunes I'd never realized even had them.

Poppy sat near me and watched me play, and the bright gleam in her eyes did something to me. Not lascivious, either—for the first time in my life, the way a woman looked at me hit me in the heart, made me want to…to be someone I'd never considered being.

I wanted to play for her just so she'd look at me like that, like I hung the moon and stars.

Later, once the jam session was over and the crowd had dispersed, Poppy and I were sitting alone once more on the top deck away from the spray, in the stiff wind, huddled under my blanket together.

"Why'd you stop playing?" she asked, after a time of silence. "You're so good."

I rolled a shoulder. "A lot of reasons, really. It hurt too much, for one. The fiddle was Dad's. The music was Dad's. The couple of years I tried filling in for him, I was constantly reminded, mainly by O'Brien, that I wasn't him."

"You were a kid, and a kid going through hell."

I let out a gruff sigh. "I know. And I think he knew, too. But O'Brien was—is—one of the old guard. An Irishman from the countryside, who grew up brawling with anyone who looked at him cross-ways. He played the bodhran, the hand drum thing, and his family connection to that goes back farther than mine with the fiddle. He's just…a stone wall of a man. He didn't know how to deal with Dad dying any more than I did, and knew even less how to show it, let alone deal with me, his mate's kid, a hurting kid lashing out and acting a fool. I don't blame him. Not now, leastwise. I hated his guts then, and it felt mutual. But now, with time and distance and a bit of understanding? I get it. I could never be my father. And the shit of it all was that I was too fucked up to properly try, and me failing at that meant the band that had been their livelihood and their life for the last twenty-some years died with Dad, because I couldn't hack it as his replacement."

"That's too much pressure to put on yourself."

I shrugged. "Yeah, I know that…now. But then, it was all just too tangled up. The easiest way through it for me was to put music behind me." I blamed the sting in my eyes on the wind and the sea spray. "There were other reasons, too, things I've come to figure out since. I was never given a choice about the fiddle. I'm a Sylvain, and Sylvains play the fiddle. But he was never home, so the teaching fell to Mum, who didn't play. She got me lessons in Christchurch, which I hated. But I just…I couldn't bear the thought of Dad coming home and him asking me what I've learned and not having shit to show him. It was the only way I knew to get his attention, to make him proud of me. I think…I think I always thought, deep down, that if I got good enough, maybe he'd stay. Or, stay longer." Blink hard, breathe deep. "Never worked. And then Mum died and Dad was all I had, and since I'd been playing since I was old enough to hold a kid-sized fiddle, meaning four or five, it was expected that when I was on the road with Dad and the guys, that I'd play. It was never discussed, just expected. Get on stage and play. And when there's a pub full of half-pissed adults watching you, you don't dare freeze up. You don't dare embarrass your dad or his mates. Once a year on Christmas, the whole band would get together, so I knew them all too. Sometimes in the summer between gigs they'd all stop off in Christchurch and they'd have a great old piss up."

"You never had a choice."

"That's why I ended up in photography, even though my talent and experience and training is actually more in the music world. There's enough folks out there who know my dad, the guys, the band, even me to a small degree, that I could get a gig fiddling. But I chose photography, because I had the freedom to *choose* it. And I put music aside because it was…it never felt like mine. I couldn't bring myself to get rid of the fiddle, and I still play sometimes. Alone, off in the middle of nowhere, when there's no one listening and no one watching, just because I guess it's in my blood." I sighed. "Today was the first time I've played with anyone or in front of anyone since Dad died, actually, except for you at the lake, and I think playing for you is the only reason I was able to play today."

"How's it feel?" she asked.

A shake of my head. "Dunno, really. Good, and painful at the same time."

"You know, my…I'm not going to say in-laws. The family, the big group of people we're going to be with…I don't know how to quantify their relation to me. Mom's boyfriend's family. Mom's adopted family? Not adopted like legally, more emotionally…" she laughed. "Whatever. A lot of them are musicians."

I growled. "Great. I'm going to be expected to play."

She shook her head, rested a hand on my arm. "No, that's why I'm letting you know. I don't want you to feel obligated. Mom has told me several times that jam sessions just happen, a lot. So if you ever feel like joining, you can. But I'm not going to put it out there that you're a musician."

I laughed, a strange, bitter, confused sound. "Musician. I've never claimed that title."

"Well, you are, and an incredible one."

"You like it when I play." It wasn't a question, more of a leading statement, I guess.

"So much. It's…it's beautiful, watching you play. You light up, Errol. You change. I don't know how to put it. It brings something alive in you, brings out this other part of you. But I understand that it's all tangled up in a lot of pain, so I'll never make a big deal out of it. You have to choose for yourself the role music plays in your life."

I held her hand. "Thank you, Poppy." I hated the constant onslaught of strong, piercing emotions that was always boiling under the surface now—now that I'd let them out, brought them up, opened the portcullis of the tower holding all the crusty, jagged wounds and pain and ghosts inside. "For seeing me."

She only squeezed my hand, and gave me space

to get some kind of a handle on this roiling crush of emotion.

"How do other people deal with feeling this much, all the time?" I asked, half laughing.

She snickered. "I think most people don't bury and suppress as much as we have, for as long as we have."

"Oh."

"It kind of sucks, doesn't it?"

"I don't mean to sound sexist or anything, but women are expected to and allowed to be all emotional. If you burst out crying in the middle of a conversation, so what? It's normal. At worst, they might figure you're on your period or something. I know, I know, you don't have to say it. Like I said, I'm not trying to sound like a sexist asshole. But for men, we're allowed anger and masculine stuff like that. Appreciation of natural beauty. Lust, and even love, I guess, but that's a confusing one. Because we have to be macho about being in love. We can't be all soft and weak about it. That's the unspoken part of it all."

She held my hand, turned to face me, brushed fingers through my hair, across my forehead and over my temple. "Well I reject that for you. Letting yourself feel emotions isn't weakness. Even the soft sappy stuff, like missing your mom and dad, or feeling, like, tender or whatever toward me. It's not weak and it doesn't make you soft. And you know what? You can be soft and strong at the same time. Like a spiderweb, you know? Soft and thin and silky and flexible, but one of the strongest substances on earth. I'm not saying be all weepy all the time, but when it comes up, let it happen."

"I'm not going to sit here and have a cry in public on a fucking ferry, Poppy," I said, growling a sarcastic laugh. "Not happening."

She sighed. "I know. I wouldn't either, honestly. But when we're alone, you don't have to, like, hide it, or feel embarrassed about it, or…or whatever. You can just let it out and let me see it, let me have that part of you, and just trust that I still know the strong, tough, capable you also."

I nodded. "I hear what you're saying, Poppy, and I appreciate it. All I can tell you is that I'll try. It's a lot of conditioning to overcome, though."

"Believe me, I understand that."

We were quiet, lost in our own thoughts as Ketchikan approached off the bow. Seagulls wheeled and called, and pine-carpeted hills rose on all sides. It was a day somewhere between cloudy and sunny, patches of blue and moments of brilliant sunlight, and leaden gray clouds scudding low and mixing with puffy white ones soaring higher up. I spotted an eagle tilting on a wingtip off in the distance, and something big splashed in the water near the shoreline.

"Beautiful country, here," I said.

Poppy nodded. "Sure is." She seemed…hesitant about something. "I see why Mom settled here."

"You've never been?"

She shook her head. "No. First time visiting her since she moved up here a few years ago." She chewed on the inside of her lip. "I'd been accepted to Columbia at sixteen, not quite seventeen—I was always a motivated student, mainly because the faster I got done with bullshit school, the more time I had to focus on art. So I crushed through high school, skipped several grades, took some dual enrollment classes at the community college. Whatever. I was shy of seventeen and acting all eager to get to Columbia, move out on my own to big bad New York City. I thought I'd be like Charlie, my oldest sister. She has not one, but two Ivy League degrees."

"No shit."

"Yeah. Look up Type-A overachiever alpha sister, that's Charlie. Goody-goody, followed the rules, the golden oldest. Look at your sister, look what she did, look at her grades. She's going to Princeton, blah blah blah." She huffed. "Granted, Mom never actually said any of that out loud to any of us, but she didn't have to."

"But you're not bitter at all."

She snickered. "Nope. Not me." A laughing sigh. "Maybe a little bitter. Because I couldn't hack it. I've been telling myself that college just wasn't for me, that I'm meant to be an artist, to hoe my own row instead of following Charlie's. But dropping out of college still feels like I failed to measure up to Charlie."

"Is she the type to lord it over you?" I asked.

"That's the hardest part—no, she's not. She's just sweet and humble, mostly. I'm lording it over myself for her."

"Well, maybe you ought to put down that burden."

"Yeah, no shit, right? I'm working on it." She gestured at the Ketchikan skyline, rising to meet us as we angled for the pier. "Problem is all of them. They're all waiting for me. They have expectations of me. Mom does, I know. I dropped out, so she expects me to make the most of being an artist. Charlie is successful, Cassie has a whole new life with this Ink dude, and that was after the car wreck ruined her dance career. She was a professional dancer, like in Europe, touring and performing for, like, royalty and shit. Then there was a car wreck and she moved in with Mom, and now she's successful at this whole new thing. Lexie is marrying a legit, bona fide superstar, and she's becoming famous herself. Torie is the only one who hasn't accomplished much, but when I talked to Mom as we were getting on the ferry, it sounded like she was with a guy and things were changing for her. So then it'll be just me with no fucking clue what I'm doing with my life."

"You're not even nineteen, Poppy."

"By the time you were nineteen, you'd been all over the world as a professional musician."

"You're not me. And you're crazy talented. You just have to figure out how to leverage it into a career. That can take time."

"You've never even seen my real art. The photographs are the just the…base, you could say."

"I'm looking forward to seeing your finished pieces, Poppy, more than I can say, really. But I don't need to have seen them to know you've got what it takes. You could make a career out of your photography alone, and I say that not as the guy who's attracted to you and cares about you, but as a professional photographer. And if, as you say, your real bag is painting, then that would mean you're even better at that. It's a no-brainer you'll be totally fucking brilliant."

She let out a breath. "Thanks. I guess I need the encouragement."

She tugged on her hair, which she wore loose today, under a floppy fedora hat. Her outfit was clearly meant to impress her family—voluminous, loose, gauzy skirt in an eye-waveringly bright pattern of yellow and red blocks, with a plain white blouse of a type you'd see "tavern wenches" wear at a renaissance fair, complete with a wide leather belt around her waist which only served to accentuate the bulging overflow of her tits, which the shirt couldn't even begin to contain. Her cleavage was mountainous, and once again she wore no bra; the thin fabric was nearly sheer, and left just enough to the imagination that I was doomed to sport a middling hard-on all day. Especially those piercings. She even had a nose ring, a diamond stud through one nostril, which I hadn't realized she had.

"What?" I asked. "You're still stewing on something."

"Just nervous. I haven't seen my whole family in a while. Last Christmas everyone was scattered across the country, and we couldn't make our schedules work to all meet. I had finals when Charlie had time off, and Lexie and Cassie were…well, it doesn't matter. We video-conferenced each other and we sent each other presents, but we weren't together. It was rough, actually. I missed them all, of course. But now I'm showing up with you, and…"

"And we're a sort of...unknown quantity. Even with each other, in some respects."

"Right. And on top of that, I'm about to meet a whole slew of new people, and from what Mom says, they're all like family to her, which means I'm expected to become part of that."

"And you don't want to?" I knew I sounded unfairly angry. "I'd give anything to have family, Pop. Especially as much as you have."

She huffed. "I know, I know. It's just...it's a lot."

"Well, you're not alone."

Her smile was relieved and thankful and intimate. "And I'm more grateful for that than I can say."

"How long until the wedding?" I asked. "Because I have to admit, I'm getting pretty well desperate for you to show me how grateful you are."

She rested her head on my shoulder, but her posture was tight, controlled. "Desperate isn't even the word, Errol."

There wasn't much else to say as the ferry slid up to the pier and tied off.

Being an orphan, I was always alone. I was always the odd man out, the newcomer, the strange face. So I wasn't nervous about meeting new people.

It was the fact that I was meeting new people as someone else's someone. I'd never been that, before.

We weren't putting ourselves in any kind of box, and I always loathed the boyfriend/girlfriend labels. They felt cheap and childish. This felt way more intense than merely being her *boyfriend*. I was her someone, and this was her family, and I had no clue how to behave, how to be, who I was in this context.

I didn't think she knew either.

We'd have to figure it out one step at a time, like everything else.

Poppy

TURNED OUT THERE WASN'T TIME FOR NERVES. IT WAS A whirlwind of doing, going, meeting. We met a good dozen people in the first few hours. Errol kept cool at all times, and seemed to be trying to find a balance between affectionate with me and not making a big deal of what we were or weren't. There were plenty of questions, of course.

The first person I saw was Torie, who was clearly hiding some kind of hurt, but set it aside out of joy to see me. And god, I had missed her.

She was changed. Physically, emotionally, she was…more there. Torie always seemed to just sort of float through life, aloof, disinterested. And it always seemed to me like she'd never finished growing up, physically. Like Dad's death had stunted her move through adolescence, both physically and emotionally.

Now, something had shifted. She'd filled out, for one thing, her butt and boobs fuller, rounder, her face more angular and adult. But her presence, her mental *here*-ness, that was the most changed. And something told me it was all due to this guy Rhys with whom she'd made her own cross-country trip.

God knows I knew a little something about that.

Then there was a monster hulk brute with killer eyes named Zane, who referred to my buttoned-up, East Coast old money, "don't swear, elbows off the table, yes ma'am no ma'am" mother as "Mama Livvie."

Then were was a tornado of humanity—massive, muscle-bound men all with the same brown eyes, each hotter and more chiseled and more impossibly macho alpha bro than the last...and all of them kind and welcoming and funny.

Annoying.

More annoying were their girlfriends and wives and fiancés. Listen, I'm not stuck on myself, okay? But I'm just not used to feeling like the ugly duckling. Any room I walk into, there's a greater than average likelihood that I'll be the objectively most beautiful woman in it.

In this crowd?

I didn't even feel like I was in the top ten. Each woman was voluptuous, with perfect hair, flawless skin, makeup on point, great clothes…and not a one was stuck-up, annoying, or arrogant.

Ugh.

Mom, you had to land here? In this?

The moment I started to get my bearings, I was yanked away from Errol and hauled off on a girls' trip to LA—on a private charter jet courtesy of Myles North, who was exactly as effortlessly rock star cool as you'd expect, and then some. There was champagne and five-star restaurants and shopping on Rodeo Drive with an unlimited credit card—and let me tell you, I was keeping track, and we racked up tens of thousands of dollars on that thing. Spa days with manicures and pedicures and massages and…

And Mom flipping out about my nipple piercings, predictably. Unpredictably, she cooled off and let it go *way* faster than expected.

On the plane ride back, I found myself sitting with Mom in the back of the jet, as alone as you could get.

She had earbuds in and dark sunglasses on, and was dozing. Or so I thought—I was texting with Errol, with whom I'd finally exchanged phone numbers.

"Tell me about him," she said, out of the blue.

"I thought you were asleep."

"No, just old lady dozing."

"That was a joke, Mom, you're not old."

She smirked. "Old enough that keeping up with you girls is exhausting." She slid her sunglasses up onto her head. "Anyway. This guy, Errol. He's from Australia?"

"New Zealand."

"Tell me about him."

I sighed. "He's a photographer for *National Geographic*, and he's just…insanely talented."

She frowned. "Isn't he kind of…young?"

I nodded. "I guess his mom was friends with an editor, and strings were pulled. He deserves it, though. He's that good."

"High praise coming from you. You've always been hard to impress, artistically."

"Well, he's good enough that I've learned things from him."

She seemed to be mulling over what to say. "I've tried to let you girls have space to figure this stuff out for yourselves without going super Mom on you."

"But."

"You haven't made the best choices where men are concerned, dear."

I laughed. "Yeah, I'm not going argue with that. It's not really been me choosing the men, per se, so much as letting myself be…"

"Used?"

I sighed. "I wish I could disagree with that, but I can't."

"You have more to offer a man than your body, my love," Mom said, her voice careful, gentle. "You need to see that, but just as important is that *he* sees it."

I gnawed on how much to tell her. "He sees it," was all I said.

"He does? How do you know? How is he showing you that, Poppy?"

"How real do you want this talk to get, Mom?"

"As real as it can get, Popsicle."

I snickered at that. "You haven't called me that in years." I eyed her. "You want it real?"

"Yes."

"When we first met, honestly, it was just…"

"Sex?"

It was weird to talk about this with my mom. I wasn't sure how much she really knew about that side of me. "Yeah." I hesitated. "Mom, this is awkward."

She put her AirPods back in the case, and the case in her purse at her feet. "Poppy, I know I wasn't always there for you when you were younger. I know there's been a lot of stuff all of us have swept under the rug, not talked about. And I'm done. Give me the truth, and there's no such thing as TMI. Not anymore."

"You were struggling with Dad dying. We all were."

"Doesn't excuse it."

I sighed. "No, it doesn't."

"So, I'm sorry, Poppy. I should have been a better mom."

"I forgive you."

She rested her head on my shoulder. "So?"

"I've spent a lot of time looking for attention in all the wrong ways, in all the wrong places."

"Men. And sex, at what I imagine was far too young an age."

"Honestly, yes. But it's all I've had. Dad dying messed us all up. For me, it's…not understanding what love is. How to…to love, and be loved."

"Sex was the only way you could conceive of it."

"Yeah."

"And Errol? Is he different?"

"Totally. Completely, and in every way." I laughed, a soft huff. "It didn't start out that way, though. We're very much alike in that, in how we use and approach sex. So that's where it started, where it went for us, just naturally."

"So what changed?"

"We got to a point very quickly where it was obvious to both of us that it wasn't just physical. But neither of us knew how to open up. How to let anyone in."

"That's hard to do."

"Very. So we went separate ways. In Dubuque, Wisconsin."

She covered her face. "I can't believe I let you *and* Torie hitchhike across the entire continent. I'm a horrible mother."

"You're not. We're adults, Mom. What were you going to do? Ground us?"

"Went and got you, that's what I should've done."

"And you think I would've allowed it? You think Torie would've?"

Mom laughed ruefully. "No, I suppose not." She eyed me. "But you're only eighteen, not even nineteen yet. Legally an adult, but…still so young. So much could have gone wrong."

"I survived New York City alone at sixteen, Mom."

Another head shake. "Don't remind me. I feel like a bad mom as it is."

"Stop, for real. I'm here. I'm fine. Torie's fine."

"No, she's not. She misses Rhys." A sigh. "I was hoping that would work out for her. He was a wonderful young man."

"It still may. And I think this is good for her, from what I've gathered in talking to her."

"True." She laughed and patted my leg. "We're off topic. Errol. And how is he different?"

"We agreed to not have sex for a while. So we can figure out how to have a relationship that *isn't* predicated on sex."

Mom nodded, making a surprised face. "Wow. Okay." A long, meaningful look. "And? How's it going?"

I cackled. "Fucking hard as hell, that's how. You said nothing is TMI, but I think all you really need to know is that we're…*definitely* compatible in that department. A little *too* compatible, maybe. Which makes this that much harder. But it's for the best. I've learned to be vulnerable. We've talked about Dad and how his dying affected me, and all of us. We've talked about everything, honestly, big and small and in between. It's funny how much there is to talk about when sex is off the table."

"It can confuse things, that's for sure." She stared out the oval window at the dark clouds beneath, a thunderstorm below us crackling with bursts of lightning. "That was a very complicated thing, for Lucas and me."

My impulse was to gag and make jokes, but this was a side of Mom I'd never seen—Mom as a woman, not just Mom. "Yeah?"

She nodded. "Oh yes, very. It was complicated enough for me as it was. Your father and I…um…things had been…difficult, even before his death."

"You said nothing under the rug, Mom."

She nodded. "I did." A pause. "He wasn't healthy, for one thing, and that made things difficult. But our relationship was…"

"He may have been present, as in he didn't move away, but he left us all the same, Mom."

She nodded. "Exactly. And that includes me, his wife. Romantically, sexually, he just…gave up. Which left me in a very confused place until I moved here. And that was when I met Lucas, and I felt so confused about being attracted to him."

"Like a betrayal of Dad, even though Dad had given up on you *and* had died?"

A nod. "Yeah, exactly. Knowing something logically doesn't make it any easier, emotionally. So, it took time to let myself…feel things." She smiled at me. "This is where things might be TMI, but I made the rule, so…here goes. Lucas made me feel things I'd never felt, Poppy. Not with your father, not ever. And that was extra confusing, because I was with Darren my whole adult life. I thought I understood myself, sexually. Turns out, I didn't. Lucas showed me things about myself that…well, that make me feel more myself and more alive than ever before."

"You do seem happier than I've ever known you."

"You know why?"

"Um. Sex?"

She laughed. "No, honey. Well, yes. But not the act of sex. I think you've discovered that you can do that with anyone, and generally speaking, it's all pretty much the same, right? A little better this way or that way, with this one or that one, all factors being equal. But generally, sex is sex."

"Yeah, I'll agree to that."

"The difference is in *meaning*, Poppy." She held my gaze. "In letting it be love."

I choked on a lump in my throat. "We're not there yet, Mom."

"What's stopping you?"

"I've known him, like, not even a month."

"Does it feel that way?"

"No. It feels like I've always known him."

"Does he respect you?"

"Yes."

"Does he take care of you?"

"Yes." It was becoming more and more difficult to get the words out.

"He's willing to shelve sex for you, for your relationship, and that says a lot. Has he shown you his heart, though?"

I nodded. "He has. He was the first to open up, actually." I ducked my head. "We went separate ways, but he went back and looked for me. Covered hundreds of miles over a whole day, looking for me. I guess it was fate that brought us together, because he'd given up. He was eating at a truck stop diner at midnight, one a.m., and the truck driver I'd hitched a ride with dropped me off at that diner. And that was when things really sort of…started."

"Wow," Mom breathed. "That's really cool, honey. That means something."

"I know."

"So what's stopping it from being love?" She shook me, both hands on my bicep. "You can't let it pass you by, Popsicle. It's scary, it takes a lot of courage to take something from merely meaningful and emotional and let it be love."

"What does love even mean, Mom? Saying it? Reed told me he loved me. It meant nothing."

"If Errol said it, would it mean something?"

"I'd probably freak out if he did."

"You're right that merely saying it doesn't necessarily mean anything. Would you believe him? Did you believe Reed?"

I chewed on that one. "I knew Reed was just saying it because he thought I wanted to hear it, that it would…get him something from me, I guess. What, I don't know. But no, I didn't believe him."

"And Errol?"

"I don't want him to say it." I leaned forward and

put my face in my hands. "I want him to show me. I need to feel it."

"In order to feel it, you have to be open to it."

"Yeah."

"So, are you?"

"I don't know." I sighed. "Love. Can you be in love with someone you've known less than a month?"

"Love is not dependent on time. Love is about your heart recognizing something in the other person. Something that makes it impossible to live without them. You just...recognize it. Know it. Deep down, you know. The hard part is making that into a life together. That's the hard part, Poppy. Just loving someone, being in love, doesn't make it easy to live with them all the time. It doesn't mean having a healthy relationship is easy. It's not. It takes work. But you can love someone instantly. I think I was in love with Lucas from the moment I saw him. Before he lost weight, before he got all muscular and sexy as he is now. I loved the man I saw inside him, probably even before he knew that man was in there. My heart saw something in who he was, and wouldn't let go. And that was instantaneous. What took longer was for my mind and my body and the messed-up chaos from Darren and our marriage and him dying and guilt and desire and all that...for all that, for him to fix his life and his bullshit so it was possible for us to even…match, I guess. For his life to fit into the shape of mine, you might say. Our lives don't always fit right away. It takes adjustment."

I considered what she was saying. "So…I could love him, and he could love me, but that doesn't mean we have to, like, be ready to get married, or know how our future will work."

She leaned closer to me. "Lucas and I aren't married. I love the hell out of that man, and I'd walk through fire for him. Marriage is important, but it's not everything. Marriage is just a ceremony and a legal contract if it doesn't *mean* something to you both. We'll get there, someday, Lucas and I. But that's a journey specific to everyone. For you, right now? You just need to…be open to him. To letting him love you, and seeing it when he shows you, and then accepting it for what it is, and showing him in return."

Be open. I could do that.

The rooftop wedding was so beautiful it hurt.

Lexie was radiant, and I understood what Mom was talking about in seeing the way Lexie loved Myles…the way he loved her. It wasn't in the way they touched, or not only; it was obvious their sexual chemistry was off the damn charts. You just had to see the way he looked at her to know they rocked the sheets until something caught on fire. It was... his awareness of her. Her presence around him was different. She was at peace. And for Lex, that was fucking massive. She'd told me what happened to her, the molestation and all that, and it made their love all the more significant. He'd...I didn't want to say he'd healed her—only she could do that, only she could allow herself to heal. But it had been...not his doing... god this was complicated. He was instrumental. He made her want to heal. Want to be different, so their lives would fit together.

And I saw it in everyone around me. Charlie and Crow, Cassie and Ink. The Badd brothers, all fucking ridiculous eleven of them. Each pair's love was different. Some were fiery and combustible, some were steady and cool. Each was unique, each was inspiring.

Normally, I'd have been gagging over the amount of PDA and gushy love talk, the couples all but mating behind every corner. Maybe it was because I was in the process of figuring out what was going on with Errol and me, but I wasn't as nauseated by it.

Inspired, if anything.

The issue was, the wedding was only a single day in a process of celebration that occurred over weeks.

We'd gotten to Alaska the week before the wedding, and then I'd spent the weekend in LA with all the women, and then we came back and there was a wedding and Errol seemed all…bro-y with the other guys, as if they'd been best buds all along. Which was cool, and I was thrilled he was getting along with what was, now, apparently, my extended family.

And then after the wedding, instead of going off on a honeymoon and life returning to whatever passed for normal in this crazy group, Lexie and Myles chose to continue partying. I guess it was fairly rare for every single member of the group to be in town all at once, so the group seemed to have mutually decided to make the most of it and use the wedding as an excuse to have a two-week-long summer barbecue, essentially.

It was fun.

I made friends with everyone, and there were jam sessions on the rooftop and wild late-night parties on Harlow Grace's yacht—yes, *the* Harlow Grace. There were casual gaming parties where the dudes played *FIFA* and *Madden* and *Call of Duty* and shouted at each other and wrestled and drank clobbering amounts of whiskey, while the women sat and played cards and told dirty jokes and watched the men act like idiots.

Errol was never far, and always allowed himself to be pulled into the fun.

It was just…we never got any time alone. We crashed in the van and were too tired to talk much less anything else, which we didn't have time alone to talk about…

So two weeks to the wedding turned into another two weeks, and those two weeks sort of morphed into me going to the gym with Cassie while Errol went hiking with Lucas and Ramsey, and me and Torie going to Seattle together and Errol was everywhere with his camera, and I was waiting tables with Kitty, and he was helping with a remodel and… we were just living life.

It was easy, natural.

But it was also anything but. The tension of a new normal without sex was beginning to wear on us.

Finally, a full month after the wedding, the tension snapped.

It was after midnight, and I'd been helping Torie remodel her house and Errol had been off with Brock doing something risky involving a two-seater stunt biplane and high-speed photography.

We'd parked the van in Mom's parking lot, and went in for showers once in a while but mainly lived out his van. So that's where I was, in the van, waiting for him to come back. Dozing, pretending to read a book.

Lounging in the back, reading by a clip-on light.

I woke up suddenly, and he was there in the darkness.

"Hey-a, Pop. Sorry to wake you."

I set the book aside. "I wasn't sleeping."

He snorted. "You were snoring."

"Oh." He had something to say, I could tell. "What is it?"

"D'you remember when you talked about a cabin in the woods?"

I nodded. "Yeah." I bit my lip around a grin. "I said we'd need a cabin in the woods and a week alone."

"You ready for that?"

I sat up higher. Held my breath. I could only nod, until my voice returned. "Errol, I…I need that so bad. Things have been so crazy, and two weeks has turned into a month and a half, and…how did we get here?"

"Just living, I reckon. You have a crazy family, Poppy."

I laughed. "Yeah, I do." I moved to sit closer to him. "*We*, Errol. *We* have a crazy family."

His face pinched. "I like them. A lot. They make me feel like…like I belong."

I brushed my fingers into his hair. "So why do you look like you bit into a lemon?"

"Because what *are* we?"

"We're...we're going to go find a cabin in the woods and not come back until we know."

He smirked. "Well. I happen to have found just such a place."

"You *have*?" I sounded shrill with excitement, but didn't care to try and tamp it down. I *was* excited. "Where? When can we go?"

"Brock helped me find a place, way out there, way up in the bush, the wop-wops we'd call it, back in New Zealand. Apparently your sister Cassie's man Ink owns a place, but it's a bit more remote and off-grid than I'm in the mood for, so we're renting this one I found. It's accessible only by seaplane, but has its own generator and indoor plumbing, which is a plus."

I grabbed his hand and squeezed hard. "Quit dragging it out, Errol. When do we *go*?"

"Brock is waiting as we speak. Get your things."

I packed in record time, and then, instead of driving off in the van, we went to a truck that had been waiting across the parking lot, and in it was Brock Badd, a walking GQ advertisement, and a pilot. We drove across town to the docks, where Brock's seaplane was tied up. A preflight checklist, and then we were taking off, my stomach dipping as we rose.

The moment we were airborne, Brock sat back and glanced at Errol, who was in the copilot's seat. "Go for it, bro."

Errol glanced back at me as he took the copilot's steering yoke. "You buckled?"

"Yeah?"

"The gear is stowed?"

"You did it yourself, Errol. Do what? What are you doing?"

He just grinned. "Hold on, Pop."

And then he twisted the yoke and the aircraft rolled, and we were upside down and my hair was drifting down to the ceiling, and then we were upside right, but diving, and he was punching the throttle…

I think I was screaming, but then my scream caught in my throat as we dove and dove—and pulled up abruptly, rising, rising, stomach now falling into my toes as we came up, up, upside down again, and back down again, diving faster than ever as we completed the loop.

"I may have taught your man some stunt flying," Brock said. "He's a natural."

"Of course he is," I snapped, when I could breathe or speak again. "Don't do that again."

Errol laughed. "No? I think it's fun."

"Yeah, well, you've also been skydiving. And shipwrecked. And in combat. So a little stunt flying is nothing."

Errol lifted a finger. "Never been shipwrecked.

Airplane crash, yes. Kidnapped by pirates? Yes. Shipwrecked, no."

"Kidnapped by pirates?" Brock said, eying him sidelong. "For real?"

The rest of the trip was occupied mainly by Errol telling stories. Which was honestly fine with me, because I loved hearing his stories. What I loved more was seeing him flying, at ease, Brock occasionally taking over to adjust our heading or whatever. I liked listening to Errol talk. It took my mind off other things.

Like wanting him.

The past several weeks we'd both sort of found a status quo, an uneasy truce whereby we avoided doing anything outright provocative. Sex took a back seat to just getting to know each other. Learning each other.

He hated apples, I found. Hated the noise they made eating them, hated how the skin got between his teeth.

Lots of things like that. How to just...be, together.

Without sex.

But that didn't mean I didn't think about it. I did. All the time.

I just didn't do anything about it, not even by myself. I wondered if he had—I hadn't asked, not really wanting to know the answer. Or rather, afraid the answer would instigate something.

But now, the farther we flew, the more things started to bubble up within me.

I got antsy. Uncomfortable. Impatient.

I lost track of the time, and even dozed off a little, until I felt us dropping. Apparently Brock and Errol had already made a trip out here—that's what they'd done all day. Flew out, got the cabin opened up, lights on, wood stocked, food stocked. Set some lights around the perimeter of the lake that would be our landing area. It was pitch black, and even Errol seemed a bit nervous, but Brock was cool as ice, watching his gauges and adjusting the throttle and all the pilot-y sort of things. My heart was in my throat as we descended toward a darker patch of black in the night, lit only by a perimeter of small, dull orange lights.

The dark patch grew bigger, and then the aircraft's lights lit up a glassy surface and how the fuck he managed to land a seaplane on an inland lake in near-total darkness was a mystery to me, but there we were, skidding and skipping and then settling to slow, and then gently coming to a stop at an angle, the side door facing a small cabin like something out of a fairy tale. There was even a plume of smoke rising from the stone chimney, and little squares of yellow light on either side of the door.

"There's no dock," Errol said. "Or at least not one we can tie up to. The water is shallow here, though." He grabbed all of our things. "Just wait here."

He hopped out onto the float, and then into the water, carrying our things ashore and into the cabin.

Brock eyed me. "He's a good dude, you know."

I nodded. "Yes, he is." I smiled. "Thank you for flying us here."

"No problem." He grinned back. "Have a good time out here. There's no cell reception, no Wi-Fi, no neighbors for dozens of miles…just total privacy and peace."

I shivered in anticipation. "Sounds perfect."

Brock just laughed. "I bet."

Errol returned then, and held his arms up to me. "Hop down. I've got you."

I would've dived in if it meant getting ashore faster. But a chance to finally get his hands on me, his arms around me? Yes please.

I slid out of the aircraft and into Errol's waiting arms. Right where I belonged—my legs around his waist, his hands under my ass holding me aloft. His heartbeat against my breast, his breath on my lips.

"Oooookay, well now," Brock said. "That's my cue to go. You don't have to get a room, just wait till I'm in the air. You kids have fun getting reacquainted."

I heard the door close, but I was more concerned with the scent of Errol's skin as I nuzzled his throat, the feel of his shoulders under my hands, his chest against mine. I heard the engine roar and water spray, then the quieter splash and distant buzz as he lifted off the water and banked away.

Brock was nowhere in my mind, now.

I buried my face in Errol's neck as he walked with me ashore. But I couldn't wait. I had to taste him. I kissed his neck, and sighed at the firm salt of his flesh. Kissed another spot, and another. His hands tightened on my ass, and his heartbeat quickened—I tasted his pulse under my tongue, pumping faster and faster.

Kissed his jaw, the underside. And then his stubble, or what was now more of a real beard. Scratchy yet soft, and I dearly desperately wanted to feel it between my thighs. For now, I just wanted to kiss him. I let him hold my weight, let him carry me and focused on kissing more of him. Slid my hands into his hair and caressed his scalp, over his ears, his jaw, cupped his chin and kissed his cheek.

He fumbled at the door, but with my weight in his hands couldn't quite get it. "Pop…could you—Pop—Poppy, the door." He had to dodge my lips as I greedily snapped kisses over his lips, his nose, his cheeks. "The door, Poppy, and then I'll hold still for you to kiss me all you want."

"What's wrong with the porch?" I muttered, but reached behind me for the doorknob, got it and twisted and pushed so it creaked open.

He stepped through, kicked it closed.

Firelight was the only illumination; I was still focused only and entirely on Errol, on kissing his temple and forehead and then his throat and neck and shoulder as he slid me to my feet.

"Pop." He caught at my face. Smiled down at me.

"You want me to stop kissing you?" I asked, plaintive, childishly annoyed.

He grinned wider. "No. Just the reverse. I just wanted to say…welcome home. Or, home for the next two weeks."

"*Two* weeks?"

I peered around his body—it was tiny. A kitchenette in the back right corner, a fireplace dominating the left wall, a bed on the right wall, a door that led to a bathroom in the back wall opposite the kitchenette. That was it.

But, it had plumbing, electricity, and, most importantly, a bed. But the way I felt in the moment, a bed was only a bonus. I just needed Errol.

When I'd finished taking in the cabin, I smiled up at him. "It's perfect. Thank you for setting this up."

He smiled. "We've got it for two weeks. We've got everything we need, and Brock will come back to get us in two weeks from today. Till then? It's just us."

"Two weeks alone with you?" I rested my hands on his chest. "I can't think of anything more perfect."

He gave a thoughtful frown. "I can."

"Oh? What would that be?" I glanced at the kitchen. "Food, I see a bottle of wine…did you bring condoms?"

"Only about a year's supply."

"Then what else could we need?"

He grinned at me. "You, naked, on that bed."

I bit my lip, tugged at the hem of his shirt. "Weird thing is, I seem to have forgotten how to undress. You'll have to do it for me."

His answering smile was *everything*.

Errol

IT WAS SILLY TO BE NERVOUS, CONSIDERING WE'D ALREADY been naked together, had sex. But this was different.

This wouldn't be a hookup.

This time, I wouldn't be watching for the opportunity to bug out. There'd be no dodging the deep stuff.

So, I was nervous.

Horny as a motherfucker, but nervous, too.

I wanted it to be everything it was supposed to be. I wanted this to feel like *us*, like the beginning of something.

I had her all to myself, and we were alone, and this was it—she was ready. So ready.

Throwing herself at me.

And I wasn't sure where to start. How to make it different from what it had been before.

She saw. Sighed. Took my hand, laced her fingers into mine, and led me to the bed. "Talk to me. I thought you'd be as raring to go as I am."

"I am."

"Then why am I not naked?"

"We took this time away from sex to establish a real relationship."

"Yes, and I think we have, don't you?"

"I do—we have." I sought the right words. "I guess I'm just feeling like…like isn't it supposed to be…different? Not just jumping right back into sex. But…something more?"

"Oh, I see what you mean. I was so focused on wanting you that I didn't even think about that."

I held her hand, lifted it to my lips and kissed the back of it. "I want to do this right, Poppy."

She frowned, but thoughtfully. "So…we just go…slower?" A laugh.

"I don't know. That's why I'm hesitating. I don't want you just jump you, maul you, and have you think I'm looking at this as just like…finally the wait is over, we can fuck again. You know what I mean?"

She nodded. "I do." She crawled up onto my lap, legs curled against her chest, draped her arms around my neck, hands in my hair at the back of my head. "Want to know what I think?"

I ran my hands over her shoulders, her back. "That's why you're not naked. Yet."

"I think maybe we're overthinking it. I talked to my mom a while back, on the plane back from LA. She made it seem like…how do I put it? She said so much more eloquently than I can. What I gathered from what she said was that *we* give this meaning, Errol. I don't think the pace or the…*style* of how we have sex is what gives it meaning. It's the emotions we put into it. Before, it wasn't really emotions, it was just desire. Chemical attraction. You're hot, and I want you, and I like touching you, and I want to get off with you. That's all I was really feeling. Now, though? It's way more, Errol. I've learned so much about you since the last time we did anything together. I know about your parents, how you grew up. I know, now, the sadness and the struggle that has helped shape the amazing person you are."

A pause, and she nuzzled her nose against my jawline, near my earlobe. Kissed there, softly.

"I'm rushing into this because I'm horny as hell, Errol. Make no mistake. I haven't had an orgasm since the last time you made me come, okay? And that's the longest I've gone without even giving myself one since I discovered masturbation at like twelve years old." Another pause to kiss under my chin, and then my throat, now whispering between kisses. "But… no matter how fast or slow this happens, it's going to mean something for me. Like, I'm nervous, and a little scared, because…because what if you've changed your mind? What if it doesn't work out with us? What if…" She pulled back, rested her forehead on mine, and I felt her words as much as heard them. "What if you can't or won't or don't love me?" Her voice broke. "I want to be loved, Errol. It's all I've ever wanted. I just…I never knew it. Not till you. And I'm scared of letting myself be in love with you because it's all happened so fast and it's so much and—and—"

I cut her off with my mouth on hers, silencing her words with my lips, my tongue. Slashing across her lips, tasting her tears and inhaling her whispered sob. I had so much to say to that, but I had no clue how to put it into words.

And that's when it clicked.

That what made this different than the last time—not only did I have things to say that went beyond words, things I felt that couldn't be framed in human speech, but now…now I understood how to express them.

At first I just kissed her, lips on lips, and then tongues tangling. But soon, I needed more. I cupped her face and wrapped my arm around her shoulders and turned with her. Lay her on the bed, beneath me. Now, it wasn't *just* kissing. It was…sharing oxygen, mutual breath through the lock of our lips. Tasting her, giving her myself. Opening.

It went beyond a kiss. Beyond making out. It was diving into her, sliding beautifully into discovering the us of touching, tasting, taking.

How long? Until we couldn't breathe, until we were left gasping, panting. I let her lips go, but only an inch or two. Held her gaze.

"But, I do, Poppy."

"You do?" She feathered my hair in her fingers, traced my temple, touched my lips, traced my chin. "You do what?"

"Love you," I whispered.

She sobbed, clung to me, face in the side of my neck. Legs around my waist, arms around my shoulders and hands in my hair, she sobbed my name.

"Errol…" She let her head drop back down to the bed after a moment.

I touched her lips with my finger. "Don't say anything back. Not yet. Just…let it be."

She sighed, smiled. "You love me."

"Yep."

A laugh. "Why?"

"Because…a million reasons. Mainly, though, because of who you are. You're funny, you're brave.

Fearless, really. You have such an amazing eye for beauty, for art. You're talented. You understand me. You accept me. You inspire me."

She let go of me and cupped her breasts, shook them. "And here I thought it was going to be all about these."

"Poppy, I'm being serious."

Her smile faded. "I know. I was just teasing."

"You need to understand that me loving you is… it's not about what you look like." I palmed her cheek. Captured her hands. "You being the most beautiful woman I've ever known isn't why I'm in love with you."

She gazed up at me. "I think I'm starting to understand."

"How else can I help you understand, Pop?"

She dragged her fingers through my hair, again and again. "I think…I think maybe more of those kisses would help." A smile up at me that was as tender and affectionate as it was adorable and heart-palpitating, heart-stoppingly gorgeous. "I think that might do the trick."

"I think I could manage just a couple more kisses."

"Just a couple?" A moue, faking a pout.

"I mean, if you really wanted me to kiss you, I *guess* I could manage it."

"I would love it if you did," she said. "I really do enjoy the way you kiss me. It's rather nice."

"Rather nice, hmm? Is that all?" I kissed her, and this time, there was more than just tenderness in it. "What would I have to do to get it up past 'rather nice?'"

She clawed at my shoulders over my shirt as I kissed her again, this time harder, deeper. "That's a good start," she gasped, when I released her.

Then she pushed at me, suddenly ferocious, and we rolled together and I ended up on the bottom, with Poppy straddling me.

"Now we're getting somewhere," she whispered, once she was on top. Cradling my face in her hands, she nuzzled her lips on mine without making it a kiss, nose to nose, chin to chin. And then took my mouth, demanding another searing, mind-melting kiss. "But we can do better."

And then she slashed her lips onto mine yet again, and this time the kiss was burning, devouring, starving, desperate. We clung to each other through it, hands gripping wherever they found flesh, scraping, seeking bare skin.

Finally we broke apart once more.

I pulled at the hem of her shirt. "I think maybe I could kiss you more thoroughly if this weren't in the way."

She sat up. "Oh, well, in that case, please, allow me to remove the distraction." And began to peel the shirt off.

I caught her wrists. "I think maybe I had better do it. You did say you'd forgotten how, remember."

She snapped her fingers. "You know, you're right. I just clean forgot how. You definitely had better help me."

She was wearing a long-sleeve T-shirt, deep scarlet, V-neck, made from thin, silky cotton, clinging to her skin, cut to accentuate her bust and trim waist. With it, tight, stretchy jeans and black boots with chunky two-inch heels.

I gathered the hem of her shirt in my hands. "I feel like a kid on Christmas about to open a present he's been waiting for all year."

"I'm wearing a bra and underwear, so I'm definitely all wrapped up for you." She grinned. "I woke up feeling sexy, so I put on my skimpiest lingerie. It looks so good, you may not even want to take it off."

I growled. "Oh, I will. But I just may have to make you put it back on so I can take it off you again." I lifted. Lifted, baring her tummy. "I can't wait to be skin to skin with you, Poppy."

Then I had the shirt off and she was shaking her hair out—loose, wild, black wavy curtains around the golden skin of her shoulders. White lingerie, and when she said it was her skimpiest, she wasn't kidding. The bra, such as it was, existed mainly as sheer mesh, with a scattered starburst of flowers embroidered over her nipples.

"Fuck me," I breathed. "So fucking gorgeous."

"I'd love to," she said, "but I can't until you're finished undressing me."

She rolled backward, stood up, backed away. I followed, knelt in front of her. Kissed her belly, her hip, over the waist of her tight, dark wash jeans. Helped her out of the boots, the tiny white ankle socks. Reached up, freed the button of her jeans, then lowered the zipper. She watched, gazing down at me. Tugged the jeans down—to thighs, past her knees. Around her ankles. She'd have just stepped out of them, but this was my show—my job. I gently tugged her foot free of one leg, then the other. Just to draw it out, I neatly folded the jeans and set them aside. Now she was clad in just the lingerie—and she hadn't been exaggerating. She looked so fucking incredible in all white, like an angel of lust, that I almost didn't want to strip her any further.

I held her hips in my hands and stared up at her, kneeling in front of her. "You're a goddess, Poppy."

"Your goddess," she breathed.

"Mine."

The key word a few lines up is "almost." Meaning, I absolutely *had* to have her the rest of the way out of her clothes.

Needed her naked. Needed her skin, bare, all for me.

The panties were a complicated network of straps and laces and silk mesh. I laughed, grinning up at her. "I don't even know how to get those off."

She just laughed with me. "Try getting them on."

I hooked my fingers into the topmost layer of straps and laces, and tugged down, but they snagged on the generous swell of her hips.

She bit her lip to stifle laughter. "Rip them off if you have to. I'll just make you buy me more."

"Make me?" I echoed. "Try and stop me."

I yanked them down, and she gasped, and I definitely heard a seam rip, but she only gazed down at me still as if the very sun itself revolved around me, as if I was her oxygen, her reason for breathing, for being, as if not being naked with me in the next few moments would be the worst tragedy there was.

I stood up, and her breasts brushed my chest, hard nipples pressing into my pecs, and she reached for me as I circled her body with my arms to find the clasp of the bra. I made quick work of it, and she let it slide down her arms, let me catch it. Not caring if I looked like a creeper, I sniffed it. She just laughed.

"Weirdo," she breathed. "I've been wearing it all day. It can't smell good."

"It does. Smells like you. Like what I've been missing so badly all these weeks."

Naked now, I released her and stepped back. Just stared at her. "Goddamn, Poppy. How did you manage to become *more* breathtaking since the last time I saw you naked?"

"I think that's the love you're seeing," she whispered. "Or it's your love acting like a filter."

"Ahh," I murmured. "That explains it."

"I just want to keep looking at you," I said.

She moved forward, reaching for the fly of my jeans. "You can look at me all you want," she murmured. "But I have needs too, you know."

"You do?"

"Oh yes. Quite a lot of them, as a matter of fact."

"Like what?"

She was trying to take off my shirt with one hand and unzip my jeans with the other at the same time. And bless her, but she managed to succeed. She pushed my shirt up off my head and threw it aside, and at the same time, got my jeans unbuttoned and unzipped. Once my shirt was off and my jeans were open, she shoved them down, moving with greedy desperation. I stepped and clumsily kicked free of the denim, and by the time my feet were freed, she had my black boxer-briefs down around my thighs, and then I was naked with her.

She grasped my cock in both hands, groaning in utter relief. "*This*," she moaned. "This is what I need."

"Oh *fuck*," I growled, as she stroked me with both hands, greedily, as if to make up for lost time. "Slow down, or this will be over before it starts. I haven't had myself off either, you know. So I'm sort of, uh, primed to blow."

"I don't care," she murmured, not slowing. "I just don't fucking care. You can come all over me if you want. We have all night. All day. We can rinse off in the lake. I don't want to slow down. I want to touch you. I want to taste you."

We stumbled for the bed, and I somehow landed on my back, filling my hands with the warm round globes of her ass, filling my mouth with her breasts, my taste buds with her skin. She had her hands on me, caressing my cock with both hands, kissing my chest and my chin and jaw and lips, wherever her lips landed, she kissed.

The box of condoms was under the bed, since there wasn't a bedside table—I fumbled for it blindly, with one hand. Found it. She noticed what I was doing, took the box from me. Unable to move fast enough, she tore it open, ripped open a packet still attached to the string of the rest, pulled the latex ring out. Sheathed me in it, rolling over me hand over hand.

The moment I was covered, she pressed her body against mine, cradling my face in her hands, lips to lips. "Errol, please."

I held myself in one hand, traced her opening with the other. She gasped as I nudged against her, writhed to take me. Her mouth dropped open, lips quivering against mine as we joined.

"Poppy," I groaned, grinding in to fill her, feeling her sex swallow around me, sliding in, deep, slow.

Her tremulous lips touched mine, in a half-kiss, an un-breathing touch of lips to lips, her gasp shattered as our hips met. "Oh god…*Errol.* Errol!"

She pulled away from the kiss, lifted up to brace her hands on my chest. Breasts hung, swayed as she found her balance on me. Eyes on mine, never looking away, not daring to even blink.

She held there, still fully impaled with me.

"Errol…" This time it wasn't a gasp of incredulous bliss, but a predicate, a beginning. Lips on mine again, now a brief kiss. "I love you, Errol."

I didn't bother hiding or wiping away the damp salt at the corners of my eyes. Didn't tear my gaze from hers—let her see it. She bent and kissed the tears, laughed giddily, sniffing, sobbing.

I ached within her. Didn't need to say it back. That's not how it works. You say it when you mean it. When it emerges from you unbidden.

She rolled back, and then I ached to be deeper, and she sobbed again, laughing still as well, and then we were moving together, me sliding in, deeper and deeper, and my groan was her breath, mouth shuddering on mouth. Each movement was slow, feeling each other, taking this as a measured experiment of what it was to make love. She clung to me and let herself sob out loud each time I drove into her, and I heard my own groans become broken as our hips met, as I delved into the deepest part of her.

It wasn't long.

It didn't matter.

It was us, expressing love.

Climax was a combined eruption, more of half-sobbed sighs than of screams, of whispered benedictions of gasped names than of growled expletives.

Them

BODY ON BODY IN THE MOONLIGHT. THE LAKE WRAPPED warm around us, enveloping us as we swam, splashed, laughed, naked together. Dove down into darkness and found each other, skin on skin, twisting and rising as one.

There was only we.

Dawn met us as we lay wrapped in a blanket on the porch, sharing a single chair, sipping from a single tin mug. Sated for the moment, we luxuriated in the feel of flesh and warmth of togetherness, sunrise staining the treetops pink and then the sky above salmon-orange and then the lake a brightening molten gradient of pink-to-scarlet.

He carried me inside once the sun had risen, and we ate a breakfast of eggs and bacon and toast cooked over an open flame, and he wore only a pair of what he called "stubbies," and I stayed wrapped in his fleece blanket, which now held so many memories of us in its soft pilled surface. More coffee, and I lay on the bed with my head on his thighs as he read aloud to me from a book of classic fables he'd found on the mantel above the fireplace. The fire had melted to glowing coals by the time we drowsed, with the sun fully breaching the windows, bathing us in stunning yellow light.

I fell asleep to the sound of his voice reading to me, the soft gentle hum in his chest and that delicious accent I never tired of hearing.

He began to drowse and I half woke to feel him set the book on the floor and slide down and now it was my turn to hold him—I cradled his head against my breasts and felt his breath on my skin and knew he heard and felt my heartbeat lulling him to sleep in my arms.

We slept longer than I think I've ever slept in my life, till the sun was orange again.

He went outside and turned on the generator, and a few minutes later the narrow, cramped shower in the bathroom was wreathed in steam, and even though it was so small it barely fit me let alone us, we took turns scrubbing ourselves clean in the iron-tang of the well water.

I left my hair wet, only taking the time run a brush through the snarls, and then he took over, sitting behind me, his legs around my hips, brushing my hair. I remember him telling me how he'd done this for his mother, and I felt him connecting to that past, felt him let it wash through him, heard him breathing hard and sniffing, and gave him space to feel it and as he brushed and brushed my hair till it shone, I felt him mourning for the first time and in so doing letting the memory and the pain become less intertwined.

I lay back against his chest, removed the brush from his hands. His chin rested on my shoulder, and I twisted until I could kiss him. I tasted salt once more, and his willingness to let me see it, feel it, taste it, to let me know the depth of his sorrow made me love him so much my heart wanted to expand past the confines of my chest, and I could only show him by kissing him, clinging to him, lying on his body, my back to his front.

He shifted and shimmied, and he was naked under me. I reached up, behind my head, clutched at his neck, his head. His hands scoured my belly, cradled my breasts, and I felt him angling hard and thick against me.

"I have to get a—"

"I don't care."

I grasped him, took him into me.

"Poppy..." he whispered, shattered to be bare inside me.

"We're covered, " I whispered back. "Birth control."

"I've never felt anything like this before," he growled, desperate, wild.

"Me either."

"It feels too good," he murmured, breathless, forcing himself to move as slowly as possible, sliding into me millimeter by millimeter, savoring the enrapturing ecstasy of bare unity, skin on skin, flesh within flesh and nothing else between.

"So good," I breathed. "Too good. I want it to last forever."

"We have forever."

His palm caressed my breast, thumbed the nipple and the piercing until I ached and mewled, and the fingers of his other hand slid over my tender swollen aching center and I didn't need the help, feeling him like this was more than enough, was more than everything, but the added rough brush of his fingertips over me took me to heaven, to climax and beyond within seconds, to a place beyond climax where even screams couldn't express the full shattering nirvana of this, with him.

I cried out, I wept his name again and again as I came apart on him, his body my bed, his arms walls around me shutting out the world that wasn't us, sheltering me; his lips whispered prayers to my body, worshipped my name, sang love to me.

I came and I came, and his growling predatory snarl told me he was keeping his back, making this moment last as long as possible and I wanted it forever, to never end. To feel him impaled full and iron hard and silk soft inside me and his hands all over me touching me so I became a wild creature of savage pleasure with every instinct unlocked and unleashed, screaming on him, snarling as I came around him endlessly, pleasure waves rolling one after the other, one into another, until there was only the breathless sobbing wonder of us, of us, of us.

"Give it to me, Errol," I gasped, when I had breath to even whisper, voice shaking.

He couldn't speak, could only groan, growl, got my name out, *Poppy, god, Poppy*…

I sat up, sat forward. Tucked my feet under my shins and rose up to gyrate, rolling my hips.

He whimpered, a soft male groan of desperation, the agony of ecstasy.

He tried to sit up, but I reached back and pushed him down, braced my hands on his thighs. "Let me," I whispered. "Just let me take it from you."

He grasped my hips, caressed my ass, and held me as I moved. Helped me lift, brought me down. And then just held on to me for dear life as I began to roll my hips, faster and faster, taking him deep with each gyrating, grinding roll of my sex onto his throbbing erection.

Held me, groaning my name.

When he began to push against me, when his grip went painfully fierce, I slowed. Instead of rolling to get a full slide of his length, I spread myself apart to take him deeper, seating lower on him, leaning forward and pushing my hips backward, angling him away to draw this moment out.

He was truly crazed with need, now, trying to move, but I had him at my mercy, and my desire was to make this a moment that would be imprinted forever on his very soul. Deep, so deep. Felt him throbbing thick, and with nothing between us, I felt *everything*. He was so huge within me, stretched my sex so I felt each vein and ridge and ripple stuttering past my nether lips, felt the thick vein on the underside against the edge of me. Leaning forward like this, facing his feet, I needed only to balance with one hand on his leg, and with the other I reached between my thighs to feel where we joined. Felt his heavy soft sac and caressed it, massaged it.

He cried out, nearly weeping with the need to

explode, but I wouldn't let him. Slow shallow thrusts, a tease of a roll, so he slid through me, so he pulsed inside me, pulsed ever so slightly deeper…

"Poppy, fuck, please, my love, please."

I laughed with delight at the mad desperation in his voice. The plea. "You want to come, now, Errol?"

"Have to, Pop, fucking *have* to."

"How hard are you going to come, when I let you?" Slow, so slow. Almost not moving. Just sitting harder on him, pushing deeper and deeper yet, angled forward until he was strained to the very edge, until his erection couldn't angle any farther away without causing real pain.

"So fucking hard."

"Are you going to fill me, Errol?" I teased him again, pulling up just a touch, then slamming down. "I need you. I want to feel you fill me."

"Poppy, you don't even understand. I need to come so bad it fucking hurts."

"Do you love me, Errol?" I asked, turning to gaze at him over my shoulder, more teasing, not-quite-enough rolls of my sex around him.

"I love you so much, Poppy. So much it scares me."

"Ask me again, Errol."

"No. You give it to me when you want me to have it."

I bent forward further, and he hissed, thrust or tried to. I caressed his sac, and he groaned. Cupped him, squeezed until he cried out.

I needed it too badly, then, to draw it out anymore.

I sat back on him, lifted up. His drawn-out groan became a cry of disbelief, of raw explosive release, or what was the beginning of it. When I rose up until he nearly slid out of me, he snarled, and when I finally sank down, his voice broke, because that was when he finally received his full climax.

I felt that vein on the underside of him pulsing as he exploded, and he was trying to grind into me, but this was *mine* to give, not his to take, and I controlled the pace. I kept it slow, rising up, a series of shallow rolls, feeling him pumping inside me, feeling him fill me with thick wet heat, and then I slammed down until my ass met his thighs with a loud *slap* and now, *now* he came. Fully and truly—what he'd felt before was only the precursor, the first warning tremors, and his voice broke and he couldn't cry out, couldn't growl, was rendered mute and breathless as I gave him what he needed what I needed, what we needed—full rolling slamming unrestrained thrusts, and I held myself up and gave over to him, rode with him, let him slam up into me as hard as he could, as hard as he needed, bodies meeting with thrust after beautiful thrust, and I touched myself and I came with him, screaming with him and he came for what seemed like an eternity. I felt his seed escaping me, plunged deep and smearing around his still-sliding shaft, felt it thick and wet, felt myself so full of him, dripping with him, and I never knew such a thing could be so beautiful.

When he stopped pulsing, I kept going. Riding him and taking him until there was nothing left, until he began to soften.

He finally lifted me off of him and turned me in his arms and gathered me so he could kiss me, kissing my cheek and lips and nose and forehead, so he could kiss me until we were breathless all over again and whispering words of love…

She shuddered on me. Head on my chest, her lithe curvaceous body belonging to me, given to me. She tapped my breastbone with a finger in time to my heartbeat—*tumtum…tumtum…tumtum.*

I left her lying in the bed and returned to clean her, marveling at the privilege she'd given me, the trust she'd shown me. When she was clean, she pulled me down to the bed once more and nestled in my arms.

"Errol?"

"Hmmm?"

"What will our life look like? My family is here, but your career is out there."

"Our life is what we make it." I touched her chin, held her eyes. "What do you want our life to look like?"

She hesitated.

"Tell me," I insisted. "Whatever it is, tell me."

"I want to go where you go. And when we're not out there, we're here." She closed her eyes. Shivered. "I want our home to be here. Together. I want to watch you play the fiddle with Canaan and Aerie and Myles and Lexie and Corin and Tate. I want to develop photos in our own darkroom. I want a studio where I can paint all day, wearing nothing but one of your shirts. I want…I want to sit in airports with you. Join the mile-high club with you." She smirked up at me. "Unless you've already done that."

"Nope," was my only reply.

"Good. That's ours together, too, then." She paused to think. "I want to see the world with you. Take photos of everything. I want to go to Machu Picchu with you, and Paris, and Tahiti, and…god, everywhere. And I want us to come home here." A laugh. "Well, not *here* here. Ketchikan, here."

"I've never had a home," I whispered, the word tasting unfamiliar on my tongue. "New Zealand hasn't been home since I was twelve, since Mum passed. I've been itinerant, since."

She gazed up at me, rolled so she was on top, rested her breasts on my belly and propped her arms on my chest, chin on her hands. "I can be your home."

"You already are."

"Can I scare you a little?"

I smiled. "You can try."

"Someday, when we're ready, I want to be Mrs. Poppy Sylvain." Serious dark eyes, only a hint of a smile, watching my reaction carefully. "Is that crazy?"

"Not crazy, or scary. Or, actually, what's crazy and scary is how *not* either one it really is." I brushed hair away from the corner of her mouth. Cupped a breast because I could. "My turn to try and scare you."

"You can try," she said, grinning as she echoed my own words.

"After I've made you Mrs. Poppy Sylvain, someday, eventually, when we're ready, I want to make you a mother. I want to..." I choked back emotion. "I want to be a father who's *there*. I've thought about it a lot, actually. How, if I ever was to fall in love, if there was ever a woman who could love me enough to get me to settle in one place, I'd want to have a baby, just so I can be there for him or her. All the time. Every day. I'd read stories, and change diapers and...and make bottles, and show them how to ride a bike and catch a fish..."

"You'll be there." She touched my jaw. "I thought you were going to scare me, Errol. All you've done is make me love you all the more."

"Does *this* scare you?" I asked, pushing my renewed desire against her soft center.

"Only in how much I want it again," was her answer.

"Are we crazy to be talking about getting married and having babies already?"

She unwrapped protection and covered me with it. We lay on our sides, merged lazily and slowly, facing each other, noses brushing like butterfly kisses. "My mom told me that love is not dependent on time, it's just our hearts recognizing the other person as belonging to us."

"My heart recognizes yours," I whispered.

"We belong together, so nothing that feels right to us is crazy, regardless of the amount of time we've known each other."

"I've never belonged to or with anyone," I said.

"Me either." She pulled me on top of her and drew me down for a kiss. "Now we do. You're mine, Errol. And I'm not letting go."

"Yours," I whispered.

"Mine," she breathed.

"Ours," we murmured, together.

LIVES LIVED

A POSTSCRIPT

TWO WEEKS? TWO DAYS, TWO MONTHS, TWO YEARS. Time meant nothing. We made love a thousand times, a thousand ways.

We returned to Ketchikan, eventually.

There was a studio full of paints and canvasses, and a gallery where our art was sold, photographs and paintings and mixtures of both, even our art merged, becoming one.

There were travels all over the globe, and we made love in exotic places. In the alleys of Casablanca, on a rooftop in Marrakech as a muezzin called the faithful to prayer. On a catamaran sailboat under the shadows of ancient Greek ruins.

There were family get-togethers in Ketchikan, with an ever-growing family.

Bast and Dru ended up with three kids, Brock and Claire with two, and Bax and Eva had five. Canaan and Aerie and Corin and Tate had four each. Lucian and Joss had two kids; Xavier and Harlow waited a long time, and were the only couple to have just one.

Roman refused to be outdone by Baxter, so he and Kitty ended up with six kids of their own. Remington and Juneau had two, but those two were unholy terrors, and thus more than enough. Ramsey and Izzy had one. Charlie and Crow three, Cassie and Ink four—each of them as big as Ink, four boys with his hair and size and heart, but Cassie's attitude--god preserve their sanity. Lexie and Myles, being public figures like Harlow and Xavier, waited a while, and had two. Torie and Rhys surprised us all by having two sets of twins, which was some kind of statistical improbability considering twins don't run on either side of their family; one set was identical, both boys, and the other was fraternal, a boy and a girl.

We have three.

Bastien, Celeste, and DJ—Darren Jones.

Lives were lived.

Families were raised.

Love was created, made, cultivated, grown, adapted, matured, multiplied.

There were endings, and beginnings, and everything in between.

A NOTE FROM THE AUTHOR

Here's where I break the fourth wall. No longer the narrator, the storyteller, the author, but someone who has lived with these characters for the past four years—*Badd Motherf*cker* was published October 28, 2016.

17 books.

34 unique characters, each with their own personalities and flaws and quirks.

I can't begin to explain how we've grown as storytellers in the shaping of these books, how much we've learned.

And now? It's at an end.

Bittersweet, for us—it's the fruition, the culmination of a series that grew far beyond our wildest expectations. We hope you find this last book satisfying, that it wraps it all up, encapsulates the essence of everything Badd and Goode.

There are loose ends, threads left untied. Questions unanswered. But that's life, no? Who among us isn't living with loose threads somewhere behind us, with questions left unanswered? It's the journey that counts, I think. And what a journey! When this all started with a bedraggled bride walking into a bar and meeting a burly, tattooed, foul-mouthed bartender in Ketchikan, Alaska, we hoped people would like the series enough to let us write all eight of the brothers we originally envisioned.

It just…grew from there.

And grew, and grew.

The question I think is on everyone's mind, now that you're reading this final book, is *Will there be another spinoff?*

No.

Maybe I should write that another way: No?

I don't like dealing in absolutes, but I feel this series is complete.

I didn't write *THE END* at the bottom of the previous page, on purpose. Because while the stories we're going tell in this particular world are ended, their lives aren't. They carry on, unseen, in our imaginations.

There are new stories to be written, now. Exciting new ideas we've been working on, developing. Characters we're fleshing out. We want to try new things. And if you're a long-time reader of Jasinda Wilder stories, you know we never do exactly the same thing twice.

So what's next?

We have a fun, steamy, funny series planned, something that will feel familiar to our fans, but breaking new ground and turning tropes on their heads as we so love to do.

In our minds, though, the more exciting project is something totally groundbreaking. If you loved *Falling Into You,* and the rest of The Falling Series, you should be very, very excited for this.

It's called *The Cabin*.

Our goal with this story is to take all the elements that make a Jasinda Wilder novel feel so unique and unforgettable, and distill them all together. We're reaching for new heights with this one. There will be heartbreak and humor, romance and tragedy and redemption; there will be steam, and there will be tears. And, hopefully, at the end of it, a deeper understanding of love, and its meaning and its effect on who we are, how we live.

We want not just to tell a story, but to create new meaning.

We hope you're as excited as we are for the next adventure in Wilder storytelling.

So, get ready, Wilder readers
The Cabin releases this fall.

Thank you for your love, support,
encouragement and faith.

Happy reading!

Also by
Jasinda Wilder

Visit me at my website: **www.jasindawilder.com**
Email me: **jasindawilder@gmail.com**

If you enjoyed this book, you can help others enjoy it as well by recommending it to friends and family, or by mentioning it in reading and discussion groups and online forums. You can also review it on the site from which you purchased it. But, whether you recommend it to anyone else or not, thank you *so much* for taking the time to read my book! Your support means the world to me!

My other titles:

Preacher's Son:
Unbound
Unleashed
Unbroken

Delilah's Diary:
A Sexy Journey
La Vita Sexy
A Sexy Surrender

Big Girls Do It:
Boxed Set
Married
On Christmas
Pregnant

Rock Stars Do It:
Harder
Dirty
Forever

From the world of *Big Girls* and *Rock Stars*:
Big Love Abroad

Biker Billionaire:
Wild Ride

The Falling Series:
Falling Into You
Falling Into Us
Falling Under
Falling Away
Falling For Colton

The Ever Trilogy:
Forever & Always
After Forever
Saving Forever

The world of *Wounded:*

Wounded

Captured

The world of *Stripped:*

Stripped

Trashed

The world of *Alpha:*

Alpha

Beta

Omega

Harris: Alpha One Security Book 1

Thresh: Alpha One Security Book 2

Duke Alpha One Security Book 3

Puck: Alpha One Security Book 4

Lear: Alpha One Security Book 5

Anselm: Alpha One Security Book 6

The Houri Legends:

Jack and Djinn

Djinn and Tonic

The Madame X Series:

Madame X

Exposed

Exiled

The Black Room
(With Jade London):
Door One
Door Two
Door Three
Door Four
Door Five
Door Six
Door Seven
Door Eight

The One Series
The Long Way Home
Where the Heart Is
There's No Place Like Home

Badd Brothers:
*Badd Motherf*cker*
Badd Ass
Badd to the Bone
Good Girl Gone Badd
Badd Luck
Badd Mojo
Big Badd Wolf
Badd Boy
Badd Kitty
Badd Business
Badd Medicine
Badd Daddy

Dad Bod Contracting:

Hammered

Drilled

Nailed

Screwed

Fifty States of Love:

Pregnant in Pennsylvania

Cowboy in Colorado

Married in Michigan

Goode Girls

For a Goode Time Call…

Not So Goode

Goode to Be Bad

A Real Good Time

Standalone titles:

Yours

Non-Fiction titles:

You Can Do It

You Can Do It: Strength

You Can Do It: Fasting

Jack Wilder Titles:

The Missionary

JJ Wilder Titles:

Ark

To be informed of new releases, special offers, and other Jasinda news, sign up for Jasinda's email newsletter.

Made in United States
North Haven, CT
13 February 2023

32521965R00243